ESYLD'S AWAKENING

CWC Collaborative Fiction Novel
Written by 27 International Authors

ISBN: 1-946275-05-0
ISBN 13: 978-1-946275-05-9

ABOUT CWC

Collaborative Writing Challenge is aptly named to describe what we do. We bring aspiring writers together from all over the world to collaborate on a full-length fiction novel. We accept writers of all ages with varying degrees of experience, as we believe everyone has something to offer.

Each chapter is written by four or five different writers, and each week, one chapter is selected to form part of the ongoing novel. The experience is challenging and unique, as the writers never meet or discuss their visions for the story.

Every story is guided by a Story Coordinator, who checks names, facts, and integrity, and who works with each chapter writer to get the best results. This story has been kissed by many hands who have yet to read the completed novel.

We also introduced a new element to CWC, a short story competition, to give our writers a chance to submit a stand-alone story to be published in the novel of the same genre. At the end of this book, you will find **'Stealing the Curse'** by **J.K. Harrison**. Her story was selected as the winner and will also be featured on the CWC website. Congratulations.

For more information, please visit:
www.collaborativewritingchallenge.com

IBBY

This is CWC's sixth project. 10% of profits from the sales of this book will be donated to the charity IBBY. This is a wonderful organization, dedicated to providing children from all over the world with access to books.

We will be donating to the specific project called the **IBBY Fund for Children in Crisis,** which provides support for children whose lives have been disrupted through war, civil disorder, or natural disaster. The two main activities supported by the Fund are the therapeutic use of books and storytelling in the form of Bibliotherapy, and the creation or replacement of selected book collections appropriate to each situation.

Please see further details about this charity by accessing their website: **www.ibby.org**

DEDICATION

This book is dedicated to all the writers who dared to get involved in a CWC collaboration. The interest in each new project is phenomenal, allowing us to start multiple projects of varying genres. This has resulted in better-quality submissions, giving the collaborations the best chance possible at being successful.

I would also like to mention my online writing friends who have brought so much fun and inspiration into my life. This encourages me to continue growing CWC and bringing people from all walks of life together!

And, of course, our CWC Story Coordinators, who work tirelessly to make each project successful. You are all a pleasure and an inspiration.

Laura Callender - CWC Founder

THE WRITERS

We had over 78 writers sign up for Esylds Awakening, resulting in 52 different writers sending in submissions. 79 chapters were submitted in total, 36 of which were selected for the story. The authors came from 5 different countries: America, UK, Greece, Austria and Australia.

Rather than fill these pages with details about all 27 authors, all their pictures and bios can be found on the CWC Website. Please stop by and learn more about our talented contributing writers. Some have very little writing experience, and some have reels of accomplishments under their belts. I think you would be hard-pressed to identify their individual chapters, and it's just possible that your favorite chapter could have been written by a fresh-faced, up-and-coming writer. There are certainly a few names that we will be looking out for in the future.

With CWC projects, it is inevitable that some writers will have their chapters rejected. We had some incredible submissions that we just couldn't use. These chapters are always integral to shaping the story, as the variety in chapters gave us the chance to find the best fit. These writers are as much a part of the teamwork that brought this project to completion, so to those who go unnamed: Thank you for your wonderful contributions and effort!

ACKNOWLEDGMENTS

This project has brought together so many talented people. I would like to thank **T.S. Dickerson** who did an outstanding job of keeping the project on track. She did the first edit with finesse and has sculpted an absolutely wonderful offering by CWC.

As always, our Chief Editor **Kathrin Hutson** has done an outstanding job getting Esyld's Awakening ready for publication. It is a pleasure working with you, my friend.

My biggest thanks must go to **all of our writers** who agreed to participate in this project. With each new project, demand increases, but so far, we manage to find a place for everyone. Some writers are not always proficient in the genre we are writing, but often their creative minds produce work so wonderful, they surprise themselves. We are very proud of all your work.

A NOTE FROM THE STORY COORDINATOR

I initially signed up to be a writer for CWC's sixth collaboration, and I was among those who voted for the starter chapter. When Esyld's Awakening was chosen, part of me was thrilled to be writing what I thought was the most fascinating of the submitted chapters, and part of me was daunted by the it's potential to be a complex and challenging project. I remember thinking, 'Wow. The Story Coordinator will have their work cut out for them.' Now, I look back and laugh at myself, knowing that two weeks into the project, I became that Story Coordinator when the original Coordinator could no longer devote the needed time.

I knew it would be a challenge, and I expected it to be fun and exciting. What I didn't anticipate was the great respect and admiration I would come to have for all these wonderful, dedicated writers from across the globe, none of whom I'd ever met. It was a pleasure to work with such talented people. My fondest hope throughout the project was to combine things in a way that would both please the writers and interest readers. Holding their hard work in my hands was an honor and an intimidating responsibility.

I never knew what to expect from the submitted chapters. It was always a thrill. It was also always tough. I can't recall a single week in which one chapter stood out immediately as the obvious choice. Instead, there would be three or more great choices, multiple intriguing directions for the story to take. Some weeks, I combined chapters, and it amazed me how well the ideas worked together despite the authors never having discussed the project. In some cases, each chosen writer had focused on a different group of characters, challenging me to fit both visions in without blowing out our goal for final word count.

We also had some rough weeks—writers dealing with illnesses or tragedies in their lives and being unable to write. Seeing their disappointment at not being able to participate showed me how much we all cared about the project. It was so rewarding to work toward a common goal with more than 70 other writers. And there were some opportunities hidden behind those disappointing weeks when no chapter could be selected. Often, it meant I got to select more chapters the following week or, in one instance, call up a chapter I had been forced to reject previously because it now fit within the timeline.

With all the world-building and magical and character development the writers whipped up on the fly, it was sometimes a stretch to make it meld together. The ending of the book was the most difficult. As the final chapters approached, we still had so much action (all of it too good not to include) and many plot lines to tie off. Those writers involved in the final couple chapters truly managed a miracle. In the end, I think we have a wild, adventurous, and occasionally dark fantasy to share with the world.

I want to take this moment to sincerely thank the writers for their hard work and dedication, whether it was flexibility in their scheduling, willingness to rework plot points to help continuity, or stepping up when we needed emergency submissions. I learned so much from all of you and from the overall experience. I look forward to any opportunity I may get to work with any of you in the future!

And a note to the reader: Any time you pick up a novel, you are seeing years of hard work, heartache, passion, and commitment all neatly bound into a package of paper and ink. But, in the case of a novel like this, you are seeing that from over 70 people—the writers who sacrificed entire weekends, never knowing whether their work would be chosen, and the hardworking CWC team who handled the editing, formatting, cover design, and promotion. On behalf of all these people, I say sincerely, we hope you enjoy it!

T.S. Dickerson
Story Coordinator of *Esyld's Awakening*

CONTENTS

Short Story Winner:

CWC's Seventh Collaboration:

Chapter 1

Esyld stood at the threshold, gazing out at the night. The new moon left the woods shrouded in a darkness as thick as black ink. If she'd had eyes, they'd be useless, even if her face wasn't hidden beneath the shroud. She smiled; her other senses were at their peak, making her body tingle from head to toe. Leaving the old wooden door open, Esyld went back inside and gathered her things into a satchel. Pulling the strap over her head, she then stood in front of the broken shard of mirror hanging on the wall by the door. She lifted the shroud from the bottom edges gently brushing against her waist, then raised it up over her bald head. She didn't gaze so much as sense her reflection. Esyld, though lacking eyes, saw everything with her mind's eye. It worked just as well as, if not better than, the eyes of mortals; it opened when she needed to see and closed when she didn't. Her mind's eye opened now as she took a rare look at herself.

Her features were less than conventional—the lack of eyes, small slits with the tiniest bump of cartilage for a nose, and spiraled cartilage on either side of her head that functioned as ears. The only aspect of her features considered normal was her mouth, with full, rose-colored lips and two rows of tiny white teeth. Esyld lowered the shroud back over her face with a sigh. Though she was well hidden in the woods, she preferred to hide herself—partly because she was worried that one day, her peace might be disrupted. She also found the darkness sharpened her senses, allowing her to see the world not only as it was but also with the potential of lurking evils that sometimes infected it and its people.

Walking briskly out the door, she paused to drag it closed behind her; the air had changed during the brief time she had been inside. The night carried a sense of urgency about it now, and she felt that if she waited much longer, her opportunity would pass.

She hurried off along the path, worn by her many trips over the decades. The absence of any woodland noises disturbed her and made the sound of her footsteps on the stones beneath her feet all the louder. Feeling the incline of the ground beneath her, she knew she had neared the Sacred Well. With hands outstretched, she touched the cool, rough stone that made up the well, ran her hands reverently along the curve before her, and took a deep breath. Her hand shook when she reached into her satchel and withdrew the athame, careful to grasp it by the crystal-encrusted hilt. It was even older than she, passed on from woman to woman down the family line. Esyld was all that was left.

Holding her wrist out over the deep darkness of the well and with a quick flick of the blade, she made a small cut across it her arm. She ignored the sting as she placed the athame on the well's ledge and overturned her injured wrist, allowing her blood to spill. When she felt the ground beneath her start to vibrate, she raised both arms towards the night sky, the ancient chant almost soundlessly spilling from her lips. The vibrations intensified, and she leaned against the well's edge. She chanted faster, shifting her weight further forward until her feet lifted off the ground and her torso hovered over the dark hole. The chant came to an end, and she leaned further still, letting herself fall head-first into the depths.

She hated the sensation of falling, but after a few seconds, her body felt weightless, as though she hovered or floated, though she knew from experience her descent hadn't ended. She willed her mind's eye to remain closed, not wanting to see what reached out for her from the darkness. Esyld had no concept of how much time had elapsed before she felt her feet softly land on plush grass. Its fragrant smell made her a bit dizzy after her downward journey, but she forced herself to inhale deeply, and her mind's eye opened wide to reveal her surroundings.

She stood in the sacred grove, a place hidden from all but her family line. The trees surrounding her grew thick and tall, their tops beyond her sight. A circle of the night sky was visible directly above her, and the stars created swirls as the ground beneath them spun. Standing out from the rest of the trees was an enormous oak tree, its long branches stretching out in all directions. From the lowest branch, still out of her reach and wider than she was, hung three ropes at the end of which dangled three rectangular glass cages, each containing a face.

Esyld walked towards them until she stood before the first.

The Maiden's hair was long and flaxen, floating freely around her face before gathering like waves across the bottom of the cage. A small wreath of delicate flowers adorned her head, and her heart-shaped face was flawless with its long lashes and rosebud lips. As much as Esyld felt pulled toward the beauty of the Maiden, innocence and purity would be of no use to her—not for what was coming. She moved on to the next cage.

While still beautiful, the Mother's face had the first traces of lines around her eyes and mouth and across her brow. Her hair had darkened with age, pulled back from her face with intricate braids. Esyld understood that the Mother's energy was worldlier than the Maiden's—and while the Mother could be nurturing, she could also be fierce. The question was, would ferocity be enough? Stepping aside, she gazed up at the final face.

The Crone was heavily lined and radiated a wisdom beyond longevity. Esyld admired the wispy white hair framing the Crone's face, only just on this side of wild. By taking on the Crone, she would take on the compassion, transformation, and healing—as well as an understanding of death. Esyld nodded. Yes. The Crone would give her the strength to succeed.

As if in acceptance, the door to the cage swung open, as did the Crone's eyes. They looked left, then right, as though trying to gather their bearings, then came to rest on Esyld. She pondered what a strange sight she must be, hiding behind her shroud.

With an unexpected nervousness, she lifted the shroud and revealed herself. Not even the slightest hint of surprise or disgust swept across the Crone's face as Esyld stood before her. Instead, the face hovered out of the cage, the hair cascading as it fell out into the open. Esyld let her own vision darken as the face neared, feeling its proximity increase. The face of the Crone wrapped itself around her head, and she felt abuzz as everything the Crone had known and experienced permeated her entire being. Opening her eyes—real eyes, now—she noted how heavy it felt to blink but enjoyed the sensation.

The joy was short-lived; she felt a jolt in her core, an urgent pull from her own realm. She knew she must hurry as her surroundings disintegrated around her. First, the leaves fell from the trees, disappearing before they had the chance to reach the ground below. The branches and trunks of the trees crumbled away like ash, and the ground dropped away as though a sinkhole had opened up, encircling the grove. As the circumference of the ground on which she stood shrank smaller and smaller, Esyld closed her eyes, hoping she could depart before it was too late. She felt herself lift briefly before the sensation of falling took over, and she squeezed her eyes shut, pushing down the panic threatening to overwhelm her.

When she took a deep breath, she immediately coughed, feeling the cold water expel from her mouth. Gasping for air, she realized she was no longer falling but floating in darkness. Esyld splashed around, disoriented, trying to right herself. The circle of night sky above her confused her when she looked up, until she realized she was back in the well. She swam until her hand hit the stone wall. Then, with all the strength she could muster, she climbed until she felt the top of the well wall and hoisted herself up and over it, relieved. Lacking grace of any kind, she tumbled to the ground. Esyld pushed the wet hair back from her face and took a moment both to catch her breath and retrieve her athame. As her heartbeat settled, her hearing sharpened. She sat up with a start, looking at the trees surrounding her. There was movement through the woods, and she strained to hear the cause.

Humans.

She froze, panic immobilizing her as her imagination flooded with what they might do to her when they found her there. The wind picked up, blowing her damp hair across her eyes, and she raised her hands to touch her face. After everything, she had forgotten her appearance was now that of a mortal. Of the Crone.

When Esyld saw the first hints of torchlight pierce the darkness, she got to her feet. Leaning against the well, she felt every bit the old crone. Before she had the chance to prepare herself, men ran out of the trees and up the hill towards her. Two fell to their knees, a third draped between them. As they looked up at her expectantly, she realized the man on the ground was severely injured. The Crone's instincts kicked in, and she sank to her knees. Determining where one wound ended and the next started was a struggle, and she looked up to find the man alert and staring at her. His mouth moved, but she couldn't hear him. She gestured to one of the men beside him to make room for her, then lowered her head and held her breath as he whispered in her ear.

"They're Coming."

Chapter 2

A horse's shrill whinny pierced the evening air. Esyld knelt near the injured man, blood streaking her fingers as she desperately tried to heal him. She glanced around the base of the well and motioned to one of the other two. The man nodded silently, standing and approaching the well's base. He knelt and cut a small handful of herbs with a tiny dagger he'd pulled from behind his bearskin belt.

Returning to Esyld, he passed her the herbs and glanced at the tree line through which he and his companions had emerged. "Can you help him?" the barrel-chested man rumbled.

"Chew these," Esyld replied, passing him the leaves.

The big man did as he was told, chewing the leaves into a paste. Spitting the mixture into his palm, he returned it to the Crone.

Esyld laid her hand on the dying man's chest, spreading the paste of herbs over as many of the wounds as she could. Whispering, she steadied her hand above him, which glowed with an unearthly sapphire hue. The wounds slowly closed.

Her patient sucked in a shuddering breath and nodded. "Thank you," he breathed, struggling to stand.

Bright sparks of orange-yellow light erupted from the trees, soaring over their boughs.

The arrows thudded into the grass, the fire eating away at their shafts. "Go!" one of the men shouted at Esyld, pointing off into the trees across from the well.

Esyld nodded, hiked up her robes, and raced into the shadows of the surrounding forest. Thunder echoed from behind her, men screaming vulgarities and battle cries. Heavy breathing filled her aged ears. Esyld glanced left; one of the men—the one she'd healed—ran alongside her, his breathing labored. "This... way!" He grasped her arm, tugging her from the trail. They ducked behind an aging oak, their breath ragged in their ears.

A midnight-black horse ripped through the dense foliage, its rider bearing a wicked, serrated broadsword. The animal's breath steamed from its nostrils, white fire against the starry sky. Twelve others joined the first, some afoot. "Find the witch. Bring me her head," the first Knight roared through his encased helm.

Pressing Esyld harder against the oak, her companion passed her a small knife. She wordlessly shook her head, trying to hand it back. He clamped a soiled hand across her mouth, stopping his own breathing as the troupe of foot soldiers approached their hiding place. "Keep to the shadows," he hissed in her ear, leading her around the oak on their bellies.

The pair crept through the darkness, slithering over the cold ground like snakes, carefully pushing debris and thin, brittle branches out of their way. Horse's hooves clopped on the trail behind them. Esyld lifted her head slightly to listen, but her companion urged her forward, shoving against her calf. "Don't stop," he hissed.

"Ser Pagaene, neither of the prisoners we've captured are willing to tell us anything about the witch," another Knight said as he rode down the trail.

The Knight on the black horse sat motionless atop his steed for a moment, then twisted in the saddle and faced the newcomer. "Destroy the well."

Esyld closed her eyes, thin tears leaking from beneath her lashes. *No.* She struggled to stand, but a heavy hand pressed her back into the foliage. "Keep down and—"

"Halt!" a soldier bellowed, rushing towards them and brandishing his shortsword.

"Run, m'lady!" Esyld's companion stood to his full height of six feet and threw his dagger at the approaching soldier, catching him in the throat. The man's scream came as only a gurgle, and he collapsed to the ground.

Esyld pushed herself to her feet and bolted through the forest as Ser Pagaene's horse screeched, the man kicking it savagely in the flanks. She leapt behind another tree just as the Knight reached out torab hold of her. Ripping a fallen branch from the ground, she slammed one end into the soil.

Violet flames burst from the tip of the staff, the spell's force pushing the Knight from the beast's back. He fell with a hard thud into the dirt, rolled to his feet, and drew his sword. He leered at her, his eyes filled with fire. "King Rouaix XVII has ordered all heretics and heathens in his lands imprisoned, witch. Surrender, now."

"I will not," Esyld snarled, backing up a pace. She deflected the slash of the man's sword as the remaining soldiers hurried to surround her and cut off her escape. Clutching the branch with white-knuckled determination, Esyld faced the Knight with square shoulders, holding her head stiffly and narrowing her eyes.

"You will surrender, or you will die," Ser Pagaene growled. He slashed in a downward arc at her neck, the blade singing against the slap of the branch as it bit deeply into the soft wood.

Shoving back against the heavy blow, Esyld smashed the butt of her makeshift staff against Pagaene's chin, knocking him to the ground. The man shook himself and clambered to his feet. Blood welled from a thin scrape on the underside of his chin. He wiped it away, glaring at Esyld.

"An attack on the King's guard is an attack on the King himself. Soldiers, cut—"

A low, shrill yowl filled the brisk night air. Ser Pagaene paused, glancing at the trees as his soldiers closed ranks, weapons glinting in the moonlight. The whining howl rose in pitch, filling their ears. "Blasphemy," he hissed, his eyes widening as fear choked off his voice.

"Let me go, and they will not harm you," Esyld stated. "I warn you, knight, harm me, and they will hunt you to the end of your days."

Ser Pagaene clenched his jaw. "Any man who flees will suffer my wrath. Stand your ground." He turned briefly to glare at his twitching, nervous soldiers.

"The Great Mother will not allow my death to go unavenged, Ser Pagaene. I offer you one last chance to seek Her forgiveness." Esyld unsheathed the athame, placing the tip against her wrist. She paused, catching the man's eye. "Don't do this. You've a stout heart and a keen mind, good knight. Let me go. Please."

"I have my orders. I *must* obey my King."

Closing her eyes as a small tear escaped, Esyld flicked the blade across her wrist, letting a single drop of blood fall to the ground. "So mote it be," she whispered. From the wooded glade around them, vicious snarling and yammering echoed on the night air. Golden yellow orbs flashed in the shadows, and large, shaggy beasts padded around the encircled troupe, slathering at them. One of the soldiers turned and bolted towards the grove, screaming as he dropped his long-spear.

A bone-crunching peal ripped through the night. The soldiers huddled together, quivering. "I said stand your ground," Ser Pagaene roared. He rushed Esyld, swinging wildly with his sword. Esyld brought her staff up, deflecting the hard blow, but the sword bit through the aging wood and splintered it. A hard kick to her gut sent the old Crone to ground, clutching her midriff, gasping for breath.

Ser Pagaene scooped her athame from the ground and stuffed it into his belt, eyes gleaming. Pointing the tip of his sword at her throat, he thrust the blade downward just as a heavy threesome of shaggy fur slammed into his back, sending the man sprawling. He rolled into the soft grass, struggling to come to his knees. A paw shoved him back into the ground, a low rumbling snarl filling his ears as slobber drooled down his exposed cheek.

Clattering steel and wood surrounded Esyld as she gained her feet. The soldiers balked, backing away from the massive beast, skittering to and fro across the glade as dozens of them snapped at their heels, backing them in twos and threes against the trees. Esyld approached the largest of the animals, resting her hand on its furry shoulder and giving a gentle squeeze.

"Thank you, friend," she breathed. "It's all right. I'm fine, now. Let him go, *daos-kunne*."

The great beast swiveled its unshorn head to peer at Esyld through fiery sapphire eyes. His upper lip curled into a tight snarl, bearing canine teeth dripping with blood. Licking his muzzle, the beast whined softly, then gave a low bark and wagged its long, recumbent tail. Twin pairs of ivory-white horns jutted from the sides of its skull, curving outward to form spikes of hard bone protecting the sides of its snout. Raising its coal-black nose to the moon, the monstrous bardoul let loose its shrill yowling cry to the stars, then sat back on its haunches, tongue lolling. Esyld scratched the beast behind the ears, smiling at it. The remainder of the pack trotted toward her, nuzzling her with cold, damp noses and yipping playfully.

"Y-you speak to bardoul?" Ser Pagaene breathed, pushing himself up from the ground. "This is truly the work of evil."

"You were warned, good knight. Take the gift of your life and leave my grove." Esyld pointed off into the trees, locking her aging eyes with his. Her mouth twisted into a hard, stern line that would brook no argument from him.

Ser Pagaene panted, swallowing into his desert-parched throat, pushing his fear aside as though he might stem the flow of the tides through sheer willpower alone. He nodded, stepping away from her.

Metal scraped against leather.

The alpha bardoul turned, slathering at the jaws, and leapt at Pagaene, dragging him to the ground. Whipping its giant muzzle back and forth, the beast splattered blood across the ground as Pagaene's shriek bellowed from deep within his gut. The bardoul stepped back a pace and snarled, the man's right forearm clutched tightly in its blood-slicked jaws. Rolling onto his back, Pagaene tried to force himself to stand with a whimper, deep crimson staining his leather breastplate.

Esyld shook her head in disgust, approaching him and waving away her furry companion. She knelt and took her athame from her belt. Slicing a strip of cloth from her robes, she wordlessly bound it just below the man's shredded elbow, where the rest of his forearm, wrist, and hand had once been. "Are you incapable of using your ears? Perhaps if I shout it, you will hear me. *Do not do be so frolicsome with what you've been given, Pagaene.*"

Gritting his teeth, Pagaene forced himself to stand. "Guards, arrest this witch!"

"The man who moves in violence first is the first to die," Esyld said, glancing at the soldiers, still guarded by beasts. "Go, all of you. Return to your families and your lives. Your service to the King is over."

In pairs and then almost as one, the soldiers slinked off into the trees amongst the growls and snarling of the bardoul watching over them. Pagaene glowered at their backs, spitting curses. Grabbing the man's shoulder, Esyld guided him into the trees, away from the departing foot soldiers. "Come, we must treat your wounds."

"Take your heathen hands off me," Pagaene roared, pulling away.

Esyld shrugged. "Then walk, but you will not leave my side." She approached a spreading sycamore tree and laid her hand upon its rough bark, muttering beneath her breath.

"More spells? You truly wish to see your neck stretched, don't you?"

"Great Mother, I thank you for the gift of this child of Earth and Water, Light and Shadow. May its finger heal with the swiftness of the blessed Wind and continue to shelter and feed to Children of the Forest," Esyld said, cutting a long bough from the tree. Flicking the blade of the athame across the branch, she severed as many of the smaller, weaker twigs as she could. Placing the tip of the knife against the staff, she deftly sliced into the bark, carving half a dozen runes into the wood.

"This way, Pagaene." She led the injured Knight through the woods, along a barely perceptible path, and the great alpha bardoul kept pace with them, sloping through the twisting shadows of the early pre-dawn light.

"Halt," Pagaene pressed his back against a wide cypress, sweat stinging his bleary eyes. "I... I can go no... n-no farther." His breath wheezed from his mouth as he sank to the ground, winded.

The first few rays of the sun overhead speared through the mists and foliage, lighting their path with swaths of gold and burnished orange. Birds twittered from their lofty perches, merrily ignoring the humans and the gigantic bardoul sniffing at a feathery fern some distance away. "Get up," Esyld said. "You need travel only a few more paces. Then you may rest and make your choice."

"Why do you torture me so, witch? Why not have your beast tear out my throat?"

"That would be wrong. The Great Mother does not disregard senseless death. Every life on Her breast is sacred. Every single one. Including yours, wicked though you may be." Esyld leaned against a tree, her wrinkled lips pressed into a hard line. "I offer you healing because it is the right thing to do. Will you accept?"

"I could, and then I would leave your side and come back with a thousand men. I would hunt you down and kill you. You cannot take that risk."

"It is mine to take."

Pagaene glanced away, his lower jaw twitching as he chewed over her words. Pushing himself to his feet, he stumbled forward. "We shall see, witch." He swallowed. Then his foot caught against a small root, sending him tumbling to the forest floor and groaning in agony as his stump smashed into the ground.

Esyld bent low and grasped his other arm, pulling him back up. "This way," she muttered, guiding him into a shaded thicket.

Breaking through the dense trees and undergrowth, Pagaene froze, his mouth agape. Crystalline waves of azure water lapped against a pristine caramel shore. Snowcapped mountains rose in the far distance, clouds of puffy white straddling their crowns. A flock of ravens cawed from the sky, circling the placid lake. To their right stood a hamlet of hewn log cabins and billowing smoke from river stone chimneys. Dozens of small children scampered amongst them, giggling and laughing as they chased each other.

"Come." Esyld gently prodded the Knight towards the sleepy village. "I think you are starting to see what we… *heathens* are trying to protect from the wrath of men like Rouaix. I will take you to Freywyn's Healers, then you will have to make your choice. Do you stand in Shadow or in Light?"

Pagaene opened his mouth to respond, but Esyld turned and walked up to the village gates, ushering him through. She led him to a large log cabin on the outskirts of the hamlet, smiling as a white-robed, rosy-haired girl took the man's remaining hand and bade him rest upon a soft straw pallet.

Esyld meandered to the edge of the loch, her staff thumping against the boards of the dock upon which she stood. She gazed out across the pristine waters, lost in thought.

"Blessed Be, Honored Grandmother," a small voice called from her.

She turned and smiled gently at the girl standing before her, a pet raven balancing on the child's thin shoulder. "Blessed Be, Youngling," Esyld replied, a grin spreading across her lips.

The girl thrust out her small, pale hand. A vellum scroll lay clutched within her grasp, bound with intricately woven ribbons of elemental hues—sapphire for Water, ruby for Fire, cloud-white for Wind, russet for Earth, and a fifth ribbon comprised of the other four meant for Spirit. Esyld thanked the messenger, taking the scroll and scanning it. Once finished, she re-rolled the velum, tied it closed again with the ribbon, and sighed. *So I am summoned. So mote it be.*

Chapter 3

E syld followed the small girl to the outskirts of the village where the largest cabin in Freywyn stood on a small hillock. It held the meeting hall for the elders and was home to Muave, the High Priestess of the realm.

Esyld bowed low as the girl disappeared down a hallway. Her raven flapped his wings once in respect to the solitary robed figure standing at the head of a long table.

"Sit, Esyld. Rest after your ordeal." Muave strode to a small side table and poured water into a goblet. "Drink this. It will ease your aches and pains."

Eslyd sat, accepted the water gratefully, and took a long drink. She felt its healing powers flow through her veins, and after another sip, she sat the goblet on the table. "Why have you summoned me, High Priestess?"

"Please. Call me Muave. We've known each other much too long for formalities."

Esyld took another sip and waited.

"As you know, your familial well has been destroyed by Rouaix's men. You have no way to return to the realm within. Without your family's magic, your line will end."

Tears brimmed within Esyld's eyes at the words, but she waited without a sound.

"Rouaix's powers grow by the day. Should his dark influences become too strong, he could destroy us all. Yours is not the first Sacred Well he has ruined."

"How do we stop him? My powers will weaken without the strength of my realm."

"You must travel to Parkovia in the winter district. There you will find five stones, colored much as the ribbons binding your scroll. You must bring them here before the final blood moon of the harvest, and with proper ceremony, we shall gain the ability to rebuild the destroyed wells."

"Parkovia?" Esyld asked, trying not to yell. "How can I travel that distance? With Rouaix and his men hunting us down and my strength waning, what you ask is next to impossible."

"Nay, my dear. Your quest will be difficult, true." Muave pulled a ring from her finger. "This will help you keep your strength much longer."

Esyld stared at her right hand. An emerald band now encompassed the middle finger.

"And you shall not travel alone. My brother Carrick will travel as your guide. He is familiar with the winter district and its inhabitants."

"Carrick?"

When he stepped into the room, Esyld's eyes widened slightly in recognition of the man she had healed—who'd attempted to help her avoid Ser Pagaene and his knights. He had become quite different from the gangly boy with whom she had shared her youth.

"My Lady. It's a pleasure to see you under more civilized circumstances."

Esyld bowed. "I thought the knights found you."

A flicker of emotion crossed his face. "They killed my colleagues… my friends. When the bardoul intervened, I fled to return here so their deaths were not for naught. You saved my life. Now is my chance to repay you."

Muave refilled the goblet. "There is one other who will be joining you…" Both Esyld and Carrick looked to her as she paused. "Ser Pagaene."

Shock kept them momentarily silent. Esyld could do no more than stare, knowing that Pagaene worked for Rouaix himself.

Carrick found his voice first. "Surely you jest."

"Nay, brother. Pagaene must join you to Parkovia. It is part of his destiny."

Esyld stood, almost knocking over the goblet. "He destroyed my property. He attempted to kill me—he did kill two of your men, and almost killed your brother. How could he possibly be part of our journey? His allegiance is with the man *set to destroy us*!"

"Pagaene keeps a secret, buried deep under his dark allegiance with Rouaix. Only he can bring it to light and banish the darkness from his soul. He will not be a willing participant in your quest, at least not at first. But he must go. You will leave in three days' time." Muave tapped her staff on the tile, letting the others know that her decision was final.

Esyld and Carrick bowed and spoke together. "So mote it be."

Muave repeated the words as she watched them walk out together. The small girl appeared at her side, and her raven hopped up on the High Priestess' shoulder. Muave spoke softly, and moments later, the bird took flight and disappeared through an open window.

Chapter 4

Tirieus bolted upright, gasping for breath. His head swam with panic and last night's alcohol. He ran his hands up and down his chest, fighting off the creatures of his nightmare.

"Snakes! Snakes! They're all over... me?" The realization that he was safe in bed above his woodsmith shop finally hit.

He wiped sweat and matted-down hair from his forehead. It had been so real. Grimacing in the dark, he stretched his arms and back, wondering what time it was. When he lay back down, his pillow was damp, so he flipped it over. "Damnit, the rooster will be calling before I know it."

A gust of wind blew his drapes, and he sat up when he remembered he hadn't had drapes since… At the foot of his bed stood a robed figure, arms crossed and silhouetted in moonlight.

"Elders!" Tirieus shouted.

"We have another job for you."

"Well, come see me in the morning, and we'll discuss it."

"Now, Tirieus. Or do you want me to continue haunting your dreams with snakes?" With a flash of light and a crack of thunder, the figure disappeared.

Tirieus rolled his eyes. "You live just down the road. Why can't you knock during business hours like everyone else?" As he grumbled to himself, the door to his shop downstairs opened with a creak. He slid out of bed, grabbing a robe and his well-worn slippers before making his way down the winding staircase without the use of a candle.

He shivered when he caught movement from the corner of his eye. Turning left, he almost jumped out of his robe when he realized how close the Elders stood in the near dark. "Do you have to scare me half to death every time you need my help?"

The three Elders remained silent, their matching hooded robes covering their faces in shadow. Only the curly brown of Aram's beard set him apart from his compatriots, and he stepped forward. "There has never been a more pressing need than this."

"It's flattering," Tirieus said, striking a flint to set the fireplace at the far wall ablaze. "But you give these cryptic compliments every time."

"Behold!" Aram said, swooshing his robe to extend his arm toward Tirieus' main worktable. Upon the table sat a thick branch of dark gray. It stretched mostly straight for about six feet save one elbow-like curve near the end.

Tirieus ran a hand along the branch. "It's sturdy stock. Comes from a special tree, I'll give you that, but I have no need for it right now."

Standing over a foot taller than Tirieus, Aram peered down. "You will build an arm for Pagaene."

Tirieus squinted. "An arm?"

"We've seen your work and we know what you can do."

"Thanks." Tirieus gave a quick bow of his head. "When can I meet this Pagaene to fit him?"

Instead of answering, the three Elders stood apart and waved their arms in clockwise circles. A dull purple haze formed between the three men. When the dim light brightened into a thick cloud, Tirieus absently scratched his forehead. "What the—"

Crackles of electricity sparkled within the cloud, moving outward and forcing the purple smoke to form a circular ring the size of the Elders' waving hands. Inside the circle, a painting formed.

"Wait…" Tirieus squinted again, disbelieving. "That horse in the painting is moving." He rubbed his eyes and shook his head, but neither did he wake from a dream nor the horse stop. It trotted out of a stable toward a fierce-looking man wearing armor shiny enough to hurt Tirieus' eyes.

The view focused on the man until he filled the entire circle from the waist up. With the help of two squires, the man removed his broad, spiked, metal shoulder armor and the chainmail underneath. He rotated, saying something to the men, which caused them to burst out in laughter. The man raised a fist in the air and pumped it. The painting froze.

Aram lowered his hands, but the vision floated in the room. "This is the man who needs an arm."

"Pardon my assertion, but his arm appears fine."

Aram pointed behind Tirieus at his workbench. "Use that branch and this image to create him a battle-ready arm."

"But how—"

"Just build it. We will handle the rest."

"First thing in the morning, I'll…" Tirieus glanced back and forth between the three men, their expressions neutral. "Get started right away, eh?"

Aram nodded. "Time grows short."

"It always does with you lot." Tirieus grabbed a chisel spike and his hammer. He focused on the branch, already seeing an arm take shape from within. He studied the wood, verifying his first instincts were correct before positioning the chisel for his first cut. "I'll send for you when—"

The three Elders now stood at the far end of his worktable, staring at him intently. Aram raised an open-palmed hand and gestured at his compatriots. The other two Elders stepped forward, each placing an item before Tirieus. "These need to be stored inside the arm."

"Why?"

Ignoring the question, Aram nodded to the Elders. "Elechim holds a scroll with a prophecy so ancient, even we cannot decipher it. Newo offers a jar of opalescent pollen."

Tirieus glanced at each of the items, but neither meant anything to him. He picked up the jar and sniffed. "What is this, shiny blue cinnamon?"

Newo opened his mouth to speak, but Aram cut in first. "There are creatures in this world so powerful, no simple blade can defeat them. This pollen allows a magic user to distract its target by…"

Tirieus had no interest in the conversation, so he peered at the branch to determine how he could fit the items inside. "Why don't you just transport them to him with some spell? What did you call it when you procured me that lathe for the throne job you needed a few years back? A… a rope spell? No, a link spell. No…uh—"

"Chain spell."

"Yeah, that's the one." Tirieus snapped his fingers. "Use a chain spell and get your guy this stuff. That way I can make this arm as strong as the wood will allow."

Aram scowled. "Pagaene's head and heart are still torn. He won't know how to use these items, much less trust the others with them yet."

In unison, the other two Elders chanted, "For the glory of the Great Mother and the end of The Purity. The prophecy must be fulfilled."

It was the first time Tirieus had heard the others speak, and it sent shivers down his spine. "All right, then." Then he added a joke to cut the tension and the lump forming in his throat. "What, Aram, you didn't bring any gifts?"

Aram nodded to the branch. "Indeed. I brought the greatest gift of all. This stock, as you called it, is indeed strong. It comes from the tallest tree in the sacred grove."

Tirieus waited for more information, having never heard of the sacred grove. Aram offered no more. Tirieus snorted. "Okay, then. I'll get started."

Aram stepped forward. "The sacred grove is a powerful place, only accessible by the caretakers of the well."

Tirieus raised his eyebrow. "Great." He glanced along the branch and then at the two items offered by the Elders.

Aram choked back words, appearing flustered, which entertained Tirieus. Having spent a lifetime watching these mysterious Elders from a distance in town, it felt satisfying to see they possessed emotions just like everyone else. He rubbed his chin and looked back and forth from the items to the branch. "Yep." He nodded, running a finger down the branch until pointing to a pebble-sized knob. "I can hollow this portion out to fit those items and use a discreet clasp to hide the secret compartment. Pagaene will still be able to count on this arm as a weapon and a de facto shield, if needed. The core strength of the wood should deflect any attacks save the strongest of blows."

Aram reached into his robe and pulled out a dagger. Its handle was a silver dragon with emeralds for eyes, rubies shooting from its mouth like flames. "Add this."

"You sure?"

Aram spread his arms skyward. "There will come a moment when all the world can slide into darkness, and—"

"Wouldn't Pagaene be better served to have this at his side, then?"

Newo and Elechim looked to Aram, apparently curious about this as well. Aram nodded to the dagger. "There is more to that dagger then a quick glance can reveal. We await your call."

The three Elders evaporated, and Tirieus grabbed a cup of mead and downed it. He circled his bench once, twice, then before completing the third trip, raised his chisel and hammer.

For hours, he chipped away at the oak branch—carving, shaping—and yet the sun never came up, nor did he grow too weary to continue. In fact, the more he completed, the more energized Tirieus became. The more he drank, the less drunk he felt.

By the time he paused to refill his cup for the fourth time, Tirieus felt ready to insert the tension rods, which would allow the fingers to flex like a real appendage. By the time he refilled for a sixth time, he had carved the tiniest version of the Pagaene family crest as he could manage just below the clasp that opened the secret compartment.

As a fifth-generation woodsmith, Tirieus knew from birth he had little chance of crawling out from beneath his ancestors' shadows, but the expert craftsmanship he used to create this arm certainly felt like an accomplishment bigger than any his family had made before. He stepped back, examining the arm, the hand, the fingers, and the secret clasp. "Not bad, if I do say so myself."

"You don't have to say it yourself."

Tirieus jolted. "What the—" He spun.

From just inside the doorway, the three Elders approached. They circled the arm, grinning. Aram nodded. "You've done well, Carver."

Typically, when someone insulted Tirieus by inferring he was a simple woodcarver, it sent him over the edge, but now that he had completed his project, he felt only exhaustion. He nodded. "So, I calculate my labor costs by the hour, but I have no idea how long this night has lasted. How about we discuss a flat fee?"

The three Elders spoke in unison, still circling around Tirieus and his worktable. "Your service is your reward!" They threw out their arms, which appeared to slither like snakes onto his chest.

***

Tirieus bolted upright, gasping for breath. His head swam with panic and last night's alcohol. He ran his hands up and down his chest, fighting off the creatures of his nightmare.

"Snakes! Snakes! They're all over... me?" The realization that he was safe in bed above his woodsmith shop finally hit.

Chapter 5

J entor was a magnificent sight to behold and a befitting capital city, the crowing jewel of which was the resplendent citadel. Perched upon a dormant volcanic edifice and surrounded by the verdant green of the forests, its ebony limestone turrets glistened in the sun, shining like a beacon to all who set their eyes upon its majesty.

Above the highest turret, pennants fluttered in the breeze. Understanding their meaning rivalled the act of deciphering semaphore—a single black lion rampant on yellow indicated the permanent throne of the House of Godfrey; a blue horizontal ankh embossed on white designated the religious centre of the monastic Prime Order; and the plain red indicated King Rouaix was in residence.

King Rouaix sat in his antechambers. Standing at his side was his personal advisor, Beltor Sparlon. Rouaix struck a casual pose in his chair, his six-foot-two frame easily filling the seat. He was lithe and wiry from a life actively lived. A full beard adorned his face below alert, sparkling eyes. He saw everything, read the scene, took decisive action—a man used to not only getting his own way but planning and executing.

Before him, fatigued and quivering, knelt a knight. His hands and face were scarred with fresh welts and bruises, his tunic ripped, and he was covered in filth and blood.

The King listened intently as the guard recounted his story of their hunt for the witch, destruction of the well, and ultimate defeat by the vicious bardoul. "Be gone. I will summon you if I require more from you," the King said when the man had finished.

The guard stiffly rose to his feet and hastily retreated from the chamber.

"Where is Pagaene?" the King demanded, his voice controlled but with building rage.

"Sire, we do not know the nature of his absence. Was it forced or voluntary? Is he bewitched?" Beltor responded.

Rouaix acknowledged the advice; it was Beltor's job to summarise and offer the counterpoint. "I understand that. However, this matter is extremely delicate. He cannot—must not—let our plans fall into the wrong hands. We must find him."

"Yes, sire. Pagaene is well trained. He will not fail us if he is of sound mind."

"I agree, Beltor. My concern is that he may not be sound, may not be rational. We have to know."

"The Prime Order may help," Beltor suggested.

Rouaix gave a sharp intake of breath. "Yes, they might… they very well might. Request an audience with His Holiness. We must move forward jointly on this."

Rouaix and Beltor walked up the oversized slate steps of the temple of the Prime Order. The King took a familiar path toward the centre of the entranceway, where he placed his hand at around shoulder height on the face of the door. A faint glow came from under his palm, a short pulse of light, and then a light click. Both doors swung open, almost floating inwards, to reveal the great hall of the Prime Order. Highly polished wooden flooring reflected the light streaming through the floor-to-ceiling windows on each side of the hall. Looking up, Rouaix saw the glazed roof. The whole room was bright, spacious, a part of the outside world yet still clean, spartan, airless, and… silent.

Rouaix bowed his head slightly and moved forward, Beltor following at his left shoulder. As they entered, the doors swung closed behind them, sealing the entrance with a barely perceptible sound. The men removed their footwear—riding boots for the King and plain moccasins for the advisor—and made their way forward barefoot. At the end of the hall was a bare, raised dais on which sat a middle-aged man, legs crossed and head bowed. The men approached the dais and paused, waiting to be invited.

Beneath the man was a small padded cushion, and he wore a tight-fitting, two-piece white robe with a high collar, which was embroidered with a blue ankh. He looked up, and the King found himself gazing into familiar, piercing blue eyes. They shined within the lean, weathered face. He beckoned the men forward, indicating they should sit to either side of him. They mounted the dais, bowed slightly, then took their places.

The King looked back down the hall; early morning rays of light streamed in diagonally, creating alternating light and dark trails. He picked out specks of dust hovering in the air, dropping, cascading, floating slowly to the floor. The air was still, and not a sound disrupted the meditation of the building. He knew he had to wait.

Minutes ticked by, slowly at first, but then time became simply another aspect of the hall's meditation. The King felt his heartbeat, the pulse of blood coursing through his veins, and the shadows in the hall appeared to pulse and change with every slow, solid beat. The dust hovered, the sun ceased to move, time stopped.

Rouaix was brought out of his trance by a soft whisper.

"Excellent, Majesty. You improve with every visit." The voice was quiet, soothing, but strong and with a hint of hoarseness to it. "How do our plans develop?" The volume increased slightly, revealing a deep, resonating voice. It was firm, calming, yet decisive. The rich velvety tone assured yet left no room for dissent.

"I have come for advice, Your Holiness," Rouaix replied.

"You do not have her."

"No, Your Holiness. A member of my regiment returned this morning. His unit has disappeared, and Ser Pagaene..."

"Ser Pagaene left with the witch," the man said, his words again flatly intoned as fact. "I warned you of her abilities, Rouaix, but you failed to heed me. I am... displeased."

Rouaix dipped his head, waiting.

"And..."

"There were bardoul," Rouaix replied.

Another meditative silence followed. The sun moved; time was barely perceptible. Outside, the day continued in the busy citadel. The hustle and bustle of commerce from the marketplace, through the streets lined with shops and businesses—blacksmiths, tanners, weavers, tailors, shoemakers, the trades of a state-supported economy. These were the key elements of industry from which food, clothing, and luxuries could be grown, manufactured and made. The world turned and toiled.

His Holiness continued. "She has unleashed a more powerful spirit this time. We have underestimated her capabilities."

Silence again filled the air.

"You will need assistance."

Rouaix remained quiet. This was why he had come, why he knew he had to come.

From the back of the dais, a server appeared and moved behind His Holiness. There was a brief whispered conversation before the server disappeared. A few moments later, another figure appeared, moving to the front of the dais to kneel before them and wait. He wore the same two-piece robe but in black. A single embroidered white circle remained the only marking. The man was young, maybe twenty-three, with an exceptionally lean, cleanshaven face beneath short-cropped hair. In this kneeling position, he placed his muscular hands upon his knees, the tendons taut across the top, leading down to neatly clipped fingernails. And on this man's hands appeared the first sign of irregularity; across the tops of his knuckles were what once must have been deep wounds, now healed but heavily scarred. Rouaix imagined the hands to be greatly calloused on the underside.

"Priest?"

"Yes, Your Holiness," the Priest replied.

"Find the witch. She was last seen at the well. Track her, bring her to me. Beware, the bardoul are in her command."

"Yes, Your Holiness."

"When you find the witch, you will also find Ser Pagaene."

"Your Holiness?" he replied.

"Kill him."

Chapter 6

P agaene sat upright in bed, a heavy wool blanket pooled around his waist. He listened to the sound of children playing outside the small cabin. Though he did not know their names, he had come to know their voices during the past two days he'd spent in this bed. They were his only connection to the world on the other side of these walls.

There was the Older Brother, who insisted they play soldiers. And then there was Little Bird and the Knight, who both shrieked in laughter and argued about whose turn it was to be the King's Soldier. From the ferocity of their arguments, it sounded to

Pagaene that no one wanted to be the King's Soldier.

He used his remaining arm to push the blanket from his lap and eased his feet onto the floor. Gripping the headboard, he inhaled and pulled himself to his feet. He made it upright, but the sudden movement threw off his balance. Out of habit, he tried to put up his other arm to counteract falling to the side, but the stump of an arm ending at its elbow was not long enough to help him regain his balance. He toppled over, smashing his ribs into the headboard.

Pagaene gritted his teeth to keep from crying out. "Better," he muttered as he sat back down. Simply losing his balance was a marked improvement from the last time he'd tried to stand. and his head had spun so fast, he nearly ended up face-down on the floor.

He grudgingly admitted that his injury had healed greatly during the course of the past two days. The witch was a talented Healer. But that did not erase the fact that she had loosed the bardoul upon him and his men.

These past days spent in solitude, apart from the Healers entering the cabin to assess his progress, afforded him time to think. He expected that his men had retreated to the Fortress at Hamlin. It was half a day's ride from the old well near where they had found the witch, easy enough for them to have traversed before nightfall. And there they would have stayed, preparing and planning to continue their mission. Because King Godfrey's soldiers never failed in their missions. And they never left their brothers- and sisters-in-arms behind.

"Good morrow, good morrow." The door across the room thudded open, and a rotund Healer garbed in a crimson tunic shuffled inside. Healer was a large man, not so much in girth or height, but large in presence. His toothy grin filled the room with warmth, banishing the chill that had weighted the air.

"Good morrow," Healer repeated. He closed the door with his hip and readjusted the basket looped over his arm. "It is the appointed time again, Pagaene." He deposited the basket on the sturdy table, humming as he dug through its contents.

"Healer," Pagaene said as he shifted back onto the bed.

"You are early."

"And you and I discussed you getting to your feet without assistance," Healer replied. "The healing charms work quickly, but they do not like to be rushed."

Pagaene bristled at the word *charms*, and Healer pretended not to notice.

"Will you tell me your name today, Healer?"

Healer removed a long, narrow object from the bottom of the basket, wrapped in a heavy, cream-colored cloth from end to end. "My name is Healer," he said, "as I told you yesterday and the day you arrived. A name bestows power on the bestowed. Therefore, all of Freywyn's Healers renounce their former names and receive the name of Healer."

"I am beginning to suspect that is not the case," Pagaene said. "I suspect that you have forgotten your name."

Healer smiled in reply and perched on the edge of the bed, laying the cloth-covered object in his lap. He motioned for Pagaene to hold out his stump.

The limb was bound and bandaged from just below his shoulder all the way down to where it ended just below his elbow. Healer untied the bandage and unwound it, revealing lily-white skin creased in places from the fabric. The stump itself was pink with red tinges. There was no scar where the skin had been sutured back together.

"Good." Healer prodded the reddish skin. "Progressing well."

Pagaene winced when Healer's fingers brushed a set of red half-moons near the inside of his elbow. It wasn't a feeling of pain, more of an ache—the kind of ache that set into muscle and skin after enough healing but far before normal strength returned. "Care to explain what you brought with you?" he asked. The smell of varnish leaking from the object in Healer's lap helped him to focus on something other than the ache.

"Since your injury has healed significantly, it was arranged for a woodsmith to construct a device for you," Healer said.

His hands dropped from the stump to the parcel and

carefully unwrapped it. From the folds of cloth emerged a false arm constructed of timber and leather. The hand had five fingers, complete with brass joints where the knuckles would be and grooves on the inside of the fingers and palms for grip. A net of well-oiled leather strings encased the back of the hand and the wrist joint before disappearing halfway up the forearm.

"It will take a fair amount of practice for you to apply this on your own," Healer cautioned as he eased the divot at the top of the device around Pagaene's stub, then fastened thick leather straps around his upper arm. "And you should not wear it for long periods of time at first."

Pagaene stared in wonder at the false arm. He cautiously reached for the smooth surface, as if nervous that it might disappear should he move too fast. His fingers brushed the cool wood and traced the lines of leather.

Healer let out a small chuckle. "Try it out."

"What do you mean?"

In response, Healer held out his hand and gestured towards it with his chin.

Pagaene concentrated on the outstretched palm. He contracted the muscles in his upper arm, bending the elbow ever so slightly, and raised the device. When he stretched to touch Healer's palm, the fingers uncurled before bending around the other man's hand. "In the name of the Prime Order," he muttered in astonishment.

"Yes, Tirieus performs supreme work." Healer's smile widened until it nearly split in half. He placed the cloth and bandage inside the basket. "You should remove it in no more than an hour's time. Your arm will need time to adjust to the device."

Pagaene nodded, his fingers still running up and down his new arm.

There was a knock on the door, which opened a second later, and both Esyld and Carrick stepped through the doorway.

"Blessed be, Honored Grandmother," Healer said and bowed his head.

"Blessed be, Healer," Esyld replied. "We seek an audience

with Ser Pagaene."

"As you wish," he said.

Healer gave Pagaene a farewell nod before slipping through the open doorway. Carrick shut the door firmly behind him.

Pagaene's hand recoiled from his new arm, and his lips curled into a sneer. "What do you want, witch?" he sneered.

Esyld did not respond. Instead she watched Carrick bring over a chair from the other side of the room. She gave him a kindly smile before sitting. "How is your arm, Ser Pagaene?"

"Missing," he replied.

A sliver of a frown creased the Crone's face, and she looked down at her hands clasped in her lap. "I cannot regret the action that led to the loss of your arm," she said. "The bardoul acted to protect me. However, I feel regret that you are now scarred for the remainder of your life."

Pagaene spat on the floor.

Carrick took a menacing step forward, but Esyld placed a hand on his arm. He stepped back behind Esyld's chair, and his gaze seared into the other man's very flesh.

"In one day's time, we will begin a journey to Parkovia in the winter district," Esyld said. "There we will gather the Five Sacred Stones in order to restore the magic in the land."

"The winter district," Pagaene mused. "The journey alone will last a month, and you will spend weeks searching for the stones. Longer, if you encounter the road's inhabitants or the king's soldiers stationed along it. You may not even return should those dangers prove too much for an old witch and a broken soldier." He let out a barking laugh. "I wish you good fortune on your journey."

"The High Priestess of the Realm has declared that you will accompany us to Parkovia," Esyld said. "And Healer has assured us you will be well enough to travel in the morning."

Pagaene's jaw dropped. He struggled to believe what he just heard. "Say that again."

"The High Priestess has decided you will join us when we leave tomorrow," Carrick said through clenched teeth.

"There is no reason for me to go with you," Pagaene said. "There is—however—a very good reason for me not to." He held up the false arm. "I will not help you."

"The High Priestess has decreed it," Esyld said. "So mote it be." She stood, ending the conversation.

Pagaene balled his fist in the blanket as he watched her and Carrick walk across the room and out the door. *How dare that witch and her kind think I would go with them?* he thought. Witches and magic had to be destroyed. It would be too much to hope that they might be killed along the road.

He paused on that thought. This little village did not have its own soldiers and certainly could not afford to send its men on a months-long journey to the winter district. The witch Esyld and the broken soldier, Carrick, would be traveling alone. And they would be vulnerable to a surprise attack.

If Pagaene could get to the Fortress at Hamlin, where his men were undoubtedly planning their next course of action, he could lead them onto the road to Parkovia, and they could lie in wait. The witch might be strong enough to call the bardoul, but no matter how strong a witch was, sleep left everyone vulnerable.

"Yes," he said under his breath. "I cannot traverse the distance on foot, but there are plenty of horses." He would simply wait for the cover of nightfall. Then he would steal a horse and ride until morning.

Pagaene touched the device on his arm. A part of him wondered what Healer would think in the morning when he entered to find Pagaene's bed empty. Healer had been kind to him, and he was a good man despite practicing magic. Should King Godfrey's plan to eliminate magic and witches from the realm come to fruition, Healer would be among those in the crosshairs.

He shook his head hard, knocking those thoughts from his mind. Now was not the time to dwell on such things. Now was the time to rest and to prepare. For he had one chance to escape, and he could not afford a single mistake.

***

Carrick leaned against the outside of the cabin where Pagaene rested. He tugged his hat down low to block the rays from the setting sun, listening intently to the sounds of the village. Fires crackled in hearths as quiet conversation seeped through open windows and doorways. Livestock crunched on dry hay. Wind whispered through the leaves still clustered thickly on the tree branches. The wind carried with it smells of cooked meat, animal dung, and damp earth.

His stomach rumbled.

A shadow crossed his limited field of vision, and he pushed back the hat. The Youngling stood before him, dressed in a simple brown frock and carrying a small basket. She held the basket out toward him, and Carrick took it with a grateful smile. "Thank you, Youngling," he said.

She smiled in response before striding back down the center of the village towards Muave's cabin.

Carrick dug through the basket and produced a soft roll of bread. He set the basket on the ground at his feet, then tore at the bread with his teeth. Then he settled back against the cabin and prepared to wait.

Chapter 7

"As you wish, Your Holiness," said the Priest. He removed his hand from beneath the shard of athame and wrapped a starched cloth around the fresh cut. His Holiness' presence faded from the Priest's mind.

After receiving his orders, the Priest had retreated to his quarters to prepare—and also to confer with His Holiness privately. His request couldn't be spoken in front of the king, and it had been granted.

The Priest stood from the floor of his quarters and removed the ceremonial robe, donning a simpler one. His hands shook when he thought of what was to come. His Holiness had granted him permission to use their enemies' tactics against them. It had been one year and twenty-seven days since he had last been permitted to use magic.

The third stone up from the corner behind his cot had stuck in place from lack of use, but with the right leverage and an ounce of desperation, he pried it free. Wrapped in a white but dust-encrusted cloth, inside the hollowed stone was the handle of the Priest's broken athame.

He held the handle and shard together and spoke the name of his long-relinquished home. "Freywyn."

A fury of wind crashed through his chambers, knocking over his desk and taking his mattress for a spin. The wind picked him apart, piece by piece, until he had no form but the thought of Freywyn.

A few dozen leagues away, just outside the town, the Priest rematerialized beside a young pine. He picked some needles that had gotten in the way of his spell out of his palm and forearm. The moon hung halfway through its path across the sky, though oddly low for the season. Muave was in Freywyn, then, beckoning the moon to bend itself to whatever mess she and her elders concocted.

A pack of beasts howled to the north. The Priest had little knowledge of creatures but great knowledge of forests and undergrowth. Plants of peculiar properties fascinated him, as well as those surviving environments in which other plant life withered. The Priest gripped the trunk of the pine beside him. It was not so young as he had thought—three rings and counting—but the soil by the road had been drained from some youngling witch practicing in secret, depriving the poor pine of its allotted nutrients.

Upon noticing a circle of painted stones and a yew wand, the Priest congratulated himself on his deduction. He squeezed the pine trunk harder, its rough bark breaking into his skin. He mustn't become distracted from the task at hand. The roots of the pine did not extend far, but they brushed against the roots of a five-ring pine, which touched a twenty-ring pine, which touched ten others, and through this method, he slipped his perception into all the pines surrounding Freywyn.

It was a trick Muave herself had taught him all those years ago, but Carrick had been better at it. Carrick was always the better one.

The Priest instructed the pine to make a seat for him of its branches, and it complied. Though it was not terribly more comfortable than sitting on the ground, the priest knew Muave favored dirt-magic and might sense his presence should he linger on the earth itself.

By the time the moon brushed the tops of the forest, the Priest was quite cold and somewhat regretted not just scrying for when they left, but Muave was the paranoid sort who might have manipulated such magic to misinform and make a fool of him. It was better to see with his own eyes.

Ser Pagaene rode out from the town on horseback, alone. Pagaene must have been a traitor indeed to be allowed to roam freely in these lands. Just as Pagaene turned the bend, two more riders left Freywyn—Carrick and the Crone. The Priest's grip on the pine tightened, reopening his latest cut.

So Carrick was one of the prophesied three. A decade-long disdain burned through the Priest's arm and into the tree. The pine cried out, and he released it.

"My apologies, young one," said the Priest. "But I have one more sacrifice in mind for you this night."

He imbedded the handle of his athame into the pine and said, "Flight." Sections of ground radiating out from the tree collapsed as it retracted its roots. The branches twisted into two flat limbs to help pull itself from the ground. Shorter roots gathered together to form two stubby limbs with claws, and the rest of its roots fanned out like tail feathers.

The crown of the three-ring pine split to form a beak. The confused creature let out a silent shriek through its functionless mouth. The Priest mounted his tree-bird and bade it fly low above the other pines, following the three on horseback.

Ser Pagaene dismounted at the crossroads and guided his horse beside him into the northern woods. No sooner had he disappeared from sight than Carrick and the Crone emerged from the shadows to follow Pagaene's tracks.

The Priest knew that shortcut through the forest led to Hamlin. Perhaps Pagaene was not a traitor after all, but it was no concern. A declared traitor as collateral damage would bring the Priest no admonishment from His Holiness. He landed his tree-bird and disenchanted it, where it collapsed into a mound of sticks and decay. Kneeling in the undergrowth, he called to mind one of his favorite flowers to focus the spell. His Holiness would likely admonish him for using magic to excess, but he could not pass over the opportunity to lay Carrick low.

***

Ser Pagaene halted at the edge of a meadow coated in a soft blue flower with opalescent pollen. It was hardly the climate or season for such vibrant flowers, and more to the point, this was supposed to be a forest. His horse bucked and strained against the reins.

"Don't go in," said Esyld.

Ser Pagaene startled and dropped the reins. His horse bolted south, nearly trampling Carrick, who sidestepped behind a tree to save himself. "Oh, are these flowers poisonous to witch-folk, then?" said Ser Pagaene with a victorious smirk. He took three quick steps backward into the meadow. The opalescent pollen stained his boots, and a scent of cinnamon and milkweed filled his nostrils.

The flowers cushioned his fall when he looked up to see the bluest sky. Ser Pagaene sat on a plane of stone, scattered arches, and crumbed corners of buildings, all the same grey. He leaned back to bask in the sight of the open sky.

"You idiot," said Esyld.

Ser Pagaene closed his eyes. "Why must you ruin such a nice day?"

"It's not a nice day," said Esyld. "It's a spell, and we've got to get out before—"

"In the name of the Great Mother," said Carrick. "Where are we?"

"I told you to stay in the forest," said Esyld.

"I did," said Carrick. "But I looked away for a second, and all of a sudden, the flowers were sprouting around my feet."

"Then the caster is still here," said Esyld. She strode toward Ser Pagaene and kicked his arm.

"Ow," said Pagaene, though it hardly hurt. He raised both arms to examine them and smiled at the sight of his missing hand, when it had previously brought nothing but a scowl. "What's going on here?"

"Some kind of dreamscape," said Esyld with a frown. "The trick is to fulfill its purpose and not give in to fantasies or loops."

"How do we know its purpose?" asked Carrick.

"That would be up to the caster, I imagine," said Esyld.

"You said the caster was nearby?" said Pagaene.

Carrick took a step back. It sounded like Pagaene might have been about to participate in a helpful manner, but that would be preposterous.

"Correct," said Esyld. "Unless Carrick is lying about how he came to join us in our dream."

"You don't trust me?" said Carrick.

"I'm merely being thorough," she replied, not bothering to meet his gaze.

"The caster was nearby to ensure all three of us were caught," said Pagaene. "Since the three of us were supposed to be traveling to Parkovia for your stones, it isn't a far stretch to assume the caster wishes to prevent us from this goal."

"And how is that helpful?" said Carrick. He'd wandered to an archway and inspected it for runes or a crafter's mark, finding none. In fact, the archway seamlessly melded into the stony plane.

"Who do you know who would be interested in stopping your little mission, and who has boundless resources?" asked Pagaene.

"The king," said Esyld, her anger singeing the words on their way out.

"Again, how is that helpful?" said Carrick.

"It's more helpful than asking how everything is helpful,"

snapped Pagaene, brandishing his arm toward the man.

"Those flowers," said Esyld. "Do you think it could be your brother?"

"I don't have a brother," said Pagaene. "Let alone do I have a witch-brother."

"Idiot, she means *my* brother. And she's wrong," said Carrick. "Sure, he holds a grudge against me, but he'd have no reason to impede our quest, let alone work for the king."

"You broke his athame, Carrick," said Esyld. "There's no telling what hatred he harbors."

"I didn't know you knew that," said Carrick. He looked to the distorted horizon and tried to find the words to explain himself.

Ser Pagaene sniggered. "Broke an athame! You're a better witch-hunter than most of my men."

"I—I didn't make him the way he was," said Carrick. "I did what was needed."

"So mote it be," said Ser Pagaene with a hoot.

Esyld frowned and crossed her arms. "We've taken some leaps in our thinking, but let us assume it is your brother. I studied under Muave with him. When we did labyrinths, his often required a random, drastic action to escape, which was impossible to discover without him explicitly explaining it. But he claimed that, so long as a way out exists, it's a proper labyrinth."

"And you're hoping he still employs his school-day pittances?" said Carrick.

"What else have we to go on?" said Esyld.

***

A random, drastic action, thought Ser Pagaene with his widest grin yet. He sprinted toward the flickering horizon. The farther he ran, the farther the horizon seemed to stretch. He ran farther, each stride building his confidence. The horizon flashed blue, then grey. At times, it seemed both, then for a horrific moment, it was neither. Not blue or grey or black or white, but a nauseating absence.

Ser Pagaene picked himself off the ground. He had

returned to wearing the false arm, but the forearm was rusted and the fingers chipped. He recognized the house of Healers and the stables from which he'd stolen a horse. He was in Freywyn, and it was all on fire.

Healer stumbled out of the house and collapsed on the ground. Ser Pagaene rushed to his side, but his hands passed right through his friend.

A robed Priest with scarred hands passed through the burning stables, neither flinching at the heat nor appearing singed in anyway. Ser Pagaene knew he was still in the dreamscape.

"Is this not what you also desire, knight?" said the Priest.

"I know the war against the witches is necessary. We cannot allow such chaos to run rampant," said Ser Pagaene, doubting his own words. "But must it be like this?"

"I'm going to tell you a little secret," said the Priest. "I'll play with your conscience and even the odds. It'll be fun."

"I am not some tool," said Ser Pagaene.

"Of course not, dear Knight," said the Priest. "But even so, you might like to know that while you're off gallivanting for stones, Freywyn will burn."

"I am loyal to the King," Ser Pagaene said through clenched teeth. "Telling me this will change nothing."

"We shall see," said the Priest. A great wind washed away the smoldering massacre, and Ser Pagaene awoke in the forest. A moment later, Esyld and Carrick awoke as well.

"Good thinking, Pagaene," said Esyld.

"Did either of you—between the jump and waking up, did you…" muttered Carrick.

"It's best not to discuss private visions," said Esyld.

With his companions so disoriented, Ser Pagaene seized his opportunity. He jumped to his feet and sprinted north. He was loyal to his king; he would prove it.

Esyld snapped her fingers. Tree branches swooped him up and passed him from one tree to the next and back to the witch's feet. "Friend," Esyld said to the tree, "hold this Knight in your arms. And if you would be so kind, shelter us from wind and rain, for we shall rest here."

Ser Pagaene found it quite easy to fall asleep. There was no sense in struggling. More opportunities would present themselves, and the strong, smooth branches were surprisingly comfortable.

***

From the base of her tree-friend, Esyld watched Carrick toss and turn on his bedroll. In saying they should not share their visions, she'd ignored the Crone's advice. Her vision of how Carrick had come to break his brother's athame made her uncertain about their journey together. There would be no sleep for her this night. She needed to meditate on what she had learned.

Chapter 8

Esyld dozed, unmoving, at the base of the tree. It had been her plan to stay awake, but somehow she's been tugged into the swirls of unconsciousness. The voice calling to her was foreign and unfamiliar, its sweetness like the caress of a familiar touch soothing the edges of her mind.

She floated above the trees, drifting slowly away from Carrick, who tossed and turned in his bedroll, and Ser Pagaene, who had somehow dozed off in the grasp of the thick tree limbs. What unsettled her, however, was the feeling of another presence. Someone was with her, just beyond the edges of her consciousness, and each time she reached out, it danced away.

"I can feel you there. What have you done to me?" she demanded.

Calm yourself.

Like cool water rushing over the heat of her body, the voice filled her with a sense of peace. It carried her over the tops of the trees, and her spirit drifted through the winter district—small villages of townspeople bustling around the markets, gathering wood, so used to the temperatures dropping lower the farther north one traveled.

As Esyld moved over the villages, she dipped down into trees and flinched. Somehow, her spirit dodged a snow-covered sycamore. "How much farther?"

Patience.

The clearing broke, and Esyld had just enough time to be taken aback by the magnificence of Parkovia. Even this early, people had risen to start about their day. A mother tightly grasped the mitten-clad hand of a small child, who kept looking back at a dog sitting outside the butcher's shop, its tail swooping through the fine blanket of snow upon the ground.

Esyld soared over the Cathedral of Ghest. A nun, whose only bit of exposed skin was her pale face, cheeks blood-red from the cold, looked up from where she headed toward the gate, as if she could almost see Esyld.

About two miles outside the town, Esyld slowed to a halt at the mouth of a large cave. Even with no body, she felt a gust of hot air blow from the darkness. In all her years, she had seen many things, but the feeling nestling its way into her chest like thousands of bees buzzing behind her rib cage told her to turn back. At this moment, however, she could not control her actions. Her spirit moved forward into the cave, and as another gust of heat enveloped her and darkness threatened to swallow her, she protested.

"Wait—"

I am here.

The words alone seemed to lift a large measure of unease from Esyld's chest. Once inside, it didn't take her long to adjust to the dark. In the center of the cave sat a large opening in the ceiling, where a shaft of sunlight fell amidst crystals of snow blown in on the wind. They danced in the sunlight before touching down onto the cave floor.

What occupied the majority of small cave space made Esyld tremble from the inside. A dragon half the size of Parkovia itself lay nestled in a ball. The warm air she'd felt earlier blew even hotter now, intensified when the creature inhaled and exhaled. Its white scales camouflaged it well, but the dried blood staining its claws could not be hidden.

"Great Mother," Esyld exclaimed.

The dragon's eyes flew open, dark slits in a sea of green narrowing when they found her hovering in the entranceway. A deep growl rumbled in its chest like thunder. As the dragon stood, the cave shook, bits of rock tumbling and tuffs of snow puffing down through the hole in the ceiling. The beast flexed its claws, and the transparent wings on its back shivered but didn't expand. Smoke curled from its nostrils, and the heat melted what ice and snow had collected on the ground and the walls of the cave. Just as the creature opened its mouth to expel the river of fire burning in its chest, Esyld's eyes flew open.

Carrick crouched next to her, his brow furrowed. "Are you all right?"

Esyld stumbled to her feet. She was in the clearing. Their bedrolls and belongings had been packed, and she turned around to find Ser Pagaene still in the tree, glowering down at her.

"I'm here," she muttered. She ran her hands over her face and down her neck, wiping away the sheen of sweat. There was no doubt in her mind that the Great Mother had shown her that vision. She closed her eyes and tried hard to remember the feeling of the Mother's presence. The echo of her words in Esyld's mind. All she could muster was the horrible vision of the white dragon.

"You seemed like you were having an awful dream." Carrick's voice brought her back, but Esyld thought she still felt the heat of the dragon's breath against her skin.

"I don't think it was a dream at all, Carrick. I think it was our reality." Instead of waiting from him to respond, she turned to the tree holding Pagaene and addressed it. "Friend, would you bring him closer?"

Pagaene seemed at ease in his captivity. Eyes bright,

darting between Esyld and Carrick, he seemed to have lost no sleep. "Let me go. When I get down from here—"

"You must release your illusions." Esyld gave a small sigh.

"I've had time to separate the dream world from this one. You need not worry."

Carrick came to stand by Esyld. With one hand on his chin, he regarded the soldier held in the tree's grasp. "You seemed rather adamant yesterday. How can we trust him, Esyld?"

Esyld thought of what possibly lay in wait for them at Parkovia. "We might not have a choice. Friend, let him go."

Pagaene landed with a thud at the base of the tree. Esyld gave a small bow, thanking the tree for its service. Carrick reached down and grabbed Pagaene's arm, helping him to his feet.

Esyld noted the rough way Carrick handled Pagaene and re-membered her vision. In light of it, how could she trust either companion?

Chapter 9

"**I** think this is a very bad idea," Carrick hissed.

"I heard you the first time." Esyld snapped, her eyes never leaving the sleepy hamlet before them. The village was nestled in a valley, the green hills that surrounded the settlement cradling it like the arms of a giant. It was beautiful, welcoming, and completely exposed.

"We agreed we should journey through the forest—"

Esyld turned to him and scowled, her eyes burning from the folds and wrinkles of the Crone. She indicated her borrowed face with a sweep of her hand. "*We* agreed that we need to go among the locals to hear what gossip flows with the ale."

Her tone brooked no argument, so Carrick settled into a

sullen silence as the trees fell away and were replaced by the farmsteads and fields surrounding the village. Ser Pagaene's shoulders shook with silent laughter a few paces ahead. The Knight rode point because he was less likely to bolt when he knew Esyld was watching, but it didn't make Carrick feel any better about taking him with them into a place they couldn't be sure was friendly to their cause, not to mention their kind.

Fireflies floated lazily around them, heralding the coming night. The fields they passed lay empty; the day's toil was over, and the time for enjoying the fruits of labor had come. As they entered the village, a warm glow spilled from the windows and open doorways of every dwelling, friends and family gathering to share a few words. Occasionally, a person raised a hand in greeting to the trio, but most people just went about their regular lives. They didn't act like people who were worried about conspiracies or the threat of violence, so they probably didn't harbor any of the king's knights, but until Carrick was certain, he would not drop his guard.

Worrying over the machinations of the townsfolk was a welcome distraction from his vision the night before. He knew better than most that his brother was treacherous and nothing he'd shown them could be trusted, but he couldn't help from wondering if the warning nonetheless held some truth. His sister believed Esyld would complete the quest, but she had been wrong before…

"Carrick!"

The sound of his name snapped him back to attention. Without his notice, the horses had carried them to a hitching post outside a tavern. The sky above now only hinted at sunset, and the light of the fireflies was supplemented by a scatter of stars against the darkening sky. Esyld and Pagaene were already busy tying up their mounts. The rest of the posts remained empty. Not a popular destination for visitors, then.

"Are you coming, or are you going to stay on that horse all night long?" Pagaene finished his knot and stood with his arms crossed and one eyebrow raised.

"Yes, of course." Carrick slid awkwardly to the ground and stifled a groan, his legs and back stiff from long hours swaying on horseback. He might have been able to summon the horses to him when they'd scattered after their strange experience in the meadow, but the art of wielding beast magic didn't make a saddle any more comfortable. Esyld healed the worst of his wounds after the knights had attacked, but his body hadn't finished knitting itself back together, and his scars ached with the memory.

"I, for one, am looking forward to a night in a bed. Not that a magic tree wasn't comfortable, but I'll take a bed with a pillow any night!" Pagaene leaned toward the tavern's open doorway and sniffed the air in appreciation. "Not to mention a hot meal."

"Watch what you say, knight," Esyld reminded him. "We don't know who might be listening."

"Which is exactly why this is a stupid risk," Carrick groused. "I still don't understand—"

"You don't need to understand," Esyld interrupted. "You just need to help me get inside. I feel like I'm a hundred and fifty years old." She gave Carrick a pat on the shoulder, but smile remained tense and tight.

Ser Pagaene looked thoughtful for a moment, then offered her his arm. "Come along, Grandmother," he said a little too loudly. "Let's find a nice place by the fire for you."

Carrick offered her his elbow and mumbled, "Laying it on a little thick, don't you think, knight?"

"Yes, good and thick. Just like the rabbit stew I smell! Lighten up, Carrick."

When they reached the tavern door, Pagaene dropped Esyld's arm to allow them all to pass over the threshold. The room was full of farmers and other hardworking peasants enjoying ale and a meal at the end of a long day. A few people regarded them as they passed but turned away just as quickly and returned to their neighborly banter. In the gentle, perpetual warmth of this district, the merry blaze dancing in the stone fireplace wasn't necessary, but the happy glow illuminated a small empty table in the corner.

Carrick helped Esyld to a chair and watched Pagaene from the corner of his eye, who walked the other direction. The Knight swaggered to the bar and sidled up to an empty stool, the barkeep welcoming him with a grin. Carrick couldn't make out anything they said from across the room, but his stomach dropped when he saw the Knight gesture to their place in the corner. His glanced quickly around the room, looking for hidden weapons or treacherous figures. When he found none, he watched Pagaene and the barkeep exchange a few more words before the Knight clapped the other man on the shoulder and sauntered back.

"What was that all about?" Carrick couldn't hide the suspicion in his voice.

"I was ordering us some dinner," Pagaene answered, smiling as a serving girl brought over three frothy glasses of beer. "And some refreshments."

"You're in a good mood," Esyld said with a smirk.

"I'm just happy for a chance to talk to somebody! You've both been quiet as the grave all day." The Knight raised his glass and tipped his head in a silent toast before taking a few huge gulps of ale.

Carrick caught Esyld's eye for a moment before she turned her attention to her drink. Though he couldn't read her expression, he knew she must have been fretting as much as he did over the vision she'd received. If they had seen the same thing, her silence and peevishness made sense, though leading them into potential danger did not. It made him wonder at her early-morning dream. The serving girl returned with three healthy portions of stew, and the aroma chased all thoughts of visions from his mind.

They ate their meal in companionable silence, which gave Carrick a chance to listen to the local gossip. Someone there celebrated the birth of a child. Another group discussed their plans for taking goods to market together two weeks hence. It all sounded like the normal rhythms of country life, until one gruff voice rose over the din.

"I'm having the same problem with my sweetroot crop," said a burly farmer to his friends. "There's never the right amount of water in the soil! When the plants are young, the soil is dry, and they wither. And then when I finally get some roots out of the ground, they're molding."

"That's the price we pay for trying to live on this land," agreed another man, his salt-and-pepper beard quivering while he spoke. "In the old days, we never had these problems."

"What are you saying?" asked a third.

"I'm saying that something has changed, and not for the better." The man looked around the room before hunching his shoulders and leaning in to speak in low tones. Carrick couldn't make out any more of the conversation, but what he'd heard made him uneasy. There were reports of a blight in the lands near Jentor, but they were far from the capitol now.

He turned back to his companions to see if they'd heard the exchange and realized the bartender now stood at the edge of their table. Two young men—probably the man's sons, given their black hair and strong features—stood on either side of him. When he saw fire in their eyes, Carrick's hand automatically went for the comforting weight of his weapon. He felt the tingle of Esyld's gaze as she regarded his action, and he dropped his hand.

"Good evening, gentlemen," Esyld said as she finished the last of her ale. "Come to offer me a refill?"

The tension in their corner of the room hadn't bled into the rest of the chatter yet. The bartender put his meaty hands onto their table and leaned in, speaking softly. "I think it's time for you to move on."

"And why would that be?" Carrick couldn't help but bristle. He stole a glance at Esyld, who blotted her mouth with a cloth napkin before folding it next to her empty bowl.

"You've finished your meal, so it's time to go. We don't want any trouble," the barkeep continued in a low rumble. "But we don't take kindly to witches."

"Witches, you say?" Pagaene asked loudly. Mock surprise plastered itself on his face, and he made a show of standing up abruptly. The clatter of his upset chair ensured everyone now paid them their full attention. The room hushed, and every face turned toward them. The bearded man made another hushed comment to the table of farmers, their muscles coiled for action.

Carrick was instantly on his feet and took a defensive

stance. It had been stupid and careless to sit so far from the exit, and now an entire tavern of suspicious people stood between them and the door. He leveled a smoldering glare at Pagaene. "I told you it was a mistake coming here," he said under his breath.

"It was a test," Esyld replied. "I had to know who I could trust."

"I could have told you we couldn't trust Pagaene."

"I wasn't testing Pagaene. I already knew *he* would betray us." The hint of amusement in her voice sounded utterly out of place. "I was testing *you,* Carrick."

Chapter 10

C arrick's eyes widened with the weight of Esyld's words. For a split second, she thought he might revert scolding her about what a bad idea this had been. But then his eyes narrowed, and he leaned forward, lurched toward Esyld, and enveloped her in his arms. The moment he touched her, she knew protected her now as he had before—just as Muave had asked him to do. Her vision of his betrayal would not come to pass. Not today.

"Predictable is so boring, Pagaene," Carrick said.

"You didn't think I was going to let you lot drag me to the winter district, did you?" Pagaene asked.

Esyld surveyed the room. A small group of locals, led by

the burly farmer, had gathered in the middle of the tavern and now prowled toward the table, forming a human wall behind the barkeep. A very human wall, Esyld thought.

"I suggest you—whatever you are—get out of here and keep your evil magic away from our land," the farmer snarled.

Esyld knew they needed to get out of there with Pagaene. And clearly, the use of magic would only deepen the townspeople's belief that the witches had caused the blight. Clearly, it would only help their quest to discover the true cause for the dying crops.

Pagaene backed away from the table, immersing himself in the bristling group of farmers. "I would agree with the kind barkeep, here. I think you two should be on your way."

Esyld felt Carrick's temper bubble beside her, and she squeezed his arm, signaling for him to be silent. "We thank you for your hospitality, kind sir. We'll be on our way," she said.

Carrick nodded, pushed Esyld behind him, and backed toward the door, keeping her grizzled Crone body between him and the wall. She sensed the angry group's desire to attack, radiating from them like the heat from the fire. She tried to remain calm so as not to add to Carrick's frantic heartbeat, which she felt pounding through his back.

When they reached the door, Esyld spoke softly. "Get us outside."

Carrick turned his head toward her and, barely moving his lips, said, "What about Pagaene? We can't let him get away."

"Trust me."

Carrick pushed back against the door, keeping his eyes on the mob as he and Esyld slipped outside. As soon as they reached the dark shadows of nearby trees, he turned toward her again. "Now what?"

But Esyld was already chanting, twisting the green emerald ring Muave had given her as tightly as her grizzled fingers would allow. Curious about the light, fireflies approached as twilight breathed its last breath into the night air.

Then Pagaene burst out of the tavern door and ran toward

them. His face was screwed up with surprise and anger, but could not speak. Carrick seized his arms and pinned them behind his back as Esyld smiled and let out a long breath.

"What did you do?" Carrick said, realizing the Knight gave no resistance.

"Like I said, I knew I couldn't trust him, so I used Muave's ring to put a silent cuff on his wooden arm when he walked me into the tavern. It's one of the many gifts the ring possesses. As soon as I call him with the chant, the cuff drags him to me like a leash." Pagaene writhed but could not move away from Esyld. "And I gagged him, for good measure." She winked at Pagaene.

Carrick burst into laughter.

They moved farther into the trees, Pagaene following obediently. When they heard voices coming out of the tavern, Carrick held his hand up to Esyld, signaling for her to stay hidden as he slipped away. He returned a few minutes later with their horses, and they walked silently into the cool cloak of the forest.

"How long will the cuff and gag remain?" Carrick asked.

"I'm not sure. The ring is new to me, but it still feels warm. So a while yet, I think," Esyld said.

They walked deep into the forest, ensuring they were well out of the town and away from danger. Heavy gray clouds hung in the sky, visible through the occasional opening in the canopy. Esyld stopped and searched with her mind's eye to assure herself this was a safe place to stop for the night. The old Crone's body tired easily. They would need some rest for their trek to Parkovia.

"I guess I'm wondering why you didn't use it to just get us all out of there. Those men were out for blood," Carrick said as he pulled blankets from the horses.

"I don't think using powers in front of them would have helped our cause. They believe our magic spas the earth and causes the blight," Esyld said.

"That's preposterous," Carrick said.

"Yes, but someone or something is depleting the earth's power at a larger magnitude," Esyld said.

"And that's why Muave called you."

"Yes. But the restoration of the wells took precedence. It is difficult to find and defeat a darkness without power of our own. She suspects the imbalance has something to do with the king. Since they raised the flag of the Prime Order at equal standing to the House of Godfrey, things have felt unstable. You heard the talk in the tavern. The blight seems to be emanating from Jentor."

"So we're going Parkovia to try to figure it out. It feels a little blind, doesn't it?" Carrick asked.

Esyld regarded him. Muave hadn't told him about the stones, only that he had to guide her and Pagaene. She wondered if there was a reason Carrick should not know. The tavern incident proved he could be trusted. She put her head in her hands, feeling the wrinkled skin around her eyes and pushing the bent fingers through the course gray hair. She felt exhausted and overwhelmed.

"We're going to have to take turns sleeping to keep watch on Pagaene." She glanced at his slumped body nestled in the blanket she had given him, wondering why he had to make this journey with her. Was the Great Mother trying to tell her the reason with the vision of the white dragon?

"You sleep first, Esyld," Carrick said.

She nodded and drifted into a dark, dreamless sleep.

***

Esyld woke to a scuffle. Carrick wielded his athame in one hand, the other on Pagaene's arm.

"I just have to piss," Pagaene grunted.

The gag had worn off, so Esyld knew the cuff was gone now, too. She didn't want to continue binding him with Muave's ring; she wanted to save as much power as she could for Parkovia. Recognizing, finding, and retrieving the stones would be difficult.

After releasing Pagaene, Carrick sat with Esyld, never taking his gaze from the knight. "I guess he had more beer than I thought."

They waited until he finished and lay down again. His alacrity surprised Esyld. The binding along with the beer must have exhausted Pagaene, and soon his snoring came as regularly as the soft beat of the forest nightlife.

"You should get some rest now. I'll watch him," Esyld said.

Carrick nodded and lay down, still watching Pagaene. Esyld heard the red fox resume his prowling and the mice their scampering on the forest floor.

"Why don't you trust me?" Carrick asked, his voice low.

Esyld drew a long breath. "I just had to be sure. But I should have known Muave chose you to accompany me for a reason."

"If it was your vision that caused doubt, remember it was my brother controlling what you saw," Carrick said, his voice unsteady.

Esyld could feel his pain in the darkness. Carrick and Muave's brother had somehow lost his way and his purpose in Jentor. He had been warped by some force, perhaps the same power depleting the land. And now, that same evil had destroyed the wells, the portals that her people—the Abdita—used to connect to the earth's magic.

"I know, Carrick. Your brother's actions are not your responsibility," Esyld said.

"But they are. And as soon as you do what you intend in Parkovia, I'm going to find him and stop whatever he's doing," Carrick said.

Esyld wanted to tell him to stay focused, but she understood his guilt and shame. The same feeling overcame her when she wished she hadn't been a Meta, one of the Abdita chosen to guard the Sacred Wells.

Pagaene turned and groaned, causing Esyld and Carrick to freeze.

"Wretched scum gwaldrannag… King brrrang… arm will defeaterer…" Pagaene mumbled.

Carrick froze, and Esyld listened, trying to decipher what Pagaene's dreams through his words; perhaps they would give a clue to his purpose. Concentrating, she used her mind's eye to break into his dreamscape, to search his buried subconscious. But just as she felt the light, it went black, and the snoring began.

After a long silence, Esyld and Carrick relaxed.

"Why are you the one Muave called?" he finally asked. "What about the others?"

She knew he referred to the other Metas—those chosen from each of the original witch families. They'd been born like Esyld—no eyes, nose, ears, or hair—so they could use their senses to guard the wells and transform when it became necessary. Their destiny was to serve the Great Mother.

"I'm not sure, Carrick. I am the oldest of the Metas, and perhaps my power is best suited to retrieve the stones. I have to trust in Muave's choice to send both of us."

"Do you enjoy being a Meta?" Carrick asked.

Esyld knew so many wanted to ask her this question. And while she should have felt powerful and superior, in reality, she often wondered what life would bring had she looked like any other human without changing. To have her own face and hair and life. To be a protector, like Carrick, or a messenger for Muave. To carry out any one of the number of duties her people fulfilled to keep the balance—the earth with humans, magic with nature.

When she'd worn the Maiden's face in the past to do her work, she'd felt men's longing eyes upon her. She'd giggle with the other girls as she sat among them to grind grain and cook the daily meal. As the Mother, she'd soothed babies with her nurturing touch, make healing decisions, and enjoyed the satisfaction of a day's work.

Visiting the well and calling on the bardoul brought confidence and peace; she had the power necessary to defend the necessary equilibrium. But sometimes, she longed for those moments that really never truly belonged to her—those ordinary moments that felt like rare gemstones.

Esyld hoped Carrick had fallen asleep in the silence, but he turned toward her, waiting for her answer.

"It is a great honor, fulfilling in ways I cannot describe."

"The rest of us were young and stupid all those years ago," Carrick said. "You know I'll protect you with my life."

Esyld smiled, remembering her tenth birthday when she'd been presented as her family's Meta. Abdita had traveled from across the land to honor her role, but she'd decided she'd rather run around with the children instead of talk with the adults, so she joined a game of tag. Amidst the running children, her shroud fell from her face, and all the other children stopped. They were too young to have seen a Meta and really didn't know any better. They found her different and ugly, screaming and throwing rocks and sticks at her. She pulled her shroud back up and ran into the forest. It was Muave who had found her, letting her weep as long as she wanted.

Of course, those children had come to understand Esyld, even looking upon her with respect, but there had always been a separation between them. Esyld touched Carrick's shoulder and felt him drifting into sleep, allowing his apology to take the edge off his guilt.

"This is all very touching," Pagaene said.

Carrick shot upright, pulling out his athame. Esyld stiffened, then pulled herself up as straight as the old Crone's body would allow. The night left the early dawn behind and poked its way through the forest canopy, adding tension to the moment. Pagaene unfolded his muscular body from the ground and stretched, testing his false arm and fingers.

"We'll leave now," Esyld said.

It would be two long days' journey with unknown obstacles to confront. And they would need to stop and rest the horses. She searched through her mind's eye for any hint to Pagaene's purpose, but all she saw was that they would have a visitor today.

Chapter 11

Esyld's unease grew as they traveled, each step bringing them closer to Parkovia. Pagaene trailed behind them, still miffed about the gag. The trees along the trail thinned and gave them a better view of the brown fields.

Esyld murmured, "I wish we knew what was killing the land."

Carrick looked around. "Maybe it has something to do with the stones." He gave her a sideways glance.

She snapped out of her thoughts. "How do you know of the stones?"

"When we spoke last night, you mentioned your powers were best suited to retrieve the stones. You haven't told me everything. Still no trust?"

Esyld cursed herself for the slip. She looked at Carrick and decided the truth would be best. "We are to retrieve five stones in Parkovia. I do not know their powers, only that we must return them to Muave before the final blood moon of the harvest. It's our chance to save the wells."

"I don't understand the secrecy." The crestfallen slump of his shoulders tugged at Esyld's heart.

A shout from Pagaene prevented her reply. The Knight pointed to an area in a field where the crops had not died. Before their eyes, a patch of healthy corn withered and fell. A startled rabbit attempted to run, but the ground beneath it turned brown. The animal froze, then shriveled, its lifeless body crumbling to the earth.

The ground rumbled and trembled, reminiscent of the night Esyld was almost trapped in the Sacred Grove. The trio glanced at each other, and the horses pranced nervously. A geyser of water sprayed from the ground near the corn, small rainbows forming and disappearing as the droplets plummeted to the earth. The trio dismounted to investigate further, and Carrick grabbed the reins to secure the horses to a tree.

Pagaene plowed ahead, determined to be the first. He hesitated at the edge of the cornfield, then moved forward and raised his good arm to reach the makeshift fountain just as a wave of danger took the breath from Esyld's body.

She stumbled as she tried to shout a warning. "Stop! Don't touch the water!"

The first drops splattered onto Pagaene's skin, and he cried out in pain. Esyld shrugged away from Carrick's hold, who had come up from behind to stabilize her, and rushed forward. She grabbed Pagaene's wooden arm and yanked him away from the geyser, careful to avoid getting wet herself.

The water changed as they backed away. It undulated and twisted, the colors of the rainbow convoluting until only black reflected. Esyld felt the evil permeate from the mass, an old yet ageless depravity. A featureless form shaped from the darkness and moved toward them with feminine fluidity.

"What the hell is that thing?" Pagaene held his arm, several painful burns scorched across his skin.

Esyld took a step forward. Carrick grabbed her shoulder. "Where are you going?"

"We have to face this… thing."

The figure stopped when Esyld approached it. "Who are you? *What* are you?"

'I am the Purity,' the voice boomed, but it took Esyld a moment to realize it was in her head.

"What is the Purity?" Carrick stepped forward, careful not to touch the water.

'The cleansing of this world. The existence of supremacy.'

Esyld's voice cracked in anger. "Your *cleansing* is killing our food, our lands. Our people will starve. The world is dying."

'Not all. Jentor will prevail.'

Pagaene stepped forward. "Why?"

'When Rouaix built his citadel, he released me from my prison of fire and ash. For that, I assured him Jentor would be spared.'

"You were imprisoned." It was not a question, yet now Esyld knew exactly how the pieces fit together.

'By your Great Mother,' the Purity seethed. *'My appetite has grown since she locked me away. I will feed my powers on her earth, and your precious wells will be destroyed.'*

"Even if you spare Jentor," Pagaene began, his fists clenched, "one kingdom cannot survive if the rest of the world has died."

'Perhaps your great king should have considered his actions with more care. The deal is in place.'

Pagaene drew his sword and moved toward the figure. "You can't do this."

Esyld twisted the ring and mumbled, casting an invisible dome around Pagaene and blocking his advance on the target. With a splash, the entity shattered into a million drops of water and disappeared into the ground.

"Why did you stop me?"

Esyld grabbed Pagaene's arm. "You cannot fight that which is not there. These burns would have encompassed your body had you engaged that thing in battle."

He lowered his head while Esyld healed his wounds. "Then once again, you have saved me from myself," he said.

Carrick scoffed. "And we know how you repay her." He glanced toward where the creature had been. "Where do you think it went?"

"Apparently, it moves through the soil, like a river underground, depleting the land instead of feeding it. The question is how to stop it."

Pagaene pulled his nearly-healed arm away. "How could Rouaix do this to his own people?"

She shook her head sadly, unable to answer. Carrick went to retrieve the horses, and it seemed no one had the presence of mind to say any more as they continued their journey.

After a few minutes, Esyld rode up next to Pagaene. "Rouaix turned his back on you. Why are you so concerned with Jentor?"

A flash of hidden emotion crossed his face. Esyld reached out with her mind, but the image of a steel door flashed up and blocked her probe. Without a word, Pagaene urged his horse forward.

They rode for a few hours in silence, then stopped for a tense lunch. Relieved by the opportunity to rest, Esyld slid from her horse and stretched. Pagaene stepped toward the thicker trees without a word.

"Where are you going?" Carrick asked.

Turning briefly with a grimace, the Knight replied, "Nature calls. I'm not going anywhere. I promise."

Esyld and Carrick returned their attention to unpacking their food, having to take Pagaene for his word. Not a minute later, a shout echoed from the forest, disturbing the natural quiet. Esyld leapt to her feet and took off toward the noise. Pushing through the foliage, Carrick soon caught up with her, and they paused in the shadows just outside a small, dark clearing. There they witnessed their companion sprawled on his back, eyes locked on a lithe, hooded figure. It stood over him, pale hand raised and clutching the hilt of a keris.

"Why have you come to our lands?" The voice was crisp and light, holding an arid tone.   Silently,   Esyld   walked through the surrounding trees, hoping to get a better look at the attacker as Carrick readied his sword.

"We are traveling through." Pagaene's eyes moved just slightly, spotting Carrick in the trees.

"For what reason? He has said you would come, and He has spoken of a creature bearing masks." A cloud of frost came from the hooded figure's face, causing the Knight to scuttle backwards. The figure lurched forward. "Have you seen a creature bearing the false face of The Crone?"

Esyld stepped into view, and the figure turned, leaving Pagaene enough time to scramble away and gather himself. The figure raised its head, and in the dim light, Esyld made out bright-green eyes set within pasty skin. The figure removed its hood, exposing short-cut, snow-breezed hair and thin, blackened lips. "Are you that whom He has sent me to find?"

Esyld tensed but found Carrick at her side, eyes drifting down the curves of the creature's blade. Green eyes narrowed at the pair, demanding an answer. "If you've come to hurt her, you won't get far," Carrick warned, readying his own blade while Esyld remained still.

Behind the figure, Pagaene reached for his blade and finally grasped it. Without turning, the hooded stranger directed an open palm toward the knight, who let out a yowl of pain. Pagaene dropped his blade to nurse his arm, which had been burned once more. The figure turned its head toward the fallen man. "I would not suggest attempting that again."

Carrick took that opportunity to lurch forward and plunge his blade toward the rough, brown fabric of the creature's cloak. Soundlessly, the figure faced him and disarmed the man with a flick of its wrist. Its eyes flashing, the creature forced him to his knees.

"Carrick." Esyld stepped forward.

"Do not make me ask again."

Remembering her vision of a visitor, Esyld raised her hands to the figure, signaling peace, and took a breath. "We're just traveling through on our way to Parkovia," she explained, glancing from Carrick to Pagaene. "We have been sent to heal the magic unrest developing across our lands."

The figure stepped closer but made no violent movements. "He has spoken of magic's powerful presence within you." A fine, clouded mist left the creature's lips when it spoke, and its eyes reminded Esyld of the white dragon; shining green and slitted like those that had tried to set her aflame in her dream. White knuckles gripped the hilt of the figure's blade. "He does not take kindly to outsiders in our lands. But He has received a message convincing Him to allow you passage. How do you intend to correct this unrest?"

"We search for stones," Esyld said.

The figure stood absolutely still, nothing but its emerald eyes fluttering as it scrutinized the old woman standing before it. "Stones?"

Reaching down, Esyld pulled the scroll from her bag and held it up just long enough for the stranger to note its presence. She did not give the figure a chance to reach for it.

The hooded thing lowered its blade. "I know the stones of which you speak." Its hand disappeared into the brown robes, sheathing the dagger beneath the cloth. "You will require company into our city. I am Khati." The figure extended a hand, pale skin outlined with swirling, grey marks imbedded deep into the skin.

Esyld took the hand in peace, realizing suddenly that Khati was female.

"Are you telling me we're bringing this…" Pagaene stumbled to his feet, still caressing the redness of his arm, a blaze of anger in his eyes. "This miscreant with us?" His eyes fell onto Esyld.

Carrick looked to her as well, equally skeptical. "Esyld…"

Esyld closed her own eyes and stretched out with her senses. "It is best that Khati accompany us. She did not attack in malice or with intent to harm."

Furious, Pagaene approached Khati. Carrick stepped between them. "An attack is an attack," the Knight shouted. "How is that not malicious intent? Why do we care about whoever sent this thing? We're capable without its aid." Carrick's eyes leveled with Pagaene's, and the Knight clenched his wooden fist and backed away, cursing quietly under his breath.

Khati's eyes never turned toward the men but instead remained on Esyld, silently establishing a respect for her presence. "I do not enjoy traveling with a haughty, armored boar, either," Khati said. "However, it is necessary for both our purposes. Come." She turned toward the path again, lightly stepping over roots. "We must travel before dark."

Scowling, Pagaene begrudgingly followed with Carrick. Trailing behind, Esyld could not shake the resemblance between Khati and the white dragon. Her magical presence was obvious and well-exerted—a clear threat. Khati exhibited an ancient sort of magic associated with the dragons, and she spoke plainly, as did the great beasts.

Approaching Esyld's black mare, Khati gently brushed her fingers over the animal's mane. She then passed all the tied horses, raised her pale fingers to her mouth, and whistled. From the darkness, a stark white horse emerged, a cold fog flowing from the tips of its mane and settling in small, cold patches on the ground. With obvious ease, Khati leaped astride the steed and said, "I shall lead."

"She will not," Pagaene said.

"He has a point," Carrick agreed as he helped Esyld onto her horse.

"Carrick and Khati will lead side by side," Esyld said, hoping to ease the tension. "Followed by Pagaene and myself."

And so it was, though the question of what true motives lay behind Khati's new contribution hung in the air.

***

Darkness fell with no further conflict, and the party secured another safe place to rest for the night. Khati retired separately from the others, situating herself on the outskirts of the firelight. She sat cross-legged and closed her eyes. The gray marks on her skin glowed, wrapping around the contours of her face and dipping into the corners of her eyes, vibrating with an ancient power.

Carrick moved to sit beside Esyld as they shared more of their provisions. Between bites, he confessed, "I am not sure this arrangement is best, Esyld."

"I had a vision."

"Of her?"

"Of a visitor."

Khati's eyes opened. "He had a vision," she said. "A visitor in the night—in His dreams." Her voice crackled like ice spreading across a lake. "And He received a message about you."

"From whom?" Esyld asked. Her mind filled with the sound of flapping wings and a might caw. She closed her eyes and saw a flash of memory not her own—a raven landing on a boulder near the white dragon. She smiled as she recognized Muave's messenger and opened her eyes, still smiling. "The dragon," she said.

Pagaene, who had been leaning against a tree trunk, sat up. Carrick's jaw dropped. Khati nodded once, green eyes flashing in amusement, though the smile never reached her lips.

"If He is to help us," Esyld asked, "why did I dream of Him burning me?"

"What you saw was an attempt to protect you from danger."

Esyld nodded. "You will be powerful allies. I am relieved that I do not need to fear you."

Khati said nothing.

"Do you know the location of the stones?" Carrick asked.

"They lay within the Shrine of Verity, built on the Lake of Destiny at the northern end of Parkovia. But there is something more pressing you must know."

Esyld raised her brow. "What is that?"

"Pagaene must be the one to retrieve the stones."

Esyld's heart sunk. It was as she had feared. Pagaene was as essential as Muave had predicted and yet untrustworthy—unconvinced of their mission.

"Why?" Carrick asked.

"How do you know my name?" Pagaene asked.

Ignoring all the questions, Khati said, "For the stones to be released, he must face himself."

Khati closed her eyes again, and no amount of questioning from Carrick or threatening from Pagaene would induce her to open them again.

As the night darkened, Esyld turned to Pagaene. "You have many secrets, my friend."

Pagaene glanced at her over the fire. "Friend?" He laughed. "Any secrets are my own."

"This quest is about you. You must face your past for us to succeed."

Pagaene turned away with a huff and focused on spreading out his bedroll.

"Maybe he's too weak to do the right thing." Carrick stared at the knight.

Before Pagaene could respond to Carrick's barb, a new voice joined their conversation, and they spun around to face the newcomer. "Maybe someone like you, *Carrick*—" the name was spat out with disgust—"should be sure that you yourself are brave enough to do what's right."

The Priest approached the fire and grinned at the stunned expressions greeting him.

Chapter 12

King Rouaix paced back and forth beneath the high-arching shadow of his throne. The room would normally be filled with people seeing to his needs, but he had ordered them away. He didn't want anyone to see him now. A lump rested high in the King's throat as he stopped to look out over the land. Night fell quickly in Jentor, the air heavy and thick. Clouds seemed to have been plucked out of the sky until only the low-hanging yellow moon remained, staring down at the lonely King.

Where is he? he though, resuming his pacing. He had just learned of the dangerous results of his decision, and only one person could tell him what to do. But where was he?

The faint moonlight in the King's doorway retreated,

replaced by a pair of dark shadows. Two figures slithered into the warm glow of the torches, then recoiled only slightly from the. A cracked, rattling sound filled the air as they rose from their slinking shadows to form humanoid shapes.

"Anguis. Caedus. Where is His Holiness? I asked to speak to him directly about this matter," Rouaix said.

"He is preoccupied," Anguis replied. "He sent us instead. I believe we will suffice." He was a tall, slender man with a narrow face beneath a full head of mangled black hair.

"No, you will not," Rouaix said shortly. "I asked to see him personally, because this is a personal matter. And very important."

"And you presume that His Holiness just goes wherever you want him to go? I think he would enjoy hearing of that farce. If we will not suffice, perhaps we should instead pass along your message."

"No!" The King tried to hide a choke of desperation. "I apologize. I understand he is an important person. And I am glad to see you. You two have always held my trust, so you of course be trusted in this matter." He attempted to stand tall but still failed to raise his eyes higher than Anguis' chin.

"Of course. He wouldn't have sent anyone else for such an important task, you can be assured." Anguis gestured for Caedus to join him.

"Any issues you have, Anguis and I will ensure they don't find their way to His Holiness," Cadeus added, his slicked-back white hair contrasting with the rough terrain of his scar-ridden face. His large, lumbering body waded from side to side, as if he felt an innate need to move even while he stood in place. "Why trouble him with a problem that's already been solved?"

"Silence, Caedus!" Anguis hissed, then looked at the King once more. "What requires His Holiness' time today, Your Grace?"

"I have freed something," Rouaix said.

"Something?" Anguis asked.

"To deal with our witch problem. I was told a force had been trapped in the volcanos—a force that could help us."

"You freed her?" Anguis' face tightened.

"Yes." Rouaix took up his pacing again. "I had just agreed to share control of the kingdom with His Holiness, and I felt I needed a—another option. An assurance that the witches could be dealt with should the Prime Order's aid not be enough. I was certain that once the witch problem was sorted, we could resolve this one. But the citizens are complaining. I've sent men to identify the problem, and she apparently has not limited herself to ridding this world of witches. I think she wants to rid the world of everything."

"And you would like to eliminate this entity?" Anguis asked. "I'll see what His Holiness can do."

"Well, no," Rouaix replied. "I don't wish to jump to that option too hastily. I think she can still be a valuable resource in defeating the witches, we just… need to speed up the process a bit."

"Do you have any idea how difficult it would be to stop her, even if we wished to do so?" Anguis' eyes darted from wall to wall, peering into shadow and analyzing their surroundings through every window. "Do you know how she was imprisoned in the first place? She is dangerous, and I think your plan carries more than a significant risk."

"I have no idea. That's why I've summoned His Holiness," the King said, his jaw firmly set.

"Then we haven't a moment to spare, Your Highness. We will return to His Holiness at once and apprise him of these new circumstances. If we are to use The Purity, we'd better ensure we maintain the upper hand." When the King nodded in dismissal, Anguis gave a slight bow, and he and Cadeus left him.

***

Anguis and Caedus left the Citadel with great haste, slinking back to the forest. There, they rejoiced in the shadow, away from the natural glow of the city. Anguis led Caedus into a clearing just off the path, where they found a man struggling against covers and restraints.

"Why do we need all this sneaking?" Caedus said. "You

know this isn't my strong suit."

"Not much is," Anguis said. "So do the thing you like."

Caedus cracked his right shoulder, then knelt before the restrained man. Carelessly freeing one of the man's arms, he then raised his own knife and slashed it down across the back of their captive's proffered limb. The bound man's blood spilled onto the forest floor as he let out muffled groans of pain.

"Now, just sit back and watch," Anguis said. "I'll show you why we're doing what we're doing, and then I promise I'll take you somewhere where you can break something." He leaned over the growing pool of blood before sinking his teeth into his own wrist. Globs of thick grey liquid dripped onto the normal crimson, seeming to pull the prisoner's blood from the ground before pooling around it and forming a thin, perfect circle. Anguis waved his hand, and the pool spun counterclockwise.

The ground around the circle shook. The trees surrounding the clearing wilted. The grass dried up and crumbled. From the pool of lifeblood rose The Purity. Anguis and Caedus bowed low, their heads almost touching the scorched earth.

'What have you learned?' The Purity demanded, her voice ringing powerful in their minds.

"The King knows no way to resist you and has no knowledge of learning now. His kingdom is already at your whim," Anguis said.

'What of him?' The fluid shimmered and rearranged itself to gesture at the restrained man.

Caedus ripped the cover off to expose His Holiness' terrified face. "He won't be in our way, neither."

'Good. We control his magic, but some powers still elude us,' The Purity said.

"We can get our hands on it," Anguis replied.

'No. The Abdita are too protected. The Great Mother watches over them. We require something else before we can go after them.'

"What do we need?" Caedus asked. "We'll get it."

'The faces. Bring me the faces.'

Chapter 13

"How did you get here?" Carrick asked, startled by the new presence. He instinctively reached for the hilt of his sword.

"Are you going to kill me, brother?" asked the Priest. "So much for sentimental reunions." He smirked from under his hood.

"What are you doing here?" asked Esyld.

"I came to end this little quest," the Priest replied. "Interesting that you picked the façade of the crone, Esyld. I would have never imagined you as wise."

"You are unwise, brother!" spat Carrick. "You are clearly outnumbered."

"So you say." The Priest dropped his arms to his sides and

opened his hands. The crimson pools of blood sprayed to the ground before him, which convulsed and opened abruptly. Out of the shallow gorge leapt two hounds, similar to the bardouls Esyld had conjured but taller, without fur, and whose sinister eyes glowed a fiery red.

Pagaene stepped back to assess the situation, but his body seemed not to respond, and he stood there, motionless. He had waited for a chance to escape, to complete his mission and be done with the witch. But now he doubted the reasoning behind anything. For a moment, he felt like he was miles away, too far to do anything but watch.

Carrick drew his sword and stepped in front of Esyld as a hound dashed forward and pounced. The beast opened its maw, within which fire blazed. Carrick ducked at the last moment, catching the hound in the chest with his sword. Though the beast's momentum knocked him to the ground, his blade sank into the beast's flesh. For a moment, it seemed the thing was slain.

But then it yelped and rolled off Carrick's blade. Even from a distance, one could not miss the fact that the knight's sword now glowed red-hot, like a piece of metal taken from a smith's forge. The hound's wound sealed in an instant, and snarling, the beast pounced once again at the unsuspecting Carrick.

Khati was better prepared to receive the other attacking hound. She stepped sideways as the beast pounced towards her and missed. Spinning in a fluid, almost effortless motion, she gave the animal a sweeping kick, which sent it sprawling on the ground. But it arose just as quickly and charged her again, jaws wide. Khati again stepped aside and rebuked the thing with another kick. The hound turned and raked her across the arm and leg with its claws. She bit back her pain and closed in on the beast.

Esyld grabbed her staff and pointed it at The Priest, who walked toward her. Violet flames shot forth from the end of the staff, engulfing The Priest. He only laughed and continued his approach, as if a strong wind had hit him instead of flames. Esyld backed up a couple steps and tripped on a fallen branch. In a panic, she grabbed her athame, but before she had the chance to cut her own arm, the Priest was upon her and wrested it from her grasp.

"I will take that, thank you," he said smugly. "You just stay there." Motioning with his open palm toward the ground, he sent the roots and plants around Esyld wrapping around her arms and legs, holding her still.

The Priest stepped away and walked toward Pagaene. The two hounds kept Carrick and Khati occupied, and Pagaene caught the fear in Esyld's eyes as she struggled against her binds; they were too strong for her.

The Priest looked at the prosthetic arm and said, "I see you received a trophy for your failure." He stepped around the frozen Knight in a circle, fixated on the new limb. "A rather curious arm, I must agree. Too bad the Prime Order does not tolerate failure." The Priest raised the athame to strike Pagaene in the back, and the Knight flinched but felt no wound. He turned to see that the athame had come within an inch of his flesh and stopped. It stunned him to find that Esyld had freed herself from the plants and once again saved his life with a twist of her ring.

The Priest stood in shock for a moment. That was all that Khati needed before she gestured towards him. The athame flew from his grasp, and the Priest glared at the shrouded figure, his eyes burning with hate.

Pagaene came to his senses, fighting whatever power had held him, and drew his sword. He turned to The Priest, who now backed away from him. The ground beneath his feet rumbled as the two hounds charged from behind, but he did not have enough time to evade them before they knocked him to the ground.

He turned just in time to see Khati moving toward the beasts, taking a huge breath. When she exhaled, a billowing cloud of mist flowed from her wide-open mouth, surrounding both the hounds and Pagaens. Then the strange woman blew upon them as if on a spoonful of hot soup, cooling the mist. The hounds yelped in pain as their flesh grew rigid, the fire in their eyes dimming. Pagaene scrambled backwards as quickly as he could but lost his balance with his artificial arm. The mist stopped mere inches from him, blocked by another of Esyld's shields.

Within the cloud of white, the hounds howled and cried in pain as the mist froze them to their death.

Pagaene stood and whirled around, searching for The Priest's next strike. He realized he shook, but it was not from the cold air that still lingered. He could not see the Priest through the foggy mist; he couldn't see anything. He called out for Carrick and Esyld but received no response.

Then he felt a pull in his body, calling him, and he allowed himself to follow it. Arms stretched out before him, he wandered through the blank whiteness for a few minutes. Without warning, he found himself in a clearing where the trees held back the mist. In the center of the grassy circle sat a thin, flat white rock, which he approached cautiously.

Something about the rock called out to him, and that realization made him move slower than usual. This was an unnatural relic, filling him with fear and anxiety. It also drove him mad with curiosity. If not for that, he wouldn't have moved at all.

I'm right here, dear. A voice bounced off the walls of his skull, familiar and friendly.

"I'm here," Pagaene said aloud. He approached the rock and touched it with his right hand, then looked up to see a woman staring at him from a few feet away. She was a radiant sight, with long, curly brown hair surrounding her vibrant skin and lush green eyes. He tried to move toward her, but when he took his hand from the rock, she vanished. His hand shot back to the stone, and she graced his eyes once more.

It's okay, she said.

"No, it's not. How can it be?" He reached out, bringing his wooden arm as close to her as he could while keeping his other hand on the rock. She didn't return the gesture—or couldn't. Pagaene tried to drag the rock toward her, but it wouldn't budge from the earth.

I forgive you, she said.

"I don't want your forgiveness." Dropping his hand to his side, he sat on the rock and stared up at her. "And I don't think you would really mean that, either."

I do, she said.

Pagaene stood, and her image vanished.

"That's because you must not be real," he said. Seeing that the mist had cleared away from the trees, he walked back toward the sound of Esyld's call.

The group met him when he exited the woods beside their doused campfire. "Where's The Priest?" he asked.

"Gone," Esyld said. "We were afraid he'd taken you."

"Or that you'd run," Carrick added. He was covered in dirt and blood from several gouges. Khati looked the same.

"I said I would stay. I will," Pagaene said. "He may return."

"And we will be better prepared when he does," said Carrick. "Let us recover and make ready for the dawn."

Pagaene retrieved his forgotten sword and thought of what he'd seen in the clearing, glancing over his shoulder.

"Where did you go? Did you find anything of interest?" Esyld asked.

"No, there's nothing there," he said.

Chapter 14

Two years ago

T he day was perfect. Kenyth held his athame up in the light, admiring the white and gold vines twisting about the silver handle. Today would be the day he'd relinquish his name and take on the power and role of Healer.

"Hey, little brother," Carrick greeted him as he stepped out from behind a nearby tree. "Ready for the ceremony? The other Healers are already lining up in the glade."

Sheathing his athame and tying it to his belt, Kenyth clasped a hand on Carrick's shoulder and grinned. "Aye, I'm ready, Brother."

The ceremony only took a few hours. One by one, the four Healers present kneeled before the High Priestess, performing the steps of the ritual and rising into their new lives. When it was Kenyth's turn, he stood before his older sister and winked at her. "Ready to end my life, Muave?"

She kept her face mostly expressionless, though her lips twitched and her eyes shone in amusement at his dark humor. "I'm ready to give you a new one," she whispered back. Raising her voice, she spoke loud enough for the attending crowd to hear. "Kneel, Kenyth, and in doing so, untie the bonds of your name."

He went through the same motions as the others before him. As one knee reached the ground, his hands released his athame from its sheath. He held it above his head and looked up into his sister's bright blue eyes. With the handle in his left hand and the blade in his right, he squeezed his fingers until the sharp edges dug into his palm and the inside of his knuckles. Slowly, he drew the blade downward, blood dancing across his face and dripping onto his white tunic. The drops expanded unnaturally across the fabric until the entire thing had been stained a deep crimson.

"In donning your blood, you proclaim to the Great Mother that your life is dedicated to the wounded. You are no longer Kenyth of Freywyn. You are a servant of life." Muave lifted her hand, palm up, motioning for him to stand. "Rise, Healer, and take your rightful place among us."

The Healer strolled through the woods, shuffling his feet among the brown pine needles and sparse underbrush decorating the forest floor in late autumn. His first week on the job had depleted his stock of lemon thyme, and he found himself searching the forest for more. He traveled between patches of direct sunlight beaming down through the canopy, checking for the medicinal perennial.

He sighed, standing from the latest patch of dirt empty-handed. It was weeks beyond blooming season, and finding this herb would be difficult without the helpful pink flowers to catch his eye.

A crunch in the leaf litter startled him, and he spun around, coming face to face with a large brown bear. He allowed himself a single gasp, then held his breath and slowly eased backward. *No sudden movements. Slow and steady*, he repeated to himself. *Slow and steady.*

The bear advanced as he retreated.

I wish Carrick were here. He always was better at communicating with the animals; he'd know what to do. Swallowing back his fear, the Healer carefully released the air from his lungs—but not carefully enough. The faintest of moans escaped his lips, and the bear roared.

Turning on his heels, the Healer ducked to avoid the massive claws swiping at his head and took off at a sprint through the woods. He dodged trees left and right, but the bear overtook him easily. Sharp pain shot through his arm as the animal's teeth latched around his wrist, and he tumbled down.

A waist-high stone structure halted his fall. The half-second it took him to realize he had collided with an old well was a half-second too long. Teeth sank into his shoulder, and he screamed in agony. The weight of the great beast threw him over the stones, and he went headfirst into the well, blood tinting the water red as he sank beneath the surface.

He struggled against the water, fighting to figure out which way was up. Lungs burning, he squeezed his eyes shut and forced himself to hold still, praying the laws of nature would kick in and he would naturally rise to the surface. He didn't. Against his will, his mouth opened wide, and he sucked in a breath. Stale air filled his lungs, and he coughed painfully. His eyes flew open, and he had to blink as his vision adjusted to bright sunlight. He lay in a dusty patch of gray dirt, the earth around him cracked and dry.

Wincing, he stood and looked around. It didn't take long to understand that he had stumbled into one of the sacred groves. But it was all wrong. The scene before him made his heart catch in his throat. "Great Mother... what has happened here?"

The skeleton of a wide oak towered before him, bare and lifeless. Black leaves coated the surrounding clearing with a macabre décor, and the blankets of grass had withered and died. The grove's sun-coated, yellow tone seemed unnaturally pleasant, and a hot wetness on his cheeks alerted the Healer that he was crying.

He knew he must try to use his power to heal the grove, but he could not sense the Great Mother around him and feared that her presence here had died with the tree. Still, he had to try. He reached out a hand and placed it gingerly against the trunk of the tree, withdrawing it immediately as a golden glow arced between his fingers and the dead bark, filling his hand with a shocking energy he didn't understand. Reaching out once more, he kept his hand against the bark and absorbed the golden energy it granted him until he truly felt the last life of the tree flowing into his fingertips. When he pulled away again, a charred imprint of his hand had burned into the trunk, a tiny green leaf blooming from the center. The hint of new life surprised him.

He looked down at his hands, feeling the new energy coursing through his veins. "What is this?" he whispered.

It is not for you to wield, Kenyth! The raspy voice echoed in his head, and the Healer fell to his knees.

"Get out of my mind, demon!" he shouted to the empty grove around him. "Begone from this sacred place, or the Great Mother will—"

Laughter erupted in his mind, ending in a low growl. *The Great Mother, indeed. She couldn't even contain me at her best. What will she do to me now? Soon I will be free, and she will not be gifted with the comfort of a prison. Look around you, Kenyth. This is her fate. Tell your Great Mother… I am coming for her.*

The laughter sounded again and faded to nothingness. Shout as he might, the Healer was met with silence. Looking around at the destruction of the grove, he found himself pummeled by the magnitude of the situation. If a formless creature could do this much damage, the Great Mother was truly in danger.

The Healer's eyes fluttered open. He lay in a slightly lumpy bed, staring at a ceiling he recognized as his brother's. He remembered stumbling into Carrick's yard. The room was filled with an orange glow; the sun must have been at the horizon, though he couldn't tell which direction it was headed.

"Little brother!"

Carrick's smiling face came into view, and the Healer returned the gesture. "Carrick." As he looked into his brother's relieved face, he felt the gnawing sense that he had meant to tell him something. He drew his brow down and tried to recall what happened. The memory of the grove came flooding back, and he bolted upright.

"The dem—ow! Gods..." A sharp pain shot through his shoulder, though when he reached a hand up to feel the bite, it had healed over. "How... how long have I been in bed?"

"Easy, Brother. You've been here three days. The Healers have closed your wounds but they said you'd likely be sore another week. What happened to you?"

"No," the Healer protested. "Get Muave. I have so much to tell her. It's urgent. Please!"

"I'm here, little brother," Muave said from the doorway. She stepped into the room, the orange light illuminating the concern in the lines on her face.

The Healer told them of the bear attack and his discovery of the blighted grove. He emphasized the conversation with the demon and his fear that the Great Mother was in danger. "We have to stop this evil creature before it decimates any other groves," he finished. Muave and Carrick exchanged a quick glance, but the Healer didn't miss it. "You... you don't believe me."

"It's not that," Muave began, reaching out and entwining his fingers within her own. "It's just that..." She paused, unease seeping from her shaking hands. "Brother... I feel a strange power within you. The golden energy you described... I worry it might be dangerous."

"*The demon* is dangerous, Muave! We must warn the Great Mother!" As his anger rose, golden light emanated from his hands and eyes, and Muave yanked her own hands away, stepping back in alarm.

Carrick stood and placed himself between the Healer and the High Priestess. "Brother, Sister, please. Let us be reasonable."

"She never believes me," the Healer pointed out. "But I can show you. Let me show you the power I discovered—I sparked life in the death of a tree! It might be a useful tool to help defeat the demon!" Looking around for something to use in his demonstration, he spotted his athame on the side table. He threw his legs over the edge of the bed, grabbed it, and took a deep breath, focusing his energy through his blade as he did with his healing magic. He placed his other hand on the wooden surface of the side table, and smoke rose from beneath his fingers. When he lifted his hand, the wood was charred and gray, and a small, cracked seed sat nestled in the smoldering handprint. "It's… I mean, I'm not very strong right now, but you see the seed? With practice, I can make it grow, and—"

"No, Kenyth. You are forbidden."

"Kenyth?" he asked, raising an eyebrow. "Sister, you know I have forsaken that name."

"I'm sorry, Brother. But look at what you have done. You have destroyed a gift of nature at your very touch. I do not know where you harnessed this… power… but it is evil, and you cannot wield it. The Elders will never allow it."

"It's not evil. I am a Healer, and I have been granted the ability to heal the dead! How do you not see the good in this?"

"No." This time it was Carrick who denied him. His voice shaky, he stepped forward and rested a hand on his brother's good shoulder. "The touch of a Healer should never burn. I… I'm so sorry to do this, little brother. But it's for your own good." Tears poured from Carrick's eyes as he snatched Kenyth's athame from his hands and in one swift motion launched it as hard as he could into the wooden doorframe. Before Kenyth could protest, Carrick pulled his own dagger and whispered a rushed chant to the blade, then leapt at the doorframe and sliced downward. The imbued metal sliced through Kenyth's and the hilt clattered to the floor.

"No!" Kenyth shrieked. He held a hand out to the broken blade and the two pieces flew through the air and into his open palm. After staring at the fragments in horrified wonder, he stood, his face blank.

Muave and Carrick both stepped backward, their eyes wide and unblinking.

"So this is how it shall be?" Kenyth asked quietly. Without waiting for an answer, he curled his fingers tightly around his broken athame and straightened his spine, squaring his shoulders and lifting his chin defiantly. "I can see your envy, Sister. Denying your saving grace because you aren't the one to wield it. So I will save the Great Mother on my own if I must. But stay out of my way. And you, Brother." He looked deep into Carrick's eyes, cold anger burning in his soul. "You had no faith in me. You are not my brother." Striding to the door, he turned his head and spoke over his shoulder. "I'd say merry part, but…" He smiled thinly and walked out of the house, out of the village, and away from the life he had once lived.

"*Kenyth.*" He rolled his name around his tongue, but it tasted more like a curse. He washed it down with the last swallow of his ale, then signaled the barkeep to bring him another. All his life, he'd wanted to heal, and he had been stripped of that gift when his brother destroyed his athame. A new glass was placed in front of him, and his fingers greeted it warmly, bringing it to his desperate lips in an effort to drown out his family's betrayal.

A middle-aged man sat beside him at the bar and eyed him curiously. "I know that look well. Life's been down on you, eh?"

Kenyth said nothing; he merely sipped his ale.

"What's a man like you doing in a run-down tavern in Jentor?"

He huffed and took another gulp. "I'm just passing through, old man."

"Yes, by your comfort on that seat and your familiarity with the barkeep, I can tell it's merely a short stay."

Kenyth glared at the man, his eyes drawn in thin slits and a threatening sneer twisting his lips. "What I do is none of your business."

"Very well." The man raised his hands and his brow, smiling despite the cold shoulder Kenyth had showed. He placed a calloused finger in the ring of condensation the glass had left on the table and traced a five-pointed star in the center. "What do they call you where you come from?"

Kenyth shook his head and sighed, feeling his face go slack. Turning his attention back to his drink, he stared into the depths of his glass. "They used to call me Brother. For a short time, they called me Healer. But they stole that from me. Now they say I wield evil." He tilted his head and studied the man's weathered face. He saw no sign of fear or concern. "I brought life to the dead. Tell me, does that make me evil?"

"No," the man stated. "It makes you special. Come, let us speak in my room. Where we may talk more… freely." He nodded toward the barkeep, who had been dusting the same glass for five minutes now, a little too close for comfort. Kenyth agreed and downed the last of his glass before following the man up the stairs to the rooms above the tavern.

"So. Allow me to be blunt," the man said as he shut the door behind him. "The power you wield—it is the third of the three prime powers. Life, Death, and Rebirth."

Kenyth stood awkwardly by the back wall, staring at this man who seemed to snap from tired and friendly to wise and knowledgeable. "Prime powers?"

"Indeed. Most magic is of Life. Your healing magic would have come from Life as well. But to bring life to the dead, that is special. That is Rebirth." The man stretched out an arm, and a golden light glowed in his palm, just like the one Kenyth had summoned when he healed the dead tree. "This power rests latent in the soul of every living thing, waiting for its chance to blossom."

Kenyth raised his own palm, matching the glow of the old man's. His jaw hung slack as he stared at the golden power lighting the room. "It waits for death?"

"That it does, Healer. Death is a natural part of life. We must embrace it."

Kenyth frowned. "I'm traveling to destroy death, not to embrace it." He told the old man of the sacred grove he had stumbled into and the demon that had destroyed it. When he finished, the old man smiled.

"We are on the same path, though it may not be so apparent at first. Allow me to introduce myself properly. I have given up my worldly name and am now known only as His Holiness of the Prime Order. Perhaps you have heard of me?"

Kenyth nodded slowly, sitting down on the bed but not taking his eyes off the old man. "You work for the King."

"I do. Four years ago, I felt a presence right here in Jentor. It was ancient and powerful, and much research into age-old myths revealed it to be The Purity. The Great Mother imprisoned her in a volcano beneath the earth and had the citadel constructed atop it. Her prison has cracked. She is slipping out and will soon break free entirely."

Kenyth leapt back to his feet. "You know this—you've known it all this time—and you're doing nothing to stop it?"

"Quiet down, boy." His Holiness opened the door and peered down the hallway before shutting it once more. "I have been doing plenty. I presented myself to the King as a worker of Divine Gift. You are aware of his... distrust... for *witch magic*. I revived his favored servant who had passed from sickness. Now, he believes Rebirth to be sanctioned by his one true God and has raised the Prime Order to a position of power in the kingdom. But it is not enough. I must earn a higher place for the Order. I must earn the King's unwavering trust in order to convince him to do what must be done."

Kenyth considered His Holiness's words. Could it be that the Great Mother had led him to His Holiness to serve him and destroy The Purity? Fate alone did not work so perfectly. "How can I help?"

Those four words were all it took to twist a smile on the old man's wrinkled face. His brow cast a dark shadow over his eyes with an almost sinister grin, but Kenyth was so blinded by the prospect of being right, by proving his siblings wrong, and by the rarity and strength of his newfound power that he saw nothing more than a simple shadow.

"Are you willing to do whatever is necessary to destroy the

evil of The Purity?"

"I am."

"Then relinquish your worldly name once more. Allow me to train you. I will teach you to harness your power and expand your ability. I will make you a Priest."

There was no hesitation. Kenyth got down on one knee and bowed his head to His Holiness.

The man rested his hand on Kenyth's shoulder. "Patience. There is more you must know before you make such a decision."

Kenyth lifted his head and met the older man's eyes, ready to stand as a loyal servant for the Prime Order. Anything to destroy The Purity and get back at his brother for his betrayal.

"The magic of Rebirth requires death. Which means that to fully destroy The Purity, it must die. Its prison, though weak and failing, also protects it." He paused, drawing a shaky breath. "We must set The Purity free to kill her."

"I will do what must be done."

His Holiness nodded, and Kenyth removed the two halves of his broken athame from his pocket, dragging the blade across his palm and smearing the blood across his face. "I knelt as Kenyth of Freywyn and now cast him aside for the greater good."

"The greater good… yes. Rise, my Priest, and serve me well."

The Priest stood and felt as if a massive weight had been lifted from his shoulders. He was no longer on an impossible quest but now served a great force with a wide presence who had the power to complete what he alone could not. He breathed deeply in the face of his new life. "What must I do to release her?"

His Holiness chuckled and stood, stretching his back and walking toward the bed. "You have much to learn, my Priest. We must first raise our position in the kingdom under the guise of the Divine Gift, then we shall convince the King to release The Purity of his own accord. If it is his idea, he cannot suspect our intentions." He turned down the covers and sat on the edge of the mattress to take off his shoes.

The Priest bowed again and headed toward the door, his

mind torn between the desire to rise above his siblings and the need to prove his worth for this new power. He paused in the doorway and looked back with a grin, the drying blood on his face giving him a surreal look in the lamplight. "Tomorrow will be the start of something great, I can feel it. Blessed be, old man."

Climbing into bed, His Holiness barked a laugh. "Your blessing does no good in the Order, Priest. We thrive on death, not good will."

Chapter 15

"You have returned," King Rouaix said. "And I trust you have accomplished your mission?"

"Not as yet," the Priest replied. "There was an unexpected development. They travel with a Sylth who managed to defeat my hellhounds."

The King spun around so quickly that his fur-rimmed coat flared out around him. He stalked toward his intricately carved throne, the petulant click of his heels echoing loudly off the stone floor of the cavernous room. "This is disastrous. Utterly disastrous," he muttered.

The Priest's eyes blazed for a moment before the obsequious veil descended. "Not at all. A minor setback at most.

The Sylth will be strongest through the forest. If they make it out—which, in truth, is unlikely—we will redouble our efforts on the other side. They will be no match for the combined strength of His Holiness and myself."

The King snorted. "I'm still waiting on His Holiness. I was given to understand it was a matter of utmost urgency, yet he still does not appear."

The Priest's eyes narrowed. "*What* was a matter of urgency?"

"That creature… The Purity… Anguis and Caedus were to summon His Holiness at once."

"I shall seek him." The Priest retrieved a tiny shard of broken athame from his cloak and, with a quick flick of his wrist, reopened the small cut on his hand. A few drops of blood appeared and dropped to the floor. The Priest's body grew rigid, and his eyes rolled back in his head.

The King paced the room, growing more anxious with each passing minute. "Bollocks, bollocks, bollocks."

The Priest began to shudder, his body wracked by wave after wave, each more powerful than the last. Rouaix watched with rising panic. Would he need to call his guard to fetch the court physician? He was unequipped to deal with such circumstances.

Finally, a last wrenching spasm seemed to shake the Priest back to himself. His eyelids fluttered open, the energy quite obviously drained from his body. He staggered to the nearest wall and sagged against it.

"Were you able to make contact?" the King asked.

The Priest shook his head. "I searched throughout the kingdom to no avail. He answered not. But, most perplexingly, I had no sense of him. It was as if I were enveloped in a mist that obscured my third eye as a smoke cloud might your ordinary vision."

"What does it mean?"

The Priest frowned. "I dare not hazard a guess at this stage, but it bodes ill. Ill indeed."

At that moment, a strident knock issued from the thick

chamber doors. "Enter," Rouaix commanded.

The heavy doors swung open, and one of the King's guards marched in, halting neatly with a smart tap of his heels. "Announcing Anguis and Caedus, Your Highness."

"You may show them in."

Anguis and Caedus soon presented themselves, shooting the Priest a curious glance as they made their obligatory bows to the King.

"You bring word of His Holiness?" Rouaix demanded.

"His Holiness has been made aware of the situation of which we spoke," said Anguis, looking pointedly at The Priest, "and he sends his assurances that it will be dealt with posthaste. He is working on it as we speak, which is why he did not come personally."

The King's brow furrowed. "You just came from His Holiness?"

"That's right."

"In the Temple?"

"Yes, of course."

King Rouaix and the Priest exchanged a look. "And he was… perfectly well?"

Anguis shot his own questioning glance at Caedus and replied, "Concerned, Your Highness, but otherwise perfectly well. It is a matter that should not be ignored, but neither is it calamitous. Do not worry. It is well in hand."

"I see. Excellent. Well then, I shall release you to your master. Come back when you have progress to report."

"Your Highness," said Anguis and Caedus in unison. With simultaneous bows, they took their leave.

As soon as the doors had shut behind them, the Priest was on his feet, his vigor restored. "They're lying," he declared.

"Or you are," said the King, his voice an octave higher than usual.

The Priest shot him a withering glance. "It is for you to decide whom to trust, me or the dumbletwins. I assure you, I don't know what has happened to His Holiness, but I know he is not 'perfectly well.' Which means they're lying to you."

"Wh-what do I do?"

The Priest stared at the wall for a moment. "Without His Holiness, our position is compromised. And you are much more likely to suss out their intentions and alliances if they don't suspect you are on to them. So for the time being, we will watch and wait until we are ready to make our next move."

***

As twilight fell, the group made camp for the night. Pagaene and Carrick, who had hunting duties, set off into the forest, hoping to score pheasant or deer if they were lucky and squirrel if they were not.

Khati and Esyld gathered firewood. "I'm glad you are with us," said Esyld. "Without you, we would never have defeated The Priest's hellhounds, and your knowledge of the forest is invaluable."

"I will do my best to get you through unscathed," Khati replied, "but I am powerless against the forest's greatest dangers. Those cannot be fought with sword or bow or any physical means."

Esyld frowned. "Tell me more."

"This forest is a master at preying on an individual's flaws and weaknesses, and none but the victim can save themselves through courage and strength of character. There are many traps. There are the Anobaith, deadly pits of quicksand that feed off despair and hopelessness. The more desperate and discouraged the victim becomes, the faster they will sink.

"And there are the hunger stones. When you touch a hunger stone, it will seize on your deepest need, your greatest yearning, and suck you into a different reality which promises to fulfill it. The attraction grows stronger over time, and it can become so powerful and its victims so enchanted by this other existence that many refuse to release the stone, even briefly, and die of starvation."

"Great Mother," breathed Esyld.

"Then there are the Paranoidea," continued Khati. "These

106

tiny creatures exploit any discord or distrust among travelers. They burrow into the inner ear and maintain a constant stream of fearful and suspicious chatter, sowing such doubt and division that the group disbands—making it easier for other predators to pick them off one by one. Or, in some cases, they go so far as to kill one another off themselves."

"Our group is particularly vulnerable there," said Esyld. "I'm already afraid Pagaene and Carrick are as likely to turn their weapons on one another as they are a stag."

Her fears were allayed, at least temporarily, when the men returned with the spoils of their hunt—a large badger that Carrick was not shy about proclaiming as his kill.

After a hearty meal, they made their beds beside the fire. Each alone with their thoughts, they drifted off to sleep.

Esyld awoke to find Carrick shaking her violently. "He's gone," he shouted. "I knew we couldn't trust him!"

Esyld scanned the campsite. The fire had died down to embers, but the moon was nearly full and illuminated the night. There was no sign of Ser Pagaene. "Are you sure? He could have taken off earlier if he'd wanted to," she said. "Maybe he just went off to relieve himself."

"I've checked all around," Carrick hissed. "He's nowhere to be found. And there's no sign of a struggle. No, he's taken off, all right, the miserable, maggot-infested cankerblossom!"

"Calm yourself," said Khati. "He can't have gotten far. He hasn't even taken a horse."

This brought Carrick up short—the first hole in his theory that Pagaene had left under his own power. "Still," he said, "he could have gone anywhere."

"I think we should go back to the where we were," said Esyld slowly.

"Why? Do you know something?" asked Khati.

"Nothing for sure, but when he came out of the woods and I asked if he'd seen anything, he was so curt and emphatic… I sensed he was hiding something."

"Why didn't you say anything at the time?" snapped Carrick.

"He'd just returned of his own accord. It didn't seem the right time to be taking him to task. Besides, it was merely a feeling."

"Well, it's all we have to go on, now," growled Carrick. "Let's go."

They quickly saddled the horses and backtracked their path. It wasn't long before they reached the clearing and saw Pagaene sitting in the middle of the grassy field, his hand on a flat white rock. He appeared to be talking to himself.

"Ser Pagaene," Esyld called as they approached. He did not respond but instead continued speaking to thin air. When they neared, they finally heard what he was saying.

"How long will it be? Will he come soon?"

"Ser Pagaene!" Esyld cried again. This time, he looked at her.

"Esyld. Esyld, look! Can you believe it? She's really here."

"No, Pagaene. It's not real," said Esyld.

Pagaene shook his head. "That's what I thought at first, but it's not an enchantment. It's really her. She knows things only she would know."

"It's using your own memories against you," said Khati. "Take your hand off the rock and you will see."

"No."

"Take it off!" Carrick demanded.

"I will not!" Pagaene reached for his sword with his free hand.

Before he could withdraw it from the scabbard, Carrick charged him and knocked him to the ground, where the two struggled mightily. "It's... just... a phantom," Carrick grunted as Pagaene attempted to pin him in a chokehold.

"Horseshit!" Pagaene yelled before Carrick threw him off, sending him sprawling backwards. By the time Carrick could attack again, Pagaene drew his weapon. He held it in front of him to keep the other man at bay as he scooted back toward the rock. "Leave me be," he said. "I have to know. I've waited so long, and

I'm not going anywhere until I find out."

"Find out what?" asked Esyld.

"Who my father is," he said just before Khati sprang up from behind him and hit him on the head with a rock. He went down like a sack of flour.

"Help me get him on a horse," Khati said, picking up one of his arms. "We've got to spirit him as far away from here as we can before he wakes up. He's going to keep trying to get back here. The farther we travel, the harder it will be for him to find his way and the less of a pull the rock will have."

"The rock?" Carrick asked in confusion.

"We'll explain on the way," Esyld promised.

***

Anguis and Caedus slithered through the dense forest underbrush on the outskirts of Jentor. Anguis stopped and stood, changing from snakelike shapes into his humanoid form in the shadows. Caedus followed his lead.

"Are you even sure it's here?" Caedus asked as they picked their way through a few feet of dense foliage. "I thought Rouaix's men had destroyed all the wells."

"Not this one. It hadn't been in use for over a decade when the family ended."

They reached the overgrown stone well and set about tearing away the vines and vegetation. Caedus peered down the long shaft, and Anguis swung his legs over the side to drop down the well. Caedus stared into the blackness, listening for a splash that never came. In a moment, Anguis' voice drifted up to him. "Throw down the rope."

Caedus removed the braided jute rope from his bag, secured one end to a gnarled oak tree, tied the other end around his waist, and climbed atop the well wall. Then, taking a deep breath, he squeezed his eyes shut and jumped.

When he opened his eyes, he lay on the ground even though he had felt no impact. In the dim light, he saw Anguis busily sawing through the rope holding one of the three glass cages aloft. In each of the cages, a woman's face blinked at him owlishly.

Caedus shivered. "Those are the faces?"

"Your stunning grasp of the obvious never ceases to amaze. Are you going to help me or just stand there gaping?"

Caedus withdrew his dagger from its sheath and set to cutting through another rope, trying not to look at the face within. The visage chilled him, even though it was undeniably lovely, with its alabaster skin, long, curly brown hair, and piercing green eyes.

Chapter 16

The smell of roasted potatoes, onion, and taro root wafted gently into young Pagaene's room as he slept. The early-morning sun had pierced through his bedroom window, casting its yellowed, warm glow across the thick, quilted blankets. The aromatic smoke from breakfast danced in its comforting light, the flavor of his mother's cooking suspended within.

The delicious smell made his nostrils twitch. Even in slumber, his senses were keen. He woke thinking he had dreamed the early-morning feast and enjoyed it immensely, but as the fog of sleep cleared, he realized he had yet to partake in the meal. He wondered if there would be toast with jam and fried bacon. Mother only cooked breakfast on special occasions, as they rarely had enough to eat and supper after a long day's work in the fields was more appealing to them both. But it had been a while since they'd enjoyed a morning like this. Not since his brother...

"Pagaene! Time to wake. Breakfast is ready," his mother called from the kitchen.

Their home was small and humble, as were most in the small town, and her voice carried easily into his room. They grew rooted vegetables to support themselves, and in such a profession, luxury and wealth went amiss. But their family had been satisfied; what little they had was enough.

Pagaene's father had gone off to battle when Pagaene was just a toddler and had not returned. His mother wouldn't often speak to him regarding his father, so he made up fantastical stories about the man who was hero of the land—a brave soul who slew fantastical beasts, saved the fair-haired maidens from wicked villains, and ultimately died for a fellow mate in the carnage of battle. This was why his father was no longer in his life. The tales had to be true, for in his eyes, any other reason could not justify his father's absence.

He kicked the covers off the bed and jumped down. His feet landed on the warm, knotted wood floor, polished smooth from years of wear. He shuffled to the door but stopped just before pulling on the latch. Voices came from just beyond the door in the kitchen. Peeking through one of the large cracks between the door and the frame, he saw a gray, weathered old man sitting at the dining table across from his mother. The man's face was stoic, his demeanor collected, but it was his voice that mesmerized the young lad.

A wave of calm washed over him as the man's deep, humbled tone reached into Pagaene's very soul. Before he realized it, he was sitting in a chair across from this new visitor, listening to the elderly man's stories of old.

Pagaene's mother set a plate of breakfast in front of him and touched his shoulder, awakening him from his trance. The boy's wild eyes focused as reality rushed back to him.

"This is your grandfather, Pagaene. He's traveled from the farther reaches to bring you with him to the capital city."

"For what?" Pagaene inquired, snapping off a bit of crispy, fried pork skin.

"Training," his mother replied. Her voice cracked with anguish.

"Training for what?" His mother's eyes welled with tears, and there was a moment of silence at the table before his grandfather spoke.

"War," the old man replied. His calm demeanor now reflected the slightest tinge of regret hidden behind a hesitant, crackled voice. "You're coming with me to a place where your father's name once carried meaning. He was the bravest warrior and the best of men. You'll learn, at last, of your heritage."

Time passed quickly from the day Pagaen's grandfather pulled him from the comfort of his home and dropped him at the gates of Jentor. Month after month of arduous training and conditioning in the Iron camps occupied him. Memories of hot tea before bed and chasing his chickens around the old well in the yard slowly faded, giving way to what his life would become.

Awakened before dawn, he trained with the sword and other weapons. He battled with his fellows, learning from the elder warriors. Battle readiness occupied his every waking moment, yet no war came to the land.

He and his fellow recruits were forced to run for miles carrying the full load of battle gear and shielding. During the winter months, they were made to sit out in the night for hours at a time, the cold air biting at Pagaene's exposed skin. Still, the months passed, and no war came to the land.

Punishment for misbehavior, failure, or the loss of sparring matches came heavy and harsh. Lashings were a daily part of his new life. But Pagaene's skill improved. His size and strength were unmatched amongst the recruits. He was being molded, conditioned into a fighter the likes of which the kingdom had never seen. Yet still, no war had come to the land. He had been lied to his entire life.

Abandoned by all those who had claimed to love him, he found his past had become a cloudy memory. He tried on occasion to picture his mother's angelic face, but even that grew harder every day. He could only remember the old man who claimed, with his mother's acknowledgement, to be his grandfather—a man who took him from all he knew on the promise of learning the meaning of the family name. But years passed with no mention of his father. Any inquiry was met with hostility and punishment.

Eventually, Pagaene pushed the memories and belief in his father's legacy out of his mind for good. He was becoming a warrior, both respected and feared. Whoever he'd been before had died the morning the old man appeared at his table. His life was dedicated now to the kingdom and the Knighthood. He never mentioned his past again. But still, no war came to the land.

Decades passed. His youth was spent in the art of war and bloodshed. All that remained of who he'd been were fleeting visions—perhaps memories, perhaps not. They flickered in his mind like sparks of steel clashing with steel. It became easier to let go altogether. He grew to be a man who lived for the sole purpose of protecting and completing his sworn duties of the court. But he was lonely.

Tired from a long day's guard, the Knight entered his quarters. His room remained uncluttered and barren, even for a Knight of the realm. He required very little—a warm bed, a wash basin, and a small wood stove. He stared at his soft down pillow, longing for rest but dreading his dreams. Recently, his mind's eye had painted ever more confounding images while he slept.

Many of his dreams included things in which he had direct involvement—battles, or men he'd been forced to kill. Nightmares frequently visited the warriors of the kingdom; rarely did they speak of such a plague. He was no exception. His need to suppress all emotion often caused physical ailments. He sometimes felt as if he was on the receiving end of a spike twisting and pressing into his gut.

But every so often, he dreamed of a woman. She came to

him as a creature of legend, a Hamadryad. They were said to be female nymphs that inhabited certain trees deep within the forests. More part of the tree than not, sharing its lifeforce with their own, they lived as symbiotic protectors of nature.

The creature never spoke. Her flesh morphed from gnarly bark, limbs forming from twisted branches and her flowing green hair growing of coniferous needles. From the waist down, she seemed nothing more than the pine from which she was birthed. She always appeared suspended amongst the branches, in shadow, the tree's sappy resin flowing from her grief-stricken eyes. She appeared in pain, reaching out to embrace him. He felt an overwhelming sense of loss, and guilt; he felt he was to blame for her sorrow. Then he would wake.

Why Pagaene dreamt of her, he did not know. He thought of the dreams as betrayals of his purpose, so close was this creature to the witches reviled by his King.

But the last dream of her was different than any other. It felt more real. The Hamadryad had leapt from her perch amongst the barren boughs. The roots of her feet landed heavily in the soft mud at the base of a scorched and withered pine. Pagaene stood motionless a few feet from the advancing nymph.

'She's coming for you, Knight. She's coming for us all.' The nymph's voice echoed in his head, but her splintered lips did not parse the words as she spoke. *'You have known this all along. She is coming, and alongside Him, you shall fight her.'*

"Who?" he questioned. "Who will stand with me? Who is He?"

The forest around them began to fade away into darkness. His senses signaled that his dream was waning and reality would return. There came the echo of a knock on wood.

"Your father, Pagaene," she whispered, her voice trembling.

He remembered her voice now. It was his mother. And in a blink, she was no longer a mythic creature. Her hair curly was now the brown of tree bark, her eyes the green of pine needles.

"Ser Pagaene." A voice woke him—a young Knight standing in his doorway. "We have the location of a well, Ser

Pagaene. The King has ordered us on the hunt. Ser Pagaene?"

"Pagaene..." Eslyd said again.

His confusion felt unlike anything he had ever experienced before. For a moment, he didn't know what was real or false. The sharp pain in the back of his head and the coppery taste of blood in his mouth set reality straight. Esyld knelt beside him, offering him water. Behind her, a magnificent pine tree rose up into the low-hanging mix of cloud and mist. In the darkness of night, with only the ambient glow of the full moon, he thought he saw a set of green eyes watching from the first set of branches.

He blinked, and they were gone. And all at once, he understood.

"She was one of you," he said, his voice hoarse. "My mother..."

Chapter 17

E syld cocked her head to one side. "Your mother was an Abdita?"

Pagaene nodded. "I am sure of it."

Esyld looked up at Khati, who stood behind her with her arms crossed. She then cast a quick glance at Carrick, who frowned down at Pagaene. Carrick caught Esyld's eye and shook his head. But Esyld needed to know the truth.

She lay a hand on Pagaene's shoulder and said, "If your mother was indeed an Abdita, perhaps I knew her. What was her name?"

Pagaene took a deep breath, then murmured, "Mathilde,

but to everyone who knew her, she was Tilly."

"Tilly." Esyld's lips curved into a warm smile. "Yes, I knew your mother. I knew her very well, actually, many years ago."

"Tell me about her," Pagaene said softly, and his voice cracked on the words. "Please. I didn't... I didn't get to spend much time with her."

"No." Khati stepped forward and swept a gesturing hand at the trees around them. "We shouldn't tarry. These woods hold more dangers than just the Hunger Stone."

"Please," Pagaene begged again and looked up at the Sylth. Khati seemed startled to find tears in the man's eyes. "Just a moment longer. I need to hear this."

Khati's slitted pupils contracted for a moment. Then, with a heavy breath, she nodded and said, "Hurry." To Carrick, she added, "Come. We should ensure nothing is headed our way."

With a quick nod to Esyld, Carrick joined Khati and strode away into the dense woods.

Esyld turned to Pagaene. "What would you like to know?"

Pagaene closed his eyes for a moment, then said, "Tell me how you knew her."

Esyld smiled. "She was my closest friend for many years. We grew up together in Freywyn and trained as Abdita together. Tilly had many friends, but somehow, she always made me feel special, like I was her favorite person in the world." She sighed, and her shoulders drooped. "But then, as it sometimes happens, we drifted apart. It wasn't that we stopped caring for each other. Life just got in the way. I was quite busy as a Meta Abdita, and your mother had met your father."

"My father?" Pagaene said, his eyes alighting with interest. "Did you know him, too?"

Esyld shook her head. "I'm sorry. I can only tell you that one summer Muave sent your mother as an ambassador to a far-away village. Tilly was gone for over a month, and when she returned, she had a blush to her cheeks I had never seen before." Esyld gave a small laugh. "She was in love. We all knew she would not be with us much longer. Sure enough, she was gone before winter. People who saw her during their travels always told me she was well. So I was happy for my friend, though I never saw her again. But I never knew she had a son." Esyld looked tenderly at Pagaene. "Now tell me something. Why does her memory trouble you?"

Pagaene cast his eyes to the forest floor, and it was a few moments before he spoke. "As a child, I was taken from her," he started, "and over that, I had no control. But I also abandoned her many times after that."

"What do you mean?" Esyld asked.

When Pagaene looked up, he seemed to see not the forest, but something else—a far-off place plucked from his memory. "I had been in Jentor for two years when a scullery boy found me in the training yard. He told me a woman had come to the castle and asked to see me. He said she identified herself as my mother. Immediately, the Master of the Yard slapped the boy across the face and instructed him to tell the woman to leave. Then he turned to me and said if I interrupted my training, he'd take off my ear. I was too terrified to disobey.

"The second time she came for me, I had nearly finished my training. At dinner, I had been given a place at the Second Table for the first time. Then a servant leaned over and told me my mother wished an audience. The men around me burst into laughter. This time, I was the one to slap the servant and send him away."

Pagaene paused and swallowed hard. "The third time was the last. I was a grown man, and it was very late at night. As I rounded the hallway leading to my apartments, I encountered an old woman standing outside my door. Bent and frail as a dry twig, she wore a traveling cloak, and the hood covered her face completely. As I neared, she whispered, 'Your mother wishes to speak to you.' I merely brushed the old woman aside and told her to leave. But she thrust something into my hand. 'Here,' she hissed at me. 'Read it.' Then she turned and disappeared into the shadows between the torch lights." Pagaene's voice lowered. "A month later, I received a notice from my village informing me my mother was dead."

"Oh, Tilly," Esyld whispered with a nod. She cupped a gentle hand around Pagaene's cheek. "What did she give to you that night?"

Pagaene reached through the collar of his shirt, and when he brought his hand back out, he held a folded, yellowed sheet of paper. "I've kept it in a secret lining beneath my clothes all these years. I keep hoping one day I'll discover the secret to understanding her words."

Esyld opened her hand. "May I?"

"Please," Pagaene said. She carefully unfolded the paper, and the Knight added, "I have read her note every day since I received it. But all I ever see are strange symbols and drawings of trees." He sighed. "I wish I knew what she had wanted to tell me."

"She wanted you to forgive yourself and know that she forgave you as well."

Pagaene shook his head. "No. It is impossible to forgive my actions."

"But she did. It says so right here."

Pagaene bolted to his feet. "What? What did you say?"

Esyld smiled and stood beside him, then pointed to the letter. "This is the language of the Abdita, Knight. And, as you may have guessed, I speak Abditan."

Pagaene clasped his hands together. "I beg you, tell me what my mother wrote! I've waited so long to hear her final words to me."

Esyld looked down at the brittle paper in her hands and translated it aloud for him. "My dearest son. First, let me tell you I love you. Know it was my deepest desire to keep you with me, and only because I knew that it would mean your failure did I allow you to be taken away. You probably still do not know why your grandfather took you, and more than likely, no one has provided any answers about your father. I wish I could explain everything in this letter, but I know you will have many questions. Thus, to help you understand, I have included a spell which will serve you well. The Abdita translating this letter will know what to do. I love you, Pagaene. The years apart have not changed that. I know you, my son. I know that you did not want to leave, but that once you did, you had to let me go and move on with your life. Please do not punish yourself for becoming the man others have forced you to be. Forgive yourself and know that I harbor no ill feelings toward you, my son. We all have our roles in life, and it is now time for you to discover your own." Esyld turned the paper over and scanned the page. "I've never seen a spell like this before," she said. "It appears to be a type of Chain Spell, but I see only a name in it."

"A Chain Spell?" Pagaene said. "What is that?"

"It calls something to you. Like yanking a chain, it retrieves whatever object you wish and immediately delivers it to you, no matter where in the world it sits, or how distant from you. But I've only ever seen Chain Spells used on *things*. This one names a person."

"Who does it name?" Pagaene asked.

Esyld swallowed. "A wizard. An… uncommon wizard. Your mother wanted you to call the Gray Wizard of Nightstone, one of the oldest and most powerful alive."

"Do you know him?" Pagaene asked.

Esyld nodded gravely. "Brace yourself." Then she planted her feet, spread her arms wide, and chanted in the language of the Abdita.

"Um forrenda.

"Um forr-nee-ah.

"Um por not-kay.

"Um forr-nee-ah.

She took a deep breath and closed her eyes. The name floated from her lips as she exhaled. *"Rassa Met Uul."*

A sharp crack split the air like lightning. Esyld and Pagaene spun around, searching for the source of the sound, yet they saw nothing but trees.

Then, from far away, came the sound of crunching leaves. It began as a soft whispering of the forest floor, but in just a few seconds, it grew into a tremulous roar. Something was running towards them.

"Here he comes," whispered Esyld.

***

Pagaene felt the vibrations under his feet, and he moved one foot back to steady himself just as the first black, hairy creature emerged from the trees. He barely had time to register what was happening before the creature leapt up onto his chest and knocked him flat onto his back. Then another one appeared, and another, and yet another. The creatures smothered him, all black fur and hot breath, and they were… licking him.

Long, slobbery pink dog tongues covered his face, his neck, his hair. The tongues went in his ears, his mouth, his nose, and his eyes. Pagaene could barely breathe. "Help," he cried.

A shrill whistle pierced the air, and at once, the dogs were gone, some driving their massive paws into Pagaene's stomach as they bounded off. He grunted and rolled over onto his side.

"I apologize," a gruff male voice said. "But I never travel anywhere without my dogs."

Pagaene spat twice, then wiped saliva from his eyes and looked up. What he saw took his breath away.

"Grandfather?"

Esyld, who had been gently petting two of the huge dogs, stood up straight and looked from the old, weathered man standing before her to Pagaene. "The Gray Wizard is your grandfather?"

The old man smiled. "On his father's side."

At that moment, the air filled with a loud crash as Carrick and Khati came charging through the trees. Khati had her keris in hand and looked ready to kill the newcomer. Carrick had his eyes on the half-dozen or so dogs that had all turned to face them.

"Who is this?" Khati demanded. "What was that noise?"

Esyld held up a hand. "This is the Gray Wizard of Nightstone. Pagaene and I summoned him here."

Pagaene pulled himself to his feet and faced the man with a steely look. "He is also my grandfather."

The wizard ignored Pagaene's glare and smiled at the

group. "My name is Rassa Met Uul. You may call me Uul. I've never cared for Rassa."

"As you wish, Uul," Esyld said. "Thank you for coming. You honor us with your presence."

"Well, I did not really have a choice." Uul laughed and scratched his whiskered cheek. "I made a promise to Pagaene's mother many years ago that I would watch over my grandson, and I do hate to break promises."

"Watch over me?" Pagaene shouted. "What do you mean? I haven't seen you since you left me in Jentor."

Uul nodded patiently. "I do not always take this form. When I wish not to be seen, I make it so. Trust me, Pagaene, when I say I have been watching over you your whole life." The wizard now frowned. "But we can discuss all this another time. I have come to provide the answers you have sought since you were a child and to help you understand your destiny."

Pagaene clenched his jaw. Long-forgotten feelings of abandonment welled inside him and filled his chest with a red-hot rage. He ached to lash out at the old man who had suddenly reappeared in his life, but his desire to finally hear the mystery of his father explained was more powerful. "Go on," he said.

"Thank you," Uul replied. "I will try to explain as quickly as possible. First, however, let me ask you, what do you recall of your father?"

Pagaene shrugged. "Nothing. I was barely more than a babe when he left. I used to invent stories about him, though. I imagined him slaying monsters, fighting on behalf of the oppressed, and dying a hero's death in battle."

"Your father," Uul said, "did *all* of those." He turned toward the Sylth. "Didn't he, Khati?"

All eyes turned toward Khati, and she nodded gravely. "Aye."

Pagaene stared, dumbfounded. "You knew my father?"

Khati looked deep into Pagaene's eyes. "I know him still. Your father is alive, Knight."

"But… but…" Pagaene sputtered. He spun to face his

grandfather. "Not one minute ago, you told me he died."

"What I said is true," the wizard said. "He died, and then he was reborn. Your father now lives in a cave on the Lake of Destiny, the very location to which you are headed. But if you were to see him now, you would never recognize him."

"The White Dragon," Esyld whispered, suddenly understanding. "His father is the White Dragon."

Chapter 18

Esyld's words caused a storm among the group. Pagaene stood frozen, tight-lipped and pale. Khati only nodded and re-sheathed her keris. Carrick, however, easily expressed his anger, turning it on her.

"Esyld, why did you call this wizard to us? Our people do not have dealings with his kind."

Esyld tipped her head to one side with a frown. She knew part of Carrick's problem was a personal anger—at his brother, and at himself—spilling out of him like water from an overfull cup. Still, some of the sudden hostility she had seen in him since they had traveled together appeared more like sudden gusts of wind rattling dry tree branches, and her Sight strained against the face of the Crone to look at him that she might see why. Shaking her head, she pushed the feeling back. Khati had been correct before; they did not have time to stand around in the woods, and especially not now that the Gray Wizard had appeared.

"We will continue through the forest," she said. "And speak as we walk. There is more to be said here than a day and a night of sitting by the fire could hold, and we do not have that luxury."

Khati nodded again and at once went for her mount, but Carrick was not so easily swayed. "We had plenty of time a moment ago," he growled.

"Time to answer a simple request and perform a simple spell. Not time to discuss the entire life of a man or explain the enigma of the White Dragon." Her Sight strained again, and with a sigh, Esyld closed the Crone's eyes to let it slip briefly to the fore and 'looked' more deeply into him, unsurprised when she found the way to his inner self clouded. Had something more happened to Carrick than personal tragedy and betrayal? Perhaps, but there was no time to investigate it now. And although her last memories of him prior to this journey were… unpleasant, he had still been a playmate of her childhood, and she would not expose him to the vagaries of the Gray Wizard.

Truthfully, the Abdita normally avoided contact with wizards, as dealing with them could be uncomfortable and troublesome. To say the least, some wizards fostered a great curiosity of the Meta Abdita—a curiosity which at least one of them in history had attempted to assuage by entering an un-attended Well to study the Faces. The Great Mother had not approved of this invasion, and the thorny branches of a wild rose had whipped him bloody before he had been forcibly ejected from the Well and barred from ever entering again, along with all others of his kind. That wizard had been left horribly scarred and bitter, and from this, a legacy of cautious hostility had been born between the two groups. The rest of their day's journey, she reflected, should be interesting indeed. Although perhaps not entirely in a good way.

***

The woods grew thicker the farther west they moved until the trees drew so close together that, in some places, the path was completely blocked by tangling branches, and a way had to be found around them. Uul's dogs made themselves useful for that— when they weren't clustering around their master or bouncing around the bemused Knight, begging for attention.

They were forced to send their horses away as the path became too tight for the beasts. After transferring their supplies to packs, they sent the mounts away. Khati bid hers to look after the others, and they trotted back down the mountain, trailing mist.

With the whole party now on foot, Uul moved up beside his grandson.

"They remember you," the wizard told him. "Dogs do not forget a scent, and these two—" he indicated a pair of dogs, gray-muzzled but no slower-moving than the others "—were young dogs when I came to get you." He huffed out a breath when Pagaene turned his face away from him at that. "It had to be done, Grandson. You have a destiny, whether you want it or not—and whether those rock-headed fools at the training ground wanted you to know of it or not."

Pagaene's jaw set. "You took me from my mother, and they kept me from her. You obviously care more for some prophesied destiny than you did for the woman who wed your son."

"She understood…"

"I don't. And it doesn't matter much now, does it?" Pagaene lifted his arm so the wooden hand could be seen. "This may work as the hand of a man but not the hand of a fighting knight. In time, I could train myself to fight again with one good hand and one of enchanted wood… but even if the other soldiers of the King did not kill me on sight—which in all likelihood they will—I have no time to train and no help. Do not offer yourself," he snapped when the older man opened his mouth. "I do not trust you. And my mother should not have trusted you, either. Were those tales I told myself as a child all lies? Was my father like you? Is that why none of the other knights will so much as speak his name?"

Uul made a face. The boy, now a man, had come closer to the truth than he knew—albeit from the wrong direction. "I cannot speak of that now, Pagaene. I will in time, however. Trust me on that." Pagaene scowled and stomped away, and the wizard rolled his eyes. "This won't do at all. He's too much like his father."

"Perhaps a thing you should have considered before you made your choice." The sylth's smooth voice startled him. She was very near, nearer than he'd realized, and her slit-pupiled green eyes gazed into his, then looked away. "You sent a child into the heart of coming darkness, with no warning or succor. And yet you expect him to embrace you with open arms and thank you for your games when he is a lonely, bitter, betrayed man of arms… who now has only one?"

The wizard frowned. "Why are you here?"

She huffed out a little puff of mist. "You know why I am here and who I serve." She gestured to where Carrick scouted ahead in the wake of one of the black dogs. "If you wish to reach someone, reach that one. I can feel the twisting fog inside him, but I do not know its cause—only that it was done to him by one who wished him to not see the truth."

"Muave?"

Khati shrugged. "It is possible. I have been sending the Meta Abdita urgings to use her Sight on him, but although she tried, briefly, such a thing needs time we do not have." She glanced at him again, the touch of those familiar eyes making him shiver. "Her Well is gone, destroyed by the King's men… the same men you tasked with training Pagaene."

This time he winced. "I am powerful, not omniscient," he said. "The corruption ran deep even at that time. Now, it runs in the open like a stream swelling from the spring thaw, plain for all to see."

"And it spreads across the countryside, like a flood breaking the stream's banks and bringing death and destruction," she agreed. "Befriend the Meta Abdita, if you can, but do not forget that the Face she wears is merely an aspect of the Great Mother, not the one who was born Esyld. And the Great Mother… has been strangely silent of late."

She moved away from him then, going ahead to try a different path, the white mist from hers and the horse's exhalations flowing brokenly over the damp, heavy air like ragged strips of fine linen. One of the dogs licked Uul's hand, and he stroked the black head absently, thinking on what this sylth had just said to him. He considered the Meta Abdita. He did remember Esyld, although she had been but a youngling herself when they had first met, and now he could see that the Face of the Crone did not impart the wisdom and confidence it should have; Esyld seemed unsure, grasping for what wisps of aged wisdom flowed her way.

He frowned, murmuring a word and making a small gesture, and many objects grew limned in magical light for his eyes alone—the sylth's keris, outlined in white fire tinged with red; Pagaene's false arm, ribbons of gentle blue wrapping around the ghost of the arm of flesh he'd lost to bind it to carved and polished wood; the athame in its sheath carried by Carrick, haloed in a deeper blue for some reason threaded with green as though corrupted—possibly the same something he now saw in the emerald ring worn by the Meta Abdita, a link to the power of a Sacred Grove, no doubt because she had lost her own. But strings of green ran from it to the Face of the Crone, binding the Face to the woman's head like green vines twining and binding a broken branch to the tree from which it should have fallen.

Esyld turned to look at him just then, frowning, and he dismissed the spell with a word before approaching her. "That wasn't why I was looking," he said. "Some of us learned from old Halvard's stupidity, you know. But have you any idea why strings of another's power run through the athame your old playmate Carrick carries? It glows blue, as it should, but the threads are green. And similar strings also run from your ring to your Face, like vines climbing a tree and wrapping dead branches."

She shook her head. "The ring was given to me by Muave, a source of power that I might undertake this journey. Carrick is her brother."

"She bound him for some reason," he repeated. "Strings of power, like a web. Not power shared by blood or a chain to link them, but a web of controlling."

"And a vine of binding." The Face of the Crone wrinkled deeply from her frown. "I don't know, Gray Wizard. Everything has happened so quickly—"

"That you haven't had time to process it. I realize that," he told her. "And perhaps you don't even know. But the sylth suspects something—or possibly many things—and she believes he was being kept from seeing something." He frowned down at her, lowering his voice. "She also says the Great Mother has been strangely silent of late, and the history we share tells me that in itself is strange and worrisome. The last time someone interfered with a Sacred Well… well, she reacted."

"And now Well after Well has been destroyed." Esyld bit her lip. "I don't know what to think… but I do know our only hope is to press on and reach the Lake of Destiny as quickly as we can. Will he…"

The old wizard nodded. "Of course. He may be in a different form, but he still has the heart of a great and honorable knight." He smirked. "Not to mention, he *is* my son."

Esyld might have responded to that, but before her mouth could open, Carrick called out, being at once converged upon by Khati, Pagaene, and several dogs. Esyld and Uul hurried to catch up and found themselves standing on a ridge overlooking the deep blue waters of the Lake of Destiny.

***

A thin layer of snow covered the ridge and the narrow path down to the rocky beach. They had been shielded from the precipitation while in the dense forest. Now, flakes fell softly onto the travelers' shoulders and into the calmly rippling water below.

Esyld closed the eyes of the Crone and began to speak a prayer of thanks to the Great Mother for bringing them safely to their destination. But she stopped when Pagaene made a sound half grunt, half gasp.

He had turned to face the mouth of a cave which had been all but hidden by the close-set, overgrown trees. The mouth had been blocked with stones and large branches, and across this rough barrier were chained the remains of what had most likely once been a Knight, now rotted away to little more than a parchment-covered skeleton with rags of clothing poking out from beneath rotting leather armor. Each skeletal hand clutched a short spear, tied into place that they might not be released, and both a rusted sword and several knives hung from the sagging belt.

Most notable and disturbing, however, were the metal stakes which had been driven through the corpse's eyes, pinning its head in place that it might forever face forward—forever on guard.

"A *forraens morta*," Esyld breathed in horror. "A Knight chained to his duty by death, so what he guards may never gain release."

"A *witch* did this?" Pagaene demanded. "What kind of magic demands this sort of sacrifice?"

"The very blackest kind," Uul answered. "But no witch did this. This is the work of the Symorcian Brotherhood. Shape-changing devotees who served the Purity."

"A long time ago?" Carrick asked hopefully. "This corpse is old…"

"No, he isn't," Pagaene contradicted him. "That badge on the left breast. The only Knights who wear that are especially dedicated to the King's safety. This man has been here five years at most."

"The life was drained from him through the stakes in his eyes, to power the spell of containment," Uul confirmed. "But I thought the Brotherhood had all been killed, years upon years ago. None of them were said to have survived that purging."

"Then whoever said that was a liar," Khati observed with a shrug. "Is there any way to know what lies behind this barrier of death-magic?"

The old wizard smirked. "Only if we break it open."

"We don't have time for this," Carrick said, gesturing across the lake to an island in its center, where a large stone shrine sat before another cave. "We have to get the stones."

Pagaene scowled at him. "We can't leave him here like this. *I* can't leave him here."

"Of course not," Uul agreed and waved his hand at the corpse. "Tell him, not me. He'll leave if you, as a fellow honorable Knight, agree to assume responsibility for whatever it is he's guarding."

His grandson faltered. "But we don't know what that is."

"No, we don't." Uul smirked again. "But we do know that evil wanted it locked away, and that whoever left him here wasn't able to simply kill it." The smirk fell off. "And we know that if you don't release him... his spirit remains bound here with his body, forever on watch."

"That is true," Esyld said. "A *forraens morta* is bound to duty by their very soul."

"Couldn't it be a trap?" Carrick fingered his athame's hilt. "What if the whole point was to trick a noble Knight who made it this far—" he indicated Pagaene "—into getting himself and his companions killed?"

Pagaene blinked at him. "If that is the case," he said quietly, "then you'd best prepare to run—because I will not leave my brother in arms here, no matter what his purpose." He stepped forward, looked the corpse in the eye as best he could, and stood at attention. "I am here to relieve you," he announced formally, just as he would have done had they been two living men changing the guard. "Your duty is now my duty, until I myself am relieved."

All was silent. Even the rustling of leaf and branch fell still. And then, horribly, the dead mouth opened with a sound of grinding bones and tearing parchment, and words fell from it like dust falling through the air. "*Who relieves me, and by whose order?*"

"Ser Pagaene." He hesitated. "And it is by my own authority I relieve you, fellow Knight."

An even more pregnant pause followed. "*Honorable fellow*

Knight, I cede my duty to you."

And then the body crumpled into dust, sliding off the makeshift barrier and leaving the chains dangling in impotent defeat. A rumbling began, seemingly coming from within the cave itself but vibrating the ground beneath their feet. A rock tumbled from its place, then several more, and then the entire surface heaved outward and a deep, rumbling surrounded them. Everyone dove out of the way as the barrier exploded out of the cave mouth, rocks and sticks and dirt flying every which way … and then a large black bear lumbered out, blinking. It emitted another roar, then dropped to all fours and sniffed, a curious expression on its face.

"Well, I'm waiting," it said in a deep, amused voice. "Come out, Knight, and let me see the man whose honor just bought him a very hungry companion."

Chapter 19

E ven while Uul and his dogs, Khati, Carrick, and Esyld remained sprawled on the ground, dazed by the blast, Pagaene stood. He strode toward the bear with a swagger, gravel crushing beneath his feet, and did not stop until he stood directly before the creature, well within range of a swipe from its titanic claws.

The bear sneered at Pagaene and sniffed twice. After a long, tense pause, it gave a hearty laugh. "You, little man? Are you the one who dares contain me?"

Pagaene drew his sword and crouched into a fighting stance. "I care not whether you are friend or foe. My only desire was to free my brother at arms from the black magic binding his soul, and in that I have succeeded. If fighting you is the consequence, then so be it."

The bear looked at the pile of dust lying pitifully at the entrance to the cave and let out a pained groan. "The poor soul. It was a *forraens morta*, was it not?"

Uul stood now, his dogs crouching tensely at his heels, and demanded, "What would you know of such black arts?"

"Who better to know the work of the Symorcian Brotherhood?"

Suddenly, the bear's snout began to shrink, and his shoulders pinched toward each other. The sound of bones popping and cartilage crunching filled the air as the bear's body jerked, contorted, and transformed in a fluid and practiced yet still labored motion. When the transformation was complete, a man knelt where the bear had stood, his face obscured by a black hood. He wore a tattered cloak revealing powerful and dark arms through its rips. The cloak bore a patch on the sleeve of two serpents intertwining around an hourglass.

Uul aimed his staff at the ragged man, and his dogs unleashed a fury of growls and bays. "Everyone behind me," the wizard cried. "This man is one of the unholy agents of The Purity."

The man laughed deeply. He pulled his hood back to reveal a dark-skinned face and a crackling white smile. "She's fooled you into calling her by that silly name?"

"And what might you call her?" Uul said. "Master? Savior?"

"I call that foul force what she is. The very rotting face of Death."

"What does he mean?" Pagaene asked.

Uul snarled and re-adjusted the grip on his staff, making sure to keep it aimed at the Symorcian Brother's heart. "He means that the force we call The Purity is actually one of the three Prime Forces at work in the world. He means that The Purity is—"

"Death herself," the Symorcian Brother said as he rose to his feet. He cut an imposing figure, nearly as tall in his human form as he had been as a bear. "And I have sworn to stop her and any weak-minded souls who would do her bidding."

"But," Uul said, "you wear the clothes of her servant?"

"That's exactly what I was. Until she betrayed me."

"Hold now," Carrick said, stepping to the fore and drawing his athame. "Why should we believe you?"

"I don't need you to believe me. I know the depth and granite density of my vengeance. What I do not know is who you all are and why you would be so stupid as to fool with a *forraens morta*. Unless, that is, she sent you here to finish the work my former brethren could not complete when they captured me."

"I told you," Pagaene said, "my only intent was to free my brother Knight's soul from his dark fate."

"You expect me to believe that you are simply passing by the Lake of Destiny with no ulterior purpose?"

"You are correct," Eslyd said. "We are not here by accident."

The Symorcian Brother walked casually to the pile of the Knight's bones and picked up what appeared to be a finger. "Oh," he said, "and what might that be?"

"Wouldn't you like to know?" Carrick shot back.

"I would very much," the Symorcian Brother said as he twirled the bone between his fingers. "And I intend to find out." He stopped twirling the bone and grasped it in his hand. A golden light arced out from the bone and surrounded his fist.

"By the Great Mother," Carrick said, his eyes wide.

The Symorcian Brother slammed his golden, glowing fist into the ground, and thick vines burst from the earth. Before any of them could dodge, the party was bound hand and foot by the newly birthed vines. The foliage ripped Uul's staff from his hand and muzzled his dogs. Khati, Eslyd, and Pagaene were dragged to the dusty ground and held fast there. Carrick's athame clattered to the earth as the vines suspended him, immobile, several feet in the air.

"You..." Carrick said. "You have the burning touch?"

"Aha!" The Symorcian Brother clapped his hands and pointed victoriously to Carrick. "That proves it. I have the gift of re-birth, and only those who serve death need fear my gift. It is why she cast me out all those years ago on the day I received my animal form. All my brethren had taken the forms of death—serpents, spiders, leeches, bats. But when I emerged from the ritual as a bear, a creature that nears death every winter only to be reborn in the spring, she sensed it was not only my shape that had changed but my very constitution as well. She knew that somehow, some deep magic had endowed me with this mysterious gift. And on that day, for the first and only time in my life, I saw her shrink and stammer in fear.

"She ordered the rest of my Brothers to end my life. Luckily, I escaped and avoided them for several years before they caught up with me here. But when they tried to kill me, none of their necrotic spells could harm me. So they locked me inside that cave instead. Soon thereafter, she was similarly imprisoned. I could feel it—her hunger and fear an echo of my own." He let out a huff, almost laughter. "My gift is the only thing she fears, and if you fear it, you must be for her."

Eslyd felt the vines tightening their grip around her wrists and throat. If they continued to tighten, she would soon be choked. "We…" She wriggled against the vine to create more room to breathe. "We have come for the stones…" She coughed. "In the Temple of Verity."

The Symorcian Brother turned to Eslyd. "What did you say?"

"We mean to heal the world from her plaguing touch. We have come for the stones."

"How do you know of the stones?"

"Eslyd," Carrick said, struggling against his own bonds. "Don't."

"Muave, the High Priestess of the abdita, sent us on this quest. We have one among us destined to retrieve them and restore balance to the land."

The Symorcian Brother glared at Eslyd's aged face. He glanced at the emerald ring on her finger before looking her in the eyes once again. "A clever lie always holds a bit of truth," he said. "We shall see how your tale holds up." The Symorcian Brother folded his and knelt back to the dusty earth. His shoulders spread, and his joints began to crack and crunch. Hair sprouted all over his body, and within a few seconds, he had returned to bear form. He sat on his haunches, stuck his snout in the air, and sniffed deeply, as if he were searching for some particular scent. His nostrils flared, and his head twitched inquisitively for a moment before he suddenly stopped. His eyes locked on Carrick. "How…curious?" he said, padding toward Carrick.

Carrick writhed against his bonds, but the vines held fast. The bear rose to two legs and placed a paw on either of Carrick's shoulders. "Stay back, death-lover," Carrick shouted.

The bear ran a razor claw slowly across Carrick's cheek. A ribbon of blood dribbled down Carrick's face. The bear gathered the blood on his claw, held it to his snout, and sniffed. "In another place or another time," the Symorcian Brother said, "you may have also borne the gift I bear. Your blood certainly carried the potential at one point in your life, but no longer. And yet…" The bear sniffed his bloody claw again. "We have not met before?"

"I would remember a face as evil as yours," Carrick spat back.

"The scent of your blood is so familiar." The bear shook his head. "Oh well. Perhaps it was a relative of yours." The bear tapped his heavy paw gently against Carrick's cheek twice, then fell to all fours and sloughed back towards the group.

"Halt, you vile beast!" Carrick shouted. His eyes flared with anger, and his face flushed red. "You did this to him!"

The bear did not look back. He sauntered past the rest of the group as they struggled against the vines holding them fast to the earth. He reached Uul, whose dogs whimpered in his presence. The bear reached down, clawed blood from the wizard's cheek, and sniffed it too. Then he shook his head and kept walking.

"You did this to my brother," Carrick screamed. "Your black magic made him a monster!"

The bear drew blood from Khati's cheek, sniffed, and once again shook his head. He continued to stalk amongst the group but did not turn to face Carrick as he spoke. "I may only identify those who may receive this power, not bestow the power myself. Though, sometimes, the kiss of my claws has caused the power to manifest. I claim to know neither how this works nor where it originates, but I know it is the only force capable of stopping Her." As he spoke, he reached a claw down to Eslyd and drew her blood. He sniffed it and once again shook his head.

"He performs that same golden, abhorrent trick as you," Carrick shouted.

"If what you say is true, it is neither my nor your brother's fault that you fail to see his gift for the blessing it truly is. You have only your own blindness to blame." The bear drew blood from Pagaene's cheek and looked to Eslyd. "You best hope this one bears fruit. Otherwise, I will maul your throats and leave you to rot for having been such a severe waste of my... of my..." The bear let out a joyous roar. He dropped his massive paw to his side and staggered backwards. "This one indeed does have the ability to bear the gift of Rebirth," the bear said. "But more, oh, so much more. He will heal this land. He will defeat Her. He will rein Her in and hold Her in balance with life. But there is also a darkness in him. One that may consume him if it goes unchecked or if Her forces fan its flames."

Eslyd felt the vines around her neck and arms begin to loosen. "Does this mean you will allow us to continue?" she said.

The bear nodded. "I cannot claim to trust you, nor will I offer my assistance. I have my own work to do in finding those with the potential to wield this power and learn more of its mysterious nature. But neither can I in good conscience interfere with your mission as long as one of such powerful blood travels with you. I can, however, leave you this." The bear reached into his fur and produced a quartz stone strung upon a leather strap. The stone was small enough to fit in the palm of Eslyd's hand, and it glowed with a soft golden light. "I have imbued this stone with a scrap of my power. Not enough to bring anything back from beyond death, for I have not yet mastered this mysterious art. But it should protect the wearer from Her necrotizing touch." He laid it on the ground in front of Pagaene. "I would highly suggest you have him wear it."

The bear backed slowly to the edge of the woods, his eyes constantly scanning the party for sign of action or betrayal. When he reached the treeline, he stopped. "Do not follow me," he said. "Do not speak of me. Ever. To anyone. She has eyes and ears all over this world, for wherever death exists, She is there also."

"Where are you going?" Eslyd cried.

"I would not tell you, even if I knew." The bear turned and bounded off into the woods.

A few moments later, the vines had uncoiled enough for Eslyd to wriggle her wrists free. Pagaene freed himself as well, and together, they cut free Uul and his dogs, Khati, and Carrick. Eslyd picked up the quartz and held it out to Pagaene. "Here," she said. "Take this and wear it well."

Pagaene stared at the stone in his hand and its soft golden glow.

"I wouldn't bother with such a trinket," Khati said with a puff of frost on her breath.

"Agreed," Carrick said. "I don't trust the shapeshifter."

"Maybe it's time you try," Eslyd replied. "We are close to our journey's end, and while we have come across plenty of danger, we have also met many whose only intent has been to aid us. There is more than evil in the world, Carrick."

Uul leaned on his staff and smiled. "She speaks the truth," he said.

"And what would you know of trust, wizard?"

Uul's hounds growled, but he quieted them with a wave of his hand. "I may not know of trust," he said, "but I know that we will need whatever help we can get against the evil we face. I know that the Symorcian Brother, however confused, held genuine anger against The Purity. He wanted to end her. And I know that in times such as these, we must be open to finding friends even in the darkest of places."

Pagaene looked to Uul and looped the quartz around his neck, tucking it beneath his armor. He looked up at the dusky sky, the light beginning to fade into dull orange and gray. "Let's make camp near the beach," he said, "and make our way to the Shrine in the morning."

They picked their way along the downward path to the rocky beach. On level ground again, they spotted the figures of two diminutive women near the woods. One sat clutching her ankle and howling in agony. The other taller figured hovered over the first, trying but unable to comfort her

Eslyd approached the women while the rest of the party remained at a close distance. She saw that the figure on the ground was a young maiden, her face contorted in pain. "What's happened?" she asked.

"Oh, my poor, poor daughter," said the standing woman. She wore a look of grim worry and shivered as she spoke. "If there's anything you can do... We were on our way back to Parkovia when my daughter turned her ankle. I'm afraid of what will happen if we have to stay the night out here. Predators and thieves and... oh, I fear for our very lives."

"Don't worry, ma'am," Eslyd said. "I know just the thing." She turned her gaze to forest floor and spotted a few basic healing herbs. Her head was only turned for a moment before she heard a sharp hissing, growling and barking, then several thuds from behind. She spun around and saw her companions—Uul, Khati, and Carrick—rolling on the ground, a thick green paste covering their faces and appearing to be burn them. Some of Uul's dogs were down, and the rest hesitantly attempted to attack two half-human, half-serpentine beasts standing now where the mother and maiden had been. Each held the limp face of a Meta Abdita in one hand.

Pagaene, who had dodged the green paste, drew his sword and charged the creatures.

"No," Eslyd cried. "You can't—

But the green spray cut her off cold.

Chapter 20

For a moment, Esyld struggled against the paste. It blocked her eyes, her mouth, and nose, and it burned fiercely. Her hands lifted automatically to claw the stuff away, but it only made her hands burn too.

She realized quickly that if she had any hope of fighting off their attackers, she'd need to remove the face of the Crone. It would leave her without the Great Mother's guidance, but then, she was no longer sure she had that anyway.

So before she could run out of breath, and before the acid could eat through the Crone's skin, she gripped her hair and pulled, willing it to come away in her hands. Her skin rippled as the face obligingly peeled away, returning her to her usual form.

Her hands still burned, but that was tolerable. She held the face of the Crone tightly in one hand as she drew her athame with the other and looked with the Sight.

Pagaene fought off the two half-snake attackers—Symorcians, Esyld realized. He was holding his own, barely, but Khati was already up and on her way to help. Some of Uul's dogs bounded to their aid.

Uul, too, was getting up, and Esyld could see him using magic to clean the last of the acid spray from his face. Carrick still lay on the ground, and she rushed to help him.

Grunting in disgust, he used a spell to clean the stuff from his eyes when she reached him. "What the—Esyld?"

"Here," she said urgently, offering him a hand. He opened his eyes and recoiled for a moment, then took it, and she helped him up. "Distract them if you can," she said. "We won't be able to defeat them, but we can escape."

"How?"

"Open water." She gestured at the lake, then pushed him toward the battle. "Go!" Then she turned back to the forest behind them and worked her magic.

***

Meanwhile, Pagaene gritted his teeth and thrust his sword at the snake-men. They reeled back at the force of his blows, but the blade barely so much as scratched them. Instead, it clanged against their scaly skin and rebounded without injury. The dogs around his feet had no more luck than he, and it didn't help that the sun had all but set.

"You won't succeed!" one of their attackers yelled.

He was relieved, more than he'd like to admit, when Khati appeared beside him. She gestured, and one of the snake-men screeched and lurched back, clutching his arm.

"I can't touch them," Pagaene exclaimed, blocking a strike from the other snake. He dodged to the side to avoid another spray of acid, almost tripping over one of the dogs.

"My magic is not as effective as it should be," Khati replied, even as she gestured and made her opponent screech in pain again. "Something is amiss."

"You don't know what?"

"No," she said grimly. "But focus."

"I *am*," he responded, stepping aside and swinging at his attacker's neck. What should have been a killing blow merely glanced off the snake-man's skin, though his enemy did make a sort of strangled noise and pulled back, clutching his throat.

Unfortunately, he recovered quickly and slithered forward to attack again, only to be pushed back by a blast from Uul.

"They seem to be protected by a dark force," Uul commented, urging his dogs forward.

"They can't always have been," Pagaene said, staring down his attacker; the fiend's face was covered in old scars. "Perhaps because they've shifted?"

"No, this is something else." Uul blasted the snake-man back once more. "If they are creatures of death, perhaps your Rebirth powers should be used."

"I don't how," Pagaene said stiffly. He and Uul dodged more acid and regrouped again. When he glanced away, he saw Carrick had joined Khati against the other snake. "Where's Esyld?"

"She's got a plan," Carrick called back.

"What is it?"

"I don't know!"

He focused on maintaining his position. Without the ability to harm the Symorcians, how could they possibly win? They'd be forced into a stalemate until one side or the other tired—and by the size and strength of these things, it wouldn't be *them*.

But he couldn't just accept defeat. So he kept launched everything he had at the snake-men, dodging their blows and acid with Uul and his dogs' assistance.

A rumble sounded behind them, then something shot past their battle toward the beach; they were branches.

"Carrick, with me!" Esyld shouted, and there was another

rumble followed by a flash of light. The Symorcians yelled and pulled back, and Esyld ran down to join the party. She passed them, followed closely by Carrick. "To the water," she cried, and Khati, Uul, and the dogs followed after her.

As he turned to run as well, Pagaene noticed that one of the Symorcians had dropped something furry—he bent and grabbed it as he ran toward the others, not caring enough to look at what it was. If the snake-men had had it in their possession, it had to be important; at the very least it might provide some clue as to what they were after.

He could see ahead—by the light of the moon, now—that a large raft of woven branches floated in the water, and most of the group already stood atop it. Pagaene waded into the water and clambered quickly onto the raft, and then they were off, the snake-men screeching and yelling behind them.

"You can't run from Her forever!" one yelled. Then they turned and slithered back into the forest, disappearing quickly into the trees.

Pagaene finally looked down at the thing in his hand and recoiled. It fell from his hand—a *face*, that of a young woman, with hair he'd mistaken for fur.

A deft hand caught it as it fell, and he looked up and blanched; the hand belonged to an unfamiliar body and an eyeless face, like something from a nightmare.

"Thank you for taking this, Pagaene." Esyld's voice emanated from the… thing. "I do not know how those *beasts* managed to steal the Maiden and the Mother of a Meta, but I *will* find out."

"I thought all the wells were destroyed," said Carrick.

"As did I."

Carrick did not seem particularly surprised or disturbed by Esyld's new appearance, nor did Khati. Uul looked as alarmed as Pagaene felt, however, and the dogs whined. And when Pagaene looked down, away from that hideous face, he saw yet another face in Esyld's hand—one that bore the appearance of the Esyld with whom he'd traveled all this time.

"Esyld?" he asked tentatively.

"Yes. It is I," she said stiffly. For her part, she paid little heed to Pagaene's discomfort, and Uul's, and the dogs', though she seemed quite aware of it. Instead she clenched her fists around the hair of the faces. With a sigh, she dug in her bag for healing plants and dispersed them. As the group treated their own acid burns, she explained her plan.

"We will be safe out here. Their magic won't travel over open water. On the other hand, that strength is also our weakness. It will slow us down. We won't reach the island before midnight, at the earliest."

"I'll take first watch and steer us toward the island," Carrick offered, picking up a sturdy strip of bark to help guide their drifting.

"Then I'll take second," Pagaene said.

"No," Esyld told him, and he was startled to be addressed so abruptly. "You will need your strength for whatever lies ahead at the Shrine of Verity. Sleep now, and the rest of us will have our turns."

"If you insist," he said uncertainly and laid down uncomfortably on the raft. Several of the dogs curled in around him. He was grateful for their warmth, but even so, knowing now that the true face of one of his companions was an eyeless, noseless horror, he could not sleep for some time.

***

Esyld turned to the rest of her companions.

"I'd heard of the true form of the Meta Abdita, but seeing it is something else entirely," Uul muttered.

"You won't have to do so much longer," she said, lifting the face of the Crone again. It did not react as it should, just as the other two barely responded to her touch. She could sense its presence still, but it wasn't strong enough.

She could no longer wear it.

How dare those monsters defile the Sacred Grove! She

clenched her fists around the hair of the faces, and both barely reacted to her presence. Could it be the Great Mother was weakening? They were almost to the stones, but was it already too late? "Or... perhaps you will," she said and carefully wrapped the face up and tucked it away with her belongings. It felt sacrilegious, but she had no choice for now.

"Is something wrong?" Carrick asked. "Has... has the Great Mother forsaken us?"

"No," she said firmly. "I don't believe that. The Crone may simply have been damaged by the acid. I hope that when the Wells are restored, so she shall be."

"Your ring is still bound to the face of the Crone," Uul noted.

"Then Muave likely already knows I've had to remove the face," Esyld said. "Though why it matters to her, I do not know."

The conversation lapsed, and Carrick moved to take watch as Esyld lay down to rest, turning the ring on her finger. She had used a lot of magic to enable their escape—more than she would have liked. Furthermore, they'd have to deal with the Symorcian Brothers again once they'd retrieved the stones. This was only a reprieve.

Sometime in the middle of the night, Khati woke her. "Your turn," the sylth said, passing the dripping paddle to Esyld before immediately lying down. The rest of the group huddled in the center of the raft, surrounded by the dogs.

Esyld resigned herself to a long, boring watch as they drifted across the Lake of Destiny. The only sounds were light snoring and the water lapping against the raft. She pulled the face of the Maiden from the pocket of her cloak and noted how much more awake and aware it felt than the Crone. She could better use the Crone's wisdom than the Maiden's innocence, but any face was likely better than none. Still, even the Mother would have been better.

She lifted the face regardless and let the Maiden cover her own skin, filling her with joy and curiosity. Those feelings were short-lived, given their situation, and not even the Maiden could remove the heavy weight of their task. Even so, Esyld enjoyed the reprieve, and as the positive emotions faded, she settled in to her watch.

Chapter 21

T he full moon rose steadily across the night sky, a beacon of light guiding them across the lake. Esyld murmured a spell under her breath, and the evening breeze carried it around them, magically cloaking them from sight. While she was grateful for the bright night sky, she knew it would make their approach that much more visible to anyone keeping watch. When the emerald ring glowed faintly before turning black, Esyld sighed in frustration; the last of the magic was gone. She removed it from her finger and tossed it into the darkness of the lake.

Unable to recall the last time she'd been surrounded by such stillness and quiet, Esyld decided she would let the others sleep, glad for the opportunity to attempt to process what they'd been through. The moonlight fell upon her, and the heaviness of her heart mixed with a sweeping sadness. She'd known it was there—the weight of losing her connection to The Great Mother, to the magic, as it dwindled away. Feeling lost, she gazed up at the night sky, hoping for some guidance or clarity. She was certain that the destruction of the Earth by The Purity had damaged her connection with the Great Mother. Would she ever manage to get it back? Could they defeat The Purity without Her?

Esyld's prayers were disrupted by a tremor running through the soles of her feet. Steadying herself, she looked down at the raft, surprisingly afraid of the unknown cause. It came again, the vibration running straight up her legs, and she turned to look back at the sleeping party. The tremors hadn't woken them, which confused her, and Esyld turned back towards the lake. There she saw a glowing light rising under the surface. The raft shook, but she barely noticed, too engrossed by the orb of light breaking free from the lake and hovering before her. A wave of warm yellow light swept out, enveloping her, banishing any concerns or fear, and Esyld closed her eyes with a hint of a smile. When she opened them, the light retreated, absorbed into the Priestess who had summoned it, and left Muave in its wake.

"How…" Esyld started, glancing once more at the sleeping group behind her.

"You need not worry. They won't awaken. We need to talk."

"I spent the ring's power. I cannot protect us now."

"The ring's power faded faster than expected, this is true, for no reason other than you no longer wear The Crone. The two were bound together."

"Is the Maiden bound to another source?" Esyld asked. Muave only stared in silence, and Esyld fought not to be distracted again by the sparks of light bursting from the Priestess' presence.

"I think you can sense that she is. Yet it is not for me to tell you the object of that bond. This connection you need to discover for yourself—and soon. You haven't much time at all. I have cast a spell upon the moon. The night will last for twenty-four more hours. The Symorcians abhor the light, where their vision is almost nonexistent, as I'm sure you've discovered. But they are also weakest under the full moon. If they are, by chance, waiting for you at the Shrine, your chance to defeat them is now."

"If I cannot find the Maiden's source in time…"

Muave's eyes narrowed, her lips pressed harshly together, and the warm yellow light around her turned a cold, pale blue. Esyld shivered. "Now is no time to doubt yourself, Esyld. You are as old as I, from a long line of magic. Quite simply, if you fail, Pagaene fails. You know what that will mean for all of us."

Before Esyld could reply, the light around Muave paled as white as the moon, and her image shimmered, shrank, and became the orb once more. Esyld reached out a hand, wanting more, but the orb erupted, knocking her backward with a violent shockwave and dangerously rocking the raft. Raising herself on her hands, she looked up to find only the reflection of the full moon across the lake.

Muave was right. Esyld always knew she had her own inner strength and resilience at her disposal, and that was something she could not forget. A tingle covered her face as though the Maiden, too, approved of her renewed optimism. Esyld arose and planted her feet firmly on the raft, setting her sights toward the Shrine of Verity.

***

Pagaene awoke and stared up at the starry sky above him. He felt groggy like he'd pulled out of a deep sleep too soon. As he sat up, he glanced at the others sleeping around him and wondered how much time had passed. When he stared at the moon, he couldn't tell if it had moved at all in the sky since he first lay down.

Then he saw her at the front the raft, radiating determination as the gentle evening breeze sent her long hair flying around her. As though sensing his gaze, she turned, the moonlight hitting her directly, illuminating her delicate features. Pagaene's heart thudded fiercely.

With a dry mouth, he let out a hoarse whisper. "Mother?"

***

Esyld watched the Knight in confusion, wondering what was wrong with him. Was he dream-talking? Before she could open her mouth, he scurried towards her on his hands and knees, lowering his head at her feet. "I thought I'd imagined seeing you when I touched the hunger stone! I've regretted turning away your forgiveness, and I fear that without it, I won't be able to continue down this path. I need you to know, Mother, I've never forgiven myself for killing Fritjof!"

"Pagaene—" she tried.

"No, no. You need to listen to me! It was an accident. He was my brother, my twin—I would never intentionally harm him. I don't even know how it happened. We were merely young boys playing. Then we were fighting." He paused, engulfed by a sob. "Then he was dead."

"Pagaene…"

"It's why I could never face you when you came to visit. I didn't want forgiveness. I wanted to be punished, and the harsh training I endured ensured that I was."

"Pagaene!"

He looked up at her, his tear-stained eyes wide with surprise. "Es… Esyld?"

She nodded, unsure of what to say after such a revelation.

"But… my mother…"

Esyld had to think carefully before answering, but she had enough knowledge to rapidly put the pieces together. "I'm wearing the face of the Maiden, stolen by Anguis and Caedus. I think this face must have come from the Well of your mother. I imagine she wore this face when you were a child."

Pagaene got to his feet and half stumbled, half shuffled away from her. "What I said…"

"Stays between us," she confirmed. He gave a slight nod as he looked around them, seeming disoriented, as though half of him was with her and the other half still relived his brother's death.

"I would very much like to be alone," he declared in an

attempt to project knightly conviction. "I will take my shift now."

Without a word, Esyld headed to the rear of the raft, far too awake to sleep but wanting to give Pagaene his space. She now understood why the Maiden had felt so charged; she remembered her son, the Knight. Esyld felt in her heart there was more to it, but each theory provided only more questions. Still, the truth remained that unlocking the mystery of Fritjof's death would lend clarity to Pagaene on his path… and lead her back to the magic.

***

Caedus and Anguis appeared before His Holiness, smiles flickering across their treacherous faces. Apparently refusing to degrade himself by pleading, the man struggled against his bonds but raised his head and sneered. Anguis pulled out his blade and stepped forward. With a single, violent strike, he sliced open the man's throat, blood gushing into the soil below.

The ground began to shake, and Caedus and Anguis stepped back. The earth cracked open, exposing the hot, molten lair of The Purity coursing below. Lava pulsated, fiery-red and orange as it appeared to lap up the blood flowing from above. With a frenzied hunger, the cracks spread farther, widening under His Holiness until he too became engulfed. The Purity, not wanting to waste a single drop, reveled in the newfound strength.

Neither Caedus or Anguis saw the Raven watching from a tree branch.

***

Esyld's companions began to wake, the animals instantly restless while Carrick and Khati stared at the sky, equally confused. They each took brief notice of Esyld's new face but made no comment.

"How can it still be night?" Carrick asked.

Esyld got to her feet, surprised by how agile and spritely she felt—a pleasant change from the slow pace of the Crone. Carrick and Khati listened intently to her quick recounting of her meeting with Muave.

"Well, if the Symorcians are waiting for us at the shrine, at least we know we stand a chance this time," Khati stated with a barely contained smile.

"Eat now," Esyld said. "We will need our strength, for we aren't far." Then she carefully sidled up to Pagaene. "You need to eat, too. I will take over from here."

He shook his head. "I'm not hungry. I just need to get off this raft—if I don't steer, I think I'd drive you all mad with my pacing."

Esyld gave a quick nod, feeling both Carrick's and Khati's gazes on them. She wanted to walk away, to give him space, yet the Maiden instilled an impulsiveness within her, and before she knew what she was doing, Esyld reached out and placed her hand on Pagaene's arm.

Instantly, a charge ran through her like she'd taken a blow to her gut, forcing the air from her her lungs. Her grip tightened as the charge spread through her body, and when she closed her eyes, her Sight was flooded with vivid imagery.

She found herself looking down upon two young, identical boys, like mirror images on the final cusp of childhood. They played with carved wooden toys on the floor. With no further knowledge, Esyld knew the boy on the right was Pagaene, and Fritjof sat on the left.

The boys narrated their actions as they went, one picking up where the other left off. They told the tale of a brave Knight traveling through a forest filled with danger to save the maiden. Yet the story halted abruptly when Fritjof snatched the wooden horse from his brother.

"What are you doing? Give it back!" demanded an annoyed Pagaene.

"No. An invisible dragon just ate it. Now the Knight must travel the rest of the way on foot," replied Fritjof.

"That's stupid! Dragon's aren't invisible, and even if they were, the Knight is the greatest in all the lands, and he would slay it before it takes his horse. Give it back."

"No. I'm telling the story too, and I say the horse is dead." Fritjof stashed the horse behind his back and away from his brother's grasp.

"I said give it back!"

"No!"

Pagaene dove atop his brother, and the pair wrestled for possession of the horse. Fritjof escaped his brother's grasp and jumped to his feet, the horse in hand. Angry, Pagaene picked himself off the ground and glared at his twin. Finally, he strode towards his brother, fists clenched at his side, and Fritjof hurled the horse against the wall. The head and one leg broke off with a snap before clattering to the floor.

"Look what you've done!" Pagaene screamed.

"What are you going to do about it?" Fritjof sneered.

The young Pagaene glared at his brother, his breath coming short and fast.

Fritjof laughed. "Oh, so tough, brother. Did you just remember that you're not a brave knight?"

"Shut up," Pagaene growled, his body trembling. Esyld found herself amazed to see his body taking on a faint glow.

"You're not our father, you know. You'll never be a hero." Fritjof laughed again.

"I said shut up," Pagaene bellowed, and Esyld felt the vibration of a powerful force-field erupting from him, sweeping his brother off his feet before slamming him into the wall. Fritjof's head made a sickening thump before his limp body fell into a heap on the floor, his lifeless eyes staring out at his twin.

Pagaene fell to his knees just as his mother ran into the room, her face that of the Maiden. She wailed, cradling her dead son before turning to see Pagaene on his knees. The youth rocked back and forth, his face frozen in horror. She scurried towards him and grabbed his face in her hands. "Pagaene, can you hear me? Are you hurt?" But her voice fell on deaf ears; he was drowning in his own torment. Mathilde sobbed as she wrapped her arms around her only son, rocking with him. "It's not your fault, my son. You didn't know. You didn't know…"

Esyld released Pagaene, staggering backward and gasping for air.

"You saw it, didn't you? What I did?" he asked in a morose whisper.

She could only nod over the thundering of her own heart. Finally, she asked, "Is this why your grandfather came for you? Why he took you to train as a Knight in Jentor?" He didn't answer. Instead, he gazed out over the water.

"What happened?" Carrick called, neither he nor Khati wanting to move any closer for fear of throwing the raft off balance.

Esyld held up a hand in reassurance, though her mind was raced with the new understanding. With a wizard for a grandfather and a Meta Abdita for a mother, it came as no surprise that Pagaene had magic in him—though she wondered why the knowledge had been kept from him. Surely, they hadn't intended for Fritjog's death at his brother's hands? Then it dawned on her. If Mathilde had been aware of the destiny awaiting her son, she would have known he'd need great power. And in killing his twin, Pagaene would have absorbed his brother's magic as well. Surely, though, the woman would not knowingly sacrificed one son for the other?

Esyld stared at him, seeing Pagaene for the first time in a new light. He was both a fierce Knight and a source of great power—a power she could teach him to wield as well as tap into herself as the Maiden. Pagaene trembled. "Rest," Esyld said. "We'll keep this between us, for now." She glanced at Uul's still-sleeping form as Pagaene moved carefully away, wondering if the wizard could provide any clarity.

Chapter 22

P agaene let the dogs' warmth relax his body. Seeing his mother's face on Esyld and remembering his past had taken more out of him than he had realized. As much as he had considered striking off on his own, he knew he could not face the challenges ahead without his... party? Team? Friends?

Right now, the only one he could trust was Eslyd. She'd promised to keep quiet about what she'd learned, and he couldn't help but feel a connection to her now. She'd seen his darkest secret and hadn't thought him grotesque. He cringed to think of his reaction to her true face.

He felt the rising and falling chest of the dog lying next to him and petted the dog's fur with his prosthetic hand. His eyes grew heavy, his sense of time confused by the extended night. But he continued to pet the dog, watching the movement of his fake arm. He usually tried not to look at it, but now, it eased his guilt over his brother to see the way he'd been damaged. He studied the grain of the wood, where some of the bark had been broken away during the battle.

Then he froze, catching sight of a detail he'd never before noticed. He ran a finger over the tiny carving of his family's crest in his arm. A surprise prick of pain caused him to pull his finger back, and he turned his wrist just in time to see the first droplet of blood slide down his finger.

Using his middle finger now, Pageane found the cause of his pain—a tiny metal piece jammed into the wood. Perhaps an arrowhead had broken off into the appendage during their battle with the Simorcian Brothers. That seemed the most likely thing, and yet it did not look accidental. When he felt a straight line cut into the wood, he knew there was another explanation. He pulled on the metal piece, which rose out of the wood, and when he twisted it, he realized it was a miniature clasp.

A scraping noise sounded as a section of his arm popped up and open. Pagaene peered inside the small compartment, astounded by having had no previous knowledge of it. Thick, soft cloth padded the chamber, which held three items. He peered around the raft, but no one paid him any attention.

He whistled softly, mimicking a three-note tune favored by a bird native to Eslyd's home territory. Just as he had hoped, it got her attention. She glanced around to find the source of the noise, and he gestured for her to join him.

She knelt. "What is it?"

Pagaene pulled back the cloth inside his arm's secret compartment, revealing a silver dragon. It strongly reflected the moonlight, and Esyld pulled away from the glare. "What do you make of this?" he whispered and pulled out the tied scroll. Eslyd unwrapped it, but her furrowed brow told Pagaene she was just as clueless as he as to its meaning. "Nothing?" Esyld shook her head, and her expression sent a jolt of bittersweet familiarity through him. He turned back to the arm and removed the last item, a glass bottle full of sparkling blue liquid. "More riddles."

Eslyd grasped the glass jar. "I do, however, think I know what we can do with this."

Pagaene tilted his head in question, curious what help pollen could offer.

Before he could ask, Carrick's panicked voice boomed from the front of the raft. "Brace yourselves."

Chapter 23

I t was growing late in the Citadel of Jentor, its great hall largely vacant at this hour. The only man who remained in the ominously silent room was His Majesty King Rouaix Godfrey XVII, lost amid his introspection.

It had been days since his talk with The Priest. The young but darkly intimidating man had left to seek his master. But Rouaix had had no word from him. Nor had he heard from the serpentine betrayers Anguis and Caedus. None of the followers within the temple could provide answers.

Jentor's patriarch was a patient man, but it did not mean he sat complacently through the many silent hours. Rouaix was unused to relying on the work of others. In short time, he'd been driven to near madness waiting and wondering and, fearing further betrayal, he'd grown desperate to learn more about the Priest. So he'd sent his trusted advisor, Beltor Sparlan, among the lower ranking members of the Prime Order to learn what he could of the Priest through eavesdropping and clever conversation.

He'd heard nothing back from Beltor.

The bell tower of the Prime Order's Temple sounded the hour, and the booming ring of bronze snapped the King from his consuming postulation. With his attention returned to the present, the man became aware of more worldly needs. His belly was empty, and his lips were cracked and parched. He had not taken food since that morning, though it was not uncommon for him to miss a mid-day meal. He would have some food brought to his chambers before he slept. The more pressing matter was the scratching of sand in his mouth and the back of his throat. He needed to wet his lips at once. The man reached for a splendidly polished silver pitcher on a tray beside him and poured a tall drink of crystal-clear water into a matching silver chalice. He cleared his throat and raised the beverage to his lips.

After a long draught, the man instantly felt better. After hours of tiresome aggravation, the simplicity of drinking water seemed a welcome leisure. He drank again, but what had once been cool and fresh now hit him as warm and salty-bitter on his tongue. The man choked, retching from the revolting taste, and spit the rest of the water from his mouth. Wiping the spray from his chin, he then looked in terror at his fingertips. His fear magnified when he glanced at what remained in his chalice; the water had turned to blood.

The silver cup clattered to the floor as the greatest man in Jentor panicked. Blood now stained the man's splendid white garments. Rouaix fell to his knees and clasped his hands together. "Forgive me, my Mistress. I know not what offense I have committed. I beg your mercy for my weakness and my ignorance." He sounded even to himself like a child.

'Present yourself before me immediately,' the voice called in his mind. Though the words had not been spoken aloud, they sounded like the final breath of a condemned man swinging from the gallows. The silent speech cut into the King's spirit like jagged fragments of stained glass.

"Yes, at once, my Mistress," Rouaix replied with a quivering lip.

He was grateful for the late hour and the lack of prying eyes within the halls. Rouaix did not wish for those of lesser statue to witness him in a state of anything beyond his usual poised composure. He certainly wanted to avoid an explanation of the blood stains on his fine white clothes, the planning of which would have to wait. Right now, there was nothing more pressing than the beckoning of the one who owned him.

The King kept to the back corridors and secret passages of the citadel, putting to good use the intimate knowledge of the structure's architecture acquired through his reign. He worked his way into the bowels of the citadel and trod down footpaths covered in thick layers of dust. Though certain nobody had followed, he could not keep from casting suspicious glances over his shoulder every few paces. Here, well into the nethers of the citadel, only he ever came to call. He held a small lantern in one hand, but its light was minimal. He had to feel his way through the darkness, as he always did, and made his way down the final twists and turns of the dark and crypt-like corridors. His free hand delved into the folds of his robes, and his fingers curled around the key dangling from his waist.

Within the dim, musty halls of shadow and stone, he arrived at the door to his mistresses' chamber, forged of solid iron and as heavy as one would expect. It was not an easy thing to open, and in the more recent years, his aging back amplified the difficulty of an already formidable challenge. Embossed into the door's metal face was the image of a fruit-bearing tree, stripped of any leaves or bounty and possessing only an array of bare, claw-like branches. Standing in front of the door felt to Rouaix like looking into a nightmare.

He paused, aware of wave after wave of fear washing over him. He had hoped that his fear would have lessened with each subsequent encounter, but it was not so. The man was just as frightened now as he had been the first time he'd been summoned to this room. He lingered one moment longer before he made himself slip the key into the lock of the solid iron door. The bolts inside seemed to hiss as the man turned the key. He placed his palms on the image of the tree and pushed, feeling his shoulders and chest pop, and the door swung slowly open.

It was completely dark inside the room save for the tiny sliver of light coming from the King's lantern. The familiar stench of sulfur and smoke assailed his nostrils, and he caught the bubbling, frothing sound from the far side of the room had come to expect. A gust of foul air snuffed out the lantern's flame, and Rouaix shut his eyes in preparation. Even with his eyes closed, the flash of light that bathed the room was bright enough to spin his head and force him to his knees. The moment of blinding silver disappeared as quickly as it had been intense, and the King opened his eyes.

A ghostly pale light washed the stuffy chamber, coming from the mouth of a well at the far end, made of chipped, black volcanic rock. The substance inside was not water but a swirling vortex of boiling filth. As bubbles of the cesspool popped, burst droplets of the well's contents spattered across the stone floor. The glowing speckles of silver liquid hissed and burned on the cobblestone like acid. A thin line of light shot from the well and brightly outlined Rouaix, leaving the rest of the room in the dim, flickering light. From inside the well came the voice that made Rouaix's heart stop for a moment whenever he heard it.

'When I no longer sensed the Meta Abdita moving upon the earth, I thought you'd apprehended her,' it gurgled. *'Now, I know her to be upon water. And still moving toward the stones, still intent on restoring what I've destroyed.'*

"Forgiveness, please, my Mistress. His Holiness sent his best man for her, and she evaded him. The impure one is stronger than anticipated," Rouaix said on trembling knees. "The Symorcians have betrayed us, and I fear for His Holiness' life. The Priest has gone to find him, but—"

'I feel that my faith in you is waning. You are blind.'

Rouaix spread his arms in defensive submission. "Mistress?"

'His Holiness is dead. The Symorcians are mine to command, now as always. They are a simple species, but loyal, and none so blind as you, who work with the Abdita without knowing.'

"Mistress, I would never—"

'The boy. The Priest, the voice interrupted. *He is one of them.'*

"No!" Rouaix shrank back from the well. "It cannot be. His Holiness wouldn't—he trusted—"

'His Holiness craved power. He wished for The Prime Order and the magic of Rebirth to rise above the Powers of Life and Death. He would have used any *means to obtain his goal. The Abdita... The King... even me. He thought he could control me.'*

"Oh, Mistress, it is my only wish to see you returned to your rightful glory. I only wish to serve you," groveled Jentor's King. "How can I make this right?" Rouaix broke into a nervous sweat as the well only boiled and bubbled. After a long, reflective silence, the man jumped in his skin when the room went totally dark. The only thing filling it now was the stink of rot and the babbling of boiling mire. Rouaix wondered if he was about to die.

The iron door behind him slammed shut, and the room lit up with a cruel red glow. The man threw himself to the floor in total subjugation. "Please, please, my Mistress. I meant no offense. I beg of your mercy.

'Do not demean yourself so. It is an unbecoming weakness I cannot tolerate. You must simply tell me what final secret you are hiding.'

Rouaix's eyes shot as wide as they could go, and his skin blanched as pale as a corpse. He swallowed, tasting blood still on his tongue. "Ser Pagaene," he said. "He travels with the impure one. His Holiness spoke of a prophecy about him... that he would defeat you, Mistress."

The room's red glow intensified, and a jet of orange flame shot up from inside the cylinder of wicked black rocks. *'You concealed knowledge of someone alive who could defeat me. A Knight from your own ranks, no less.'*

Rouaix quaked and cried out, "Tell me how to make it right."

The red light faded, and an eerie silver spotlight glowed in the corner of the dank chamber. Within the light crouched Beltor Sparlan, his trembling shoulders crashing against the stone wall behind him.

'A worthy servant,' said The Purity from within the well. *'It was he who learned The Priest's true lineage. He who first told me of Pagaene's prophecy—the means by which His Holiness meant to defeat me once I've rid the world of The Abdita.'* Boiling water spurted from the mouth of the well, sizzling on the stone. *'To make things right, I require no less than this worthy sacrifice.'*

Rouaix froze in terror. Time slowed as his mistress' cruel laughter overwhelmed him, echoing in the catacombs of the citadel. The King watched Beltor fold to the ground and lay in the fetal position, whimpering like a beaten dog. Hot tears trickled down his face, and only when he realized this did he also discover that it was not Beltor but he himself who whimpered.

His hand came to rest on the dagger at his side, but he did not draw it. For a moment, deep beneath his city in the darkness, with no sound save the wicked bubbling of the well, he couldn't remember why he'd chosen this. As he stared at his best man, his friend cowering before him, he lost all memory of the passion he'd felt, the drive to protect his kingdom from the evil threat of the witches. The compelling picture once painted by His Holiness faded in his mind.

"I…" he began.

'Don't worry, little King,' said the voice from the well. *'I'll do it.'*

Intense flames jetting out of the well once again lit the room. A bolt of red-hot fire shot from the caustic water and covered Beltor. The King shouted as he was splashed, fell to the floor, and backed away. Beltor screamed as he burned.

Chapter 24

T he raft suddenly ran ashore, and Esyld pitched forward onto all fours. The scroll and jar of pollen went skittering across the raft until they were stopped by Khati's foot. Somehow, the Sylth had managed to keep her balance through the abrupt stop, and she now bent forward to retrieve the two items.

She unrolled the scroll, and her two slitted pupils expanded to perfect circles as she read it through. "Where did you get this?" she hissed at Pagaene.

"Never you mind," Pagaene replied as he extended a hand to Esyld and helped her to her feet. "Those items are mine, and I beg you return them."

Khati looked down at the jar of blue liquid, then tossed it

166

into the Knight's outstretched hand. But the scroll she rolled back into a tube and shook at him. "Do you know what this says?" She closed her eyes and shook her head. "No, of course you don't. How could you?" She looked at Pagaene and Esyld. "This is Drag—"

"Tilly?" From the back of the raft, Uul groggily sat up and stared open-mouthed at Esyld's new face for several seconds. Then the dog who had been sleeping in his lap stretched his neck and licked the man's cheek. Uul absentmindedly wiped the slobber away and blinked several times, as if trying to change what he saw before him. Then, with a great sigh of understanding, he said, "Oh, Esyld. I see. You're wearing her face." Uul slumped back against his dogs for a moment, then jumped up and yelled, "You're wearing her face!"

Esyld flinched against his thunderous voice. "Yes, Uul. It was necessary. The Crone's face was ruin—"

To her surprise, Uul ran across the raft toward her and swept her up in his arms. "Do you know what this means?" he laughed into her ear as he spun her around.

"Careful," Carrick growled. "Let us disembark before you engage in such tomfoolery."

One by one, the party stepped from the raft onto the rocky beach. The raft creaked and moaned as they each took turns upsetting its balance, but it did not betray them into the cold water. When all had come ashore, Esyld asked, "What does it mean to you, Uul?"

"This can wait," Khati said. "We are too close to completing our mission to stop now."

"I apologize, but as a Gray Wizard, I am going to overrule you, Khati," said Uul. "I have information that will affect us all and may even save our lives, should they need saving."

Khati frowned at Uul, then muttered, "So mote it be, then. But hurry."

A cool breeze rustled through the tall, leafy trees lining the beach as far as Esyld could see in either direction, and with it came the spicy-sweet aroma of cloves. The curious nature of the Maiden longed to discover the source of the new smell, but Esyld put those feelings aside and turned to Uul. There was a deeper curiosity about him that needed to be sated. "Tell me everything, Uul. What does this face mean to you?"

Uul paced in front of the group. Two of his large dogs lay down to nap in the rocky sand, but the others paced with him. "As you all know," he began, "wizards and Abdita do not exactly see eye-to-eye."

"Since Halvard violated the Sacred Well," Esyld said, crossing her arms.

Uul nodded. "Yes. But it was not always that way between us. And so many years ago, I decided to form a truce between our people. I wanted to give something to the Abdita, a gift that would show them how sorry we wizards were for what our brother had done. But," he said, scratching his grizzled cheek, "before I tell you about that gift and for whom it was intended, I must tell you about the place I call home."

"Nightstone?" Pagaene asked.

Uul smiled. "Yes. Did your mother ever tell you about it?"

Pagaene shook his head. "She used to sing a song to me and Fr—" He cast a quick glance at Esyld, who nodded solemnly. "It was… it was about a powerful wizard who lived in a town called Nightstone. But I didn't realize it was about you."

"Nightstone is more than a single town, Pagaene," Uul said. "It is a collection of villages, all independent from one another, but with one thing in common. All are built over a deep, underground mine of magical rock, for which the area is named."

"Are you saying Nightstone is an actual *stone?*" Esyld asked in surprise. "I've never heard of it."

"Nightstone has only ever been used by wizards, and each only allowed one small piece. The wealth of power it provides a wizard is almost unimaginable. Therefore, it can be extremely dangerous in the wrong hands. Nightstone is never spoken of to the outside world, but young wizards from all the corners of the globe flock to Nightstone for their training." Uul's eyes sparkled in the moonlight as he spoke. From a pocket of his cloak, he retrieved a small, irregularly cut stone so black, all light seemed to sink into it. But as Esyld studied it, she realized it was filled with thousands of tiny shards, the glittery substance twinkling like stars.

Her face grew warm, and the warmth spread down her neck, into her chest, and from there it radiated to her limbs. The Maiden was reacting to the stone.

This was the source of power Muave had told her to find.

Uul smiled at her as he held the Nightstone up for the others to see. "After Halvard began the bitter feud between the wizards and Abdita, I thought that perhaps if I made a gift of this chip to one of you, it would end our bitterness toward one another. So I asked Muave to choose a worthy Meta Abdita to receive this gift."

"My mother," Pagaene whispered.

"Yes," Uul replied. "I made this chip into an amulet for her to wear, and I could tell that as soon as she put it on, it increased her powers just as it did for wizards. I explained to her that the Nightstone could only have one master and would bond to her only as long as she wore the Maiden's face. Tilly promised that while the Nightstone was in her possession, she would never change into the Mother's face. Then, just as she was about to leave my home and return to Freywyn, my son walked through the door." Uul smiled warmly. "They locked eyes, and it was another twenty minutes before Tilly remembered she was leaving."

Then Uul's face clouded, and he took a deep breath before continuing. "But wearing the Nightstone had an unintended consequence for your mother, Pagaene. Having never been used by a Meta Abdita before, no one could have predicted exactly how it would cause a surge in her powers. This power manifested itself in a most unfortunate way when your mother was with child."

"How so?" Pagaene asked warily.

Uul sighed. "Abdita are single-birth creatures. Never had an Abdita's egg split inside her womb. Every child of an Abdita has its own individual powers instilled in it upon conception. But the power of the Nightstone gave your mother two children at once, and thus the balance of power was split."

"You had a twin?" Carrick asked Pagaene, but Pagaene did not respond. He only narrowed his eyes at his grandfather and clenched his teeth.

"Muave told your mother that Nature would right itself eventually. Balance must, and always will, be restored," Uul continued. "The second child was never meant to be. Tilly knew it was only a matter of time before she lost one of her boys."

Pagaene dropped to his knees and covered his face. "I didn't mean to," he cried, and his shoulders shook.

Uul crouched beside his grandson and placed a hand on his shoulder. "Listen to me, my boy. There was nothing you could have done differently to save your brother. Only one of you was meant to live." He sighed. "I told your mother these words, as well, but they failed to comfort her. And so she asked me for help."

Pagaene looked up at the wizard. "What do you mean?"

"Tilly couldn't bear the loss of your brother, especially after losing your father as well. So she asked me if I could save Fritjof somehow."

"You have the power to do this?" Esyld asked. "You have the power of Rebirth?"

Uul shook his head. "No. But I did not earn the title of Gray Wizard for nothing." He stood and resumed his pacing on the beach. "I was not able to fully restore Fritjof, but I was able to save a piece of his soul and, from it, create a new life. I sent this new creature to live with another soul I had saved—my son."

All eyes turned to Khati, who had been standing solemnly in the shadows.

"You?" Pagaene whispered. "Fritjof?"

Khati stepped forward and spoke. "Yes, in my past life, I was human. But do not let this cloud your mind or change your feelings about me. I am no more Fritjof than Esyld is Pagaene. I have no connection to that life, as I was never meant to be born into it. The name Fritjof means nothing to me, and all I remember from that life are vague feelings of confusion and grief." She pointed a finger at Uul. "I do not even remember my creation, nor do I care for my creator. I am Sylth through and through." Khati locked eyes with Pagaene. "I never knew you and I were brothers, Knight. How strange this must be for you."

170

Pagaene blinked furiously and jumped up to face his grandfather. "You kept this information from us all this time?" he cried. "You knew who Khati was and you didn't tell us?"

"Yes and no," Uul replied. "Khati was created from a small fraction of Fritjof's soul. I knew Fritjof. I do not know Khati. And she does not know me. When I created her, I was able to leave a small bit of familial loyalty in her so she would remain a devoted companion to my son, even if she did not understand *why*. I hope that one day, her companionship all these years will help..." Uul lowered his eyes. "My son. Pierce was his name. I named him thusly, for when I first laid eyes on him, he pierced my heart. When he died, it tore me apart, Pagaene. I could scarcely bear it. Your mother asked me to save Fritjof because she knew I had done it before, with him."

"*You* turned my father into the White Dragon?" Pagaene asked.

Uul nodded. "It was the only way I could save him."

Khati strode to Pagaene and grasped his hand. "Pagaene, do not mourn your brother. He was never meant to be. But because of him, and because of your grandfather's abilities, I have been able to watch over the White Dragon all these years, and I have served him well. I have lived with him for so long, I can tell you without a doubt, there is still some human living inside him."

"What do you mean?" Pagaene whispered.

"I hear him," Khati said. "I hear his thoughts. Mostly, they are in Dragonite, but when the White Dragon sleeps, his thoughts become human. He can speak in the human tongue at times, and I believe the Dragon is still attached to his previous life. That is why he sent me to help you."

Uul held out the amulet to Esyld. "Tilly returned the stone to me after the loss of Pagaene. She told me she regretted never changing to the Mother's face and that perhaps things would have turned out differently for everyone if she had. The Nightstone is bonded to *you* now, Esyld. Please, take it."

Esyld's face tingled with excitement, but as she reached forward to grasp the mesmerizing necklace, a leathery vine shot from beneath the ground and wrapped itself around her wrist. She gasped.

"Not so fast."

Uul's dogs barked and growled as a man appeared from behind the tree line and marched toward the group.

It was Kenyth.

"You!" Carrick growled. "What are you doing here?"

With a flick of his finger, a singular vine snapped at Carrick, snatched his athame, and flipped it back to Kenyth. "Now," the Priest said, "it's time to make things right." Carrick's athame crumbled in his palm.

Chapter 25

E syld cried out, and Carrick, in silent horror, watched the pieces of his athame fall to the ground. Vines shot through the air and imprisoned the dogs when they charged The Priest. Their growls and struggles broke the silence that had descended upon the group.

"I've waited years for that." Hatred spewed from Kenyth's lips as he faced his brother.

Pagaene pulled his sword as Uul stepped toward his dogs to cut them free. More vines flew from all directions and wound around each member of the party until no one could move at all.

"Let them go, *brother.* This is between me and you." Carrick pulled at the vines. "You don't need them."

"No," Kenyth hissed, "I don't need them, but you do. You just never needed me." He pulled out a new athame and pointed it toward his brother. "But that ends now. I've waited a long time to defeat you."

Kenyth approached, and Carrick struggled to free his arms. One of Uul's dogs had managed to free itself, rending the vines with its teeth, its muzzle bloodied with the effort. The animal shook itself and darted toward Uul, setting to work on the vines entangling its master.

Carrick turned his focus back to Kenyth. "Brother, you don't want to do this." At Kenyth's scoff, Carrick added, "Not like this. What victory is there in killing me while I'm unable to fight you?" He risked a glance toward Uul. Freed, the man was running to Pagaene.

"You're still Abdita, Kenyth," Esyld said, drawing The Priest's eyes toward her and farther away from where more of Uul's dogs were freeing themselves. "You still have honor."

Carrick didn't hear his brother's reply. He watched the vines that had enclosed Khati turn white with ice, then blacken and crack, falling away. Hearing the noise, the Priest turned only to be lunged at by one of Uul's dogs.

"Go, Pagaene!" Esyld cried. "Retrieve the stones."

"I'll not leave you," he replied, but Khati had grasped his arm and now dragged him away.

"Go, grandson," Uul said as he ran to free Carrick. "Complete this task."

Seeing that all his companions would soon be free, Pagaene conceded. They disappeared into the woods.

***

Carrick had run to the mass of writhing flesh that was Uul's dogs and The Priest. There were too many of them for Kenyth; he didn't have the time or presence of mind to use a spell. Uul cut through the vines holding Esyld, and the instant she was free, she grabbed the wizard to hold him back from the fight.

The pull was too strong to ignore. "The amulet," she ordered.

He placed it over her head, and the black stone rested on her heart. A surge of power ran through Esyld's body, like liquid heat through her veins. She struggled to remain upright as she warmed from head to toe.

Then she knelt, forcing her fingers deep into the rocky sand beneath her, and connected with the power of the earth. The ground rumbled, the waters of the lake roiled as though boiling, and roots sprang up through the damp sand. The sparkles in the amulet seemed to shine in the extended darkness.

Carrick stumbled and crawled away. Uul's dogs hesitated in their attack, finally darting away from the cage of roots rising up around Kenyth. Esyld met his gaze. His arm, bloodied and the sleeve shredded, moved up to cover his face as the vines and roots closed around him. Soon, Kenyth was encased in roots, stray limbs, and driftwood. His prison was just slightly larger than the man himself and rose up from the ground like a strange tree trunk devoid of branches and leaves.

Gasping, Esyld sank down into the sand and laid her head upon her arms. Before she could regain her composure, Muave tore into her mind's eye, sending a vision from a bird's-eye view.

When she opened her eyes again, still lying on the ground, one of the dogs licked her face. Uul bent over her, and she grabbed his hand and stood.

"His Holiness is dead," she said.

The wizard grabbed her shoulder. "Dead?"

Esyld held her forehead. "Muave sent a message. The Purity killed him, absorbed him. We need those stones, and we have to hurry."

A breeze blew across the sand, again carrying the sweet smell of cloves. Esyld sniffed appreciatively, and an idea took root. "Uul, those trees. Do you think we could make clove oil?"

For a moment, he frowned at her in confusion. "Whatever for?"

"The Purity is water-based. Cloves fight off evil and

negativity. We might be able to fight her with the oil, are at least weaken her."

Understanding dawned on him. "Of course. I am at your service."

He hurried toward the trees while Esyld took a seat on a nearby log. Carrick knelt beside his brother's cage, holding the broken shards of his athame in his open palm.

***

Pagaene ran with Khati in silence, frequently turning to search over his shoulder. He flinched every time a shout or the bark of a dog carried toward them on the breeze.

"This is your destiny, Knight," Khati said, and Pagaene narrowly missed stumbling over a rock when he glanced backward. "They will be fine."

"It's cowardly," Pagaene spat between pants. "Leaving my comrades in distress."

"Is that what we are now?" Khati asked. "Comrades?"

Pagaene looked at her, but before he could reply, they reached the clearing and the Shrine of Verity within it. They paused to catch their breath for a moment.

Khati bowed to the Knight and motioned for him to continue on his own. Pagaene made it a few steps before he walked into what felt like a wall, the force of which knocked him backwards. "What—" He felt the air with his hands, finding a smooth but completely impenetrable surface in a dome around the Shrine, completely invisible to the naked eye. He finally walked back to Khati. "Do you have any ideas how we get in?"

She shook her head. "None."

"All this way, just to be stopped now. The stones are so close."

"One moment," Khati said, reaching into her bag and pulling out the scroll discovered inside Pagaene's arm. She unrolled it and read in silence, then looked back up at the Knight. "The scroll was meant for this."

Pagaene raised his brow at her. "Care to illuminate me?"

Khati reread the scroll and took his hands. "Open your mind."

"To what?"

"To what feels right."

Pagaene closed his eyes and focused on the feeling of their clasped hands. He felt a slight hum, then a thought pushed into his mind, eventually forming a voice.

'My son.'

His eyes popped open, and he yanked his hands away from Khati. She looked down at him with flared nostrils. "What are you doing?"

"What am I doing? What are *you* doing? How can I hear my father?"

"Obviously he's channeling through me, as directed in the scroll. Now give me your hands." She grabbed his hands and held tight. In defiance, he blocked his mind, unwilling to hear what his father wanted to say. After a minute, Khati let go. "You disgust me. You need help, yet you shut out the one person who can offer it. The scroll was given to you for just this purpose so your father might help you access the Shrine."

"Person? My father is *not* a person, no matter what thoughts you hear. Just as you say you're not my brother. I don't need his help."

Khati suddenly stiffened, glanced around, and backed away from Pagaene. "He's coming."

Pagaene grabbed his sword. "Who?"

A mighty roar sounded overhead, and a sudden wind whipped at their clothes. Khati moved toward the Knight and pushed down his sword. "Your father. Put that away."

Pagaene's eyes widened as he turned and found himself face to face with the White Dragon. He backed away, pinning himself between the dragon and the shield around the Shrine. Khati backed away as well, giving the dragon wide berth.

'Climb upon my back.'

The order burned into Pagaene's brain. He stood in frozen

defiance, unwilling to concede.

The White Dragon growled, grabbed the Knight's tunic in his huge maw, and tossed Pagaene over his shoulder and onto his back. Pagaene scrabbled for a hold in surprise but found himself relaxing when the White Dragon did not take flight. Instead, it shambled forward, easily penetrating the unseen wall guarding the Shrine. When they approached the building itself, the beast stopped.

'I can go no farther.'

Pagaene jumped down, embarrassed by his own hostility, and nodded. He straightened his clothes, took the few steps forward to push open the door, and stepped into the Shrine of Verity.

***

Esyld grabbed Uul's hand as they finished the first batch of clove oil. "He has entered the Shrine."

"I thought that was a good thing. He can retrieve the stones." Uul placed a cap on a small bottle.

"His father came to his aid." She looked at the wizard. "Your son is there."

Uul paled. "My son?"

Esyld shook her head. "They needed his help." She rubbed the amulet, feeling a strange presence worming its way into her mind before she recognized its evil intent. She gasped and jumped to her feet. "We must go. Hurry. Pagaene needs us."

The dogs barked at her sudden movement. Carrick stood, tucking away the broken athame. "What danger is there?"

"I don't know yet. I just know we must make haste."

Carrick hesitated, looking once more at Esyld's cage of roots and bark.

"It will hold him until we can deal with him, Carrick," she said. Carrick nodded, and the trio took off at a run, the dogs quick on their heels.

***

The door slammed shut behind Pagaene. Colored light from the stained-glass windows illuminated the Shrine, the air fresh and pristine, the walls white and pure. A pedestal, engraved with white dragons, stood in the center of the room, the five stones resting in a pillar of bright light.

There was no sound other than his own breathing, but Pagaene waited. He felt his heart beating in anticipation, but he paused to be sure all was the way it should be.

After several moments passed, he moved to the pedestal to discover that the bright light protecting the stones was actually a solid flame. He felt its heat emanating from the glow.

'The dagger, my son. Use the dagger.'

Pagaene pulled out the dagger, the dragon's emerald eyes casting sparks as they danced in the light. A narrow slit on the side of the pedestal fit the blade to perfection. As the dagger sank into the marble, the flame extinguished. Pagaene removed the special pouch Esyld had given him to carry the stones, then reached up to remove the first one.

'Well done, Knight. Now step aside.'

He spun around as The Purity moved toward him from the corner of the room.

Chapter 26

Rouaix's fingers thumped on the arm of the chair in which he'd forced himself to sit. He had paced his halls for hours until even his well-muscled legs grew weak. His mind had been just as active. Now his thoughts had no outlet but through his fingers, every muscle in his body taut with energy. Beltor Sparlan was dead. His Holiness was dead. The Priest was an imposter. The Purity would destroy Rouaix along with his enemies. It was no use trying to control her; what happened to His Holiness showed that much.

Rouaix slammed his palm down against the arm of his chair, wood smoothed and faded from years of use. He reached up to grasp his head. His brain felt split by the loss of his advisor. There was now no one to whom he could turn even for council. His soldiers remained his, but what good was an army against a force like The Purity?

Abruptly, Rouaix stood. It was decided. Hour after hour, he'd thought it through, his pride battling with his better wisdom, one side of him the King, the other the words he knew dear Beltor Sparlan would not hesitate to speak. It was his only course of action. He had to find Pagaene.

He'd feared the prophecy, and it had cost Beltor his life, but perhaps it had come to him for good reason. Perhaps he could make something out of his loss. He'd been prideful before, greedy even. His desire to achieve his own ends, his great fear of failing, had led him to release this evil upon his kingdom, a greater evil even than the witches he had sought to fight. He could see that much now. If Pagaene was the answer, Rouaix would find him. He had always been a loyal Knight. Perhaps Rouaix had been mistaken to see his actions as a betrayal. For all he knew, Pagaene was still loyal to the crown, engaged in a mission that would ensure the kingdom's safety above all and allow them to conquer these filthy witches once the lives and livelihoods of their innocent subjects were safe.

Rouaix looked down at his bandaged arm. The Purity had burned him well, but not well enough. He was in no shape to ride or fight, but what choice did he have? It was a decisive action from which he could return in victory or not at all. The Purity would no doubt return soon enough and discover his betrayal, but he was now convinced that even loyalty would never buy him his life. He was only delaying the inevitable. The longer he delayed, the more his options narrowed.

The King moved quickly to the side door of the chamber, listening for signs of anyone outside. He opened the door cautiously and peered around the corner before letting his wobbly legs melt down the stairs. When he reached the bottom, he pulled a plain hooded cloak from the pegs on the wall and threw it over himself, careful to hide his injuries. His feet grew heavy, and he sank into the familiar rhythms of the bored and battle-ready. "Out of ale. I'm going to get more," he grunted over his shoulder as he stomped past the table of lounging guards. No response came, but he heard the slick crack of a card on the table as the soldiers continued their game. By then, he was out the door.

***

"No!" Pagaene shouted and slammed his hand down over the stones.

The watery female form seemed to tilt its head. Then, she turned to face the Shrine's door. With a whoosh, a wave of water rolled from The Purity, and the doors burst outward, jets of steaming water rising into the air. Pagaene had barely had time to wonder why when he heard a scream of rage and fear, a great beating of wings, and the roar of the White Dragon.

His ears rang, damaged by the volume, and he squinted against the pain. When he opened his eyes again, a pale grey form hung over tendrils of scalding water. Khati writhed, her clothing and flesh torn and bleeding where she had surely been ripped from the White Dragon's grasp. Her skin slowly turned from grey to an odd purple as The Purity burned her skin.

His eyes returned to the liquid form, dark not so much in color but in depth. The thing seemed to shake. Could it be amused?

Then it spoke, or at least, Pagaene heard it. '*I don't mind killing her*,' it said, its tone now undoubtedly mirthful. '*I don't mind killing you, either. You'll die one way or another. But humans have an odd relationship with death. They like to put it off as long as possible, as if time will change the course of their destinies, as if they have… hope. Well, the choice is yours. Now or later.*'

'*No, Pagaene.*'

Pagaene's eyes flicked as far as they could toward the dragon—his father, the other voice in his mind—but his neck would not move, his whole focus drawn towards The Purity.

"Take them, Pagaene," Khati cried. Her voice was as shredded as her body had become. "Take them and run."

Pagaene's muscles twitched as his mind flicked between

decisions. The stones slipped cool and smooth beneath his fingers.

'She's your brother, Pagaene. Your twin.'

"I'm not your brother. I am Khati. I am a sylth."

'You killed him once already.'

"I died to give you the strength," Khati screamed, then grunted, and Pagaene finally tore his eyes from the liquid evil. With a shock, he realized that the hilt of Khati's keris protruded from her own abdomen, angled such that she had clearly stabbed herself. "It's yours. A gift. Take it," she said, her voice a struggling whisper.

A great bellow rose outside the Shrine, but he barely heard it. A strange sensation heated his core.

Khati's limp form collapsed to the floor as The Purity detached her attention from the useless hostage. She snapped her misty tentacles at Pagaene but writhed back in surprise and anger. It appeared the Symorcian's amulet had worked. In a flash, Pagaene withdrew the jar of blue pollen from his arm and smashed it on the floor before him. A shimmering blue haze rose around them, and Pagaene inhaled to fill his lungs completely.

He stared at The Purity as she coalesced. Once again, she seemed to shake in that amused way. *'So you have some tricks in your bag, little Knight.'*

"More than you know." Pagaene narrowed his eyes and his concentration. With all his might, he visualized The Purity melting, dissolving, evaporating. After a moment, the dark form stopped shaking and began to writhe. It emitted no words, but a chilling sound escaped its form. Pagaene maintained his focus, his earthly vision clouding over with his mind's eye. He saw deserts and droughts and dust. The sky withered. The earth rent in great cracks. The seas became forests of great white bones sharpened by marauding sands.

Then he blinked, and the vision was gone. The slick form of The Purity was thrashed on the ground before him, folding in on itself. He felt the muscles of his arm activate, and his hand tightened over the stones.

"We must go!" he yelled to the dragon and dove for Khati's

body. He retrieved her keris, then struggled to lift her, his grip failing in the warm water and blood. "It won't hold her for long."

A shadow passed over Pagaene, and he ducked to the side as the White Dragon, rearing, reached into the Shrine, scooped up Khati's body, and cradled it to his chest. He turned with a whoosh of wind and extended his wing so Pagaene could scramble over it and onto the great beast's back. His massive wings beat heavily, and Pagaene gripped the dragon's ridged hide firmly with his knees. They were aloft by the time the Knight shoved the pouch of stones into his false arm, and they'd landed again faster than he would have thought possible. He looked down, and there, below him, Uul, Esyld, and Carrick stood poised to attack. "Hold," he called, sliding down the crease of the dragon's leg to the ground.

"Pagaene," Carrick shouted.

Esyld ran toward him. "Do you have them?" she asked, and her voice carried with her urgency though her tone was hushed.

Pagaene gave her a quick nod. "We must leave quickly. The Purity is here."

Esyld swung around, and Pagaene lifted his eyes to Carrick, but the other man had directed his gaze elsewhere. Uul knelt before the White Dragon, and as Esyld and Pagaene approached, Khati's body came into view on the other side of one massive forepaw.

"She sacrificed herself for the stones," Pagaene said softly to Esyld.

'Remake my child, as you have remade us before.' Pagaene heard his father's voice in his mind and realized the dragon spoke to Uul.

"I am sorry, my son," Uul said aloud, his head heavy. "Your child's soul is spent. Let her rest now." The dragon seemed to curl in on himself but made no other move.

"We must go," Pagaene repeated.

"Kenyth," Esyld said. She turned and jogged back the way they had come. Pagaene followed her, Carrick close behind.

Esyld slowed as they approached the organic prison she had wrought. "Something is wrong," she said softly, and again, her voice carried on the breeze.

Pagaene approached the wooden shape cautiously, his long strides overtaking Esyld's. He circled the tree, then widened his circle. There, a few feet from its base, was a large hole—large enough for a man to crawl through to freedom. Pagaene crouched down to examine it as his companions approached.

"No," Carrick whispered.

"Look," said Esyld. Pagaene looked up and followed her voice to the tips of the wooden prison. The wood was budding with leaves.

"No," Carrick repeated, this time a growl.

"We have no time to spare. Where is Uul?" Pagaene asked, rising.

"No!" Carrick shouted. "Not without my brother."

"We must return to Freywyn," Esyld urged.

"You promised it would hold," Carrick snapped at her.

"It should have. It did. It's the earth that gave way," Esyld stammered. "I didn't want to lose him any more than you did, but we've come this far on our journey. We cannot let ourselves be distracted."

"You said Pagaene was in danger. You lured me away with false threats."

"And he was! Khati died for this. If we had only gotten there a few moments sooner—"

"He had a dragon Meta. If that could not save her, we would have surely been of no use."

"I am of more use than you think me, Carrick," Esyld said, her voice dropping low.

"We must follow him," Carrick insisted. "You ignore what he's done to us, to me. He's a traitor, and my brother!"

"More than one of us has lost a brother today in pursuit of our cause," Pagaene interjected, but Carrick turned on him.

"You didn't lose anything. You killed him. I'd wager you killed Khati too, or all but did, in that temple with no witnesses."

"Carrick," Esyld hissed, but Pagaene held up a hand.

"Your brother will be first on my list, Carrick, once these stones are safely in Muave's hands," he said.

"I won't be returning without him," Carrick countered. "You may go where you please, but this Meta owes me my brother."

"No," came Uul's voice from behind him. "She does not." Pagaene turned to see his grandfather's grief-wearied form approaching. "The price is not hers to pay. Nevertheless, the Priest is a threat to us. I will go with Carrick to hunt down the traitor Abdita. Esyld, Pagaene—the High Priestess awaits."

Pagaene was still for a long moment, sizing Carrick up with a scowl. He'd never known the man to be so rashly aggressive. Something about him seemed amiss. He turned his gaze to his grandfather, and Uul's steady demeanor comforted him, seeming to balance the younger man's rage. Pagaene turned last to Esyld, who still watched her friend Carrick, suspicion glittering in the narrowed corners of her eyes. At last, she met his gaze.

"Come," she said, and Pagaene followed her.

The White Dragon lay curled up on a low hill of dirt, and as he approached, Pagaene realized that his father had used his great paws to rend the earth and place Khati inside it.

"You must ask him to take us to Freywyn," Esyld said softly to Pagaene.

"I've cost him his child. Again. I can ask no more of him," Pagaene replied.

Esyld stopped and looked him in the eyes. "The Purity is here. We have no choice."

The Knight looked away from her, blinked, and drew a great breath as if preparing himself, but as he exhaled, a great wind made him shut his eyes and shield his face. When he opened them, the White Dragon was crouching before them.

"Will you take us to Freywyn, my father?" Pagaene asked as gently as he could, but his mind remained blank. No words came in response. The White Dragon puffed a little breeze of smoke from his nostrils and scooped first Esyld, then Pagaene onto his back. Pagaene grasped the rough ridges once more and waited. "Thank you," he said.

The dragon lifted into the air without a response.

Chapter 27

F lying on the back of a dragon—the back of his father, no less—was a strange experience for Pagaene. He felt the air rushing under the huge, leathery wings, the exhilaration and power that came with riding the winds. But he did not feel as though he should have enjoyed that feeling, nor that he should have shared it.

His brother had once again been lost by his hand. He hadn't acted to cause it this time, no; he'd been transfixed by the dark depths of The Purity, torn between the words of his newly discovered father and those of his resurrected sibling. He could have thrown the stones at The Purity… but he hadn't. Why?

Wind blew through his mind, clearing it briefly, sweeping aside everything hot and heavy. He hadn't done so because he was a trained Knight, a soldier, and because he'd known that giving the stones to The Purity would not have saved Khati. Khati had died, her life already leaking out of her burned and torn skin in quantities too vast to be replaced even by magic. What had Uul said? Her soul—the soul of his brother Fritjof—was used up.

And deep down, Pagaene had known that. Because of his training, because of his experiences. And he'd also known that there was no negotiating with the endless hunger for death and pain that was The Purity. It had, he was sure of it, been laughing at the pain it caused. Had he heeded his father's plea and given it the stones, Khati would still have died horribly. And then he would have died as well, and their father, and after them, all else living everywhere.

The Purity had to be stopped. He had slowed it, yes, bought them time. Probably not much time, but hopefully enough. Enough to stop it. Enough to ensure the sacrifices had not all been in vain.

The wind blew over and under the huge white wings, blew past his ears, filling them with sound even as it deafened him, but even if it hadn't, Pagaene knew there would be nothing to hear. His father was in mourning for Khati, having just roughly buried her broken shell in a furrow in the earth, gouged with his claws. He doubtless had no desire to speak to the one who had now twice taken his son from him and had probably only agreed to fly them so Khati's sacrifice would at least mean something.

***

Sitting before Pagaene on the white dragon's back, Esyld found it difficult to deal with what had just occurred. So many threads of destiny seemed tied to this quest, so many connections, like an old spider's web. And so many of them had been brutally cut. She felt for Pagaene, who had lost his brother twice now and blamed himself for both, could understand why he had not wished to ask his father to help them. But it had been necessary. Surely, he understood that she would not have asked it of him otherwise, or if she had had the means to ask the dragon herself.

Carrick's renewed hostility also weighed on her mind. So much anger and even hatred kept boiling up and out of him, like a geyser erupting and falling silent again. Her Sight had shown her that his inner self was clouded, but not by what; the Crone's wisdom had not managed to make sense of it, and now the Maiden's innocence could not, either. His fear and distrust ran so deep, and she could not discern the cause.

Regretfully, she did not have the time to think about it now. She could only hope that Uul, his perception of Carrick unclouded by childhood memories, might see what she could not. The present moment had to be used only for thinking about what lay at the end of this sad, glorious flight, about bringing the stones to Muave and the fulfilment of their quest. As to the future, she could not see it and was afraid to try. The Sacred Wells and Groves were gone, and those that had somehow remained had apparently been pillaged by the Symorcian Brotherhood. Yes, they had the means to restore the Wells, but could they, if the Great Mother remained silent and disconnected? And if they could not, what would happen to the Meta Abdita? A terrible thought crept into Esyld's mind. What if, at the end of all this fear and pain and loss, there was no true healing to be had?

**

It took only a few hours on dragonback to reach the hills outside Freywyn, and this was where the White Dragon landed. With a meaningful tilt of his wings, he indicated that Esyld and Pagaene were to dismount. The Knight quickly slid down, then helped Esyld down as well, letting go of her and looking away once she had her feet, as seeing the mind of another looking out through his mother's eyes was disturbing enough, to say the least. He circled around, placing himself in front of the dragon, and bowed. "Thank you," he said.

There was no response, not even a blink or a nod, and

Pagaene made to turn away. Then the soft words came into his mind. '*I do not blame you,*' the White Dragon whispered. '*I blame magic held in secrecy, and the greed and fear of men, and the gods who weave prophecies with no regard for the lives of those who must fulfil them. Forgive the words I spoke in my anguish when Khati was ripped from me, my son, and my silence after. For your brother's death was not your choice, as you were given none. On either occasion. And if I do not accuse you, let none other do so. They do not have that right.*'

Pagaene could not help himself; he threw his arms as far around the dragon's neck as they would go. "Be safe, Father," he whispered back. "If I fail…"

'*You will not, so long as you do not fear failing. Now go your way, as I must go mine. There is something I must do. I will see you again.*'

Pagaene let go and stepped back, dashing tears from his eyes with his good hand. The White Dragon crouched, then sprang back into the air, and once the beast had flown until it looked no larger than a sparrow, the Knight turned back to Esyld. He knew she wanted to be told what his father had said to him, but he was of no mind to share it with her. Those words had been meant for him alone. "He says there is something he must do. This way?" he asked unnecessarily, waving at the only visible path before them.

"Yes," she said, turning and walking away. "Follow me closely. Do not stray from the path."

He fell into step behind her and pushed all other thoughts from his mind, that he might pay close attention to their surroundings. Because although he did not think the Meta Abdita sensed it, something in this place felt very wrong. He was not sure all was as it should be with the High Priestess Muave—just as it was not with her brother, Carrick. Could whatever affected the one be affecting the other? And if so, with which one of them had it originated?

***

190

Rouaix staggered through the woods, his cloak wrapped tightly about his failing body, partly to conceal his identity should anyone see him but also because he wasn't sure he could remove or even loosen the cloak without further injuring himself. He could feel the thick wool sticking to his burned, oozing skin. The pain had become a drumbeat to which he marched, one foot in front of the other, almost mindlessly. He must find his Knight. Pagaene was still loyal. Pagaene was on a mission to save the kingdom. Doubtlessly, he would use the witches with whom he had been seen to distract The Purity so he could destroy it. Those who had seen him just hadn't understood—and he couldn't have told them, of course, not without letting the witches know as well. He was such a good Knight. How it must pain him to think his King distrusted him. Rouaix would reassure him, once he was found…

That idea introduced a stutter into his endlessly circling thoughts and the broken cadence of his steps. He lurched to a halt, frowning. If he found Pagaene and told him he knew about the Knight's task, the witches would hear it too and know they had been fed nothing but lies. And without the witches as a distraction, Pagaene would not be able to defeat The Purity. And then they would all die. He raised the hand not trapped by his cloak to rub his burning eyes. His skin felt as though it too burned, though the fitful wind was cool and the spatters of rain occasionally making their way through the trees were cold and wet. Had The Purity burned him more than he'd thought? Perhaps. It wasn't important, though. Pagaene would know who he was. Pagaene, the loyal Knight, would certainly know his King. And perhaps the witches would be fooled, seeing that The Purity had attacked him. Perhaps they would think he had come seeking Pagaene because he was on their side.

Stupid witches. Rouaix wanted them all dead, but he agreed with the Knight's plan to use them to distract The Purity. He would be glad when The Purity killed them, and then Pagaene would destroy The Purity, and they would return to Jentor together, victorious. Yes, that was what they would do, provided Pagaene didn't have to sacrifice himself to destroy The Purity. It was possible he might have to do that; prophecies were hard to understand and usually involved a lot of death. Rouaix considered it, then shrugged one-sidedly to himself and lurched back into motion. If Pagaene had to die, he would make sure the man was honored for his sacrifice and that his name was cleared. Yes, that was what he would do, because Pagaene was a good, loyal Knight, and Rouaix was a just, noble King. Pagaene might have to die, but he would die honorably and be remembered with honor. And that was what knights wanted, wasn't it? They wished to die with honor and be remembered with honor. Pagaene would want that, Rouaix was sure of it, because he was a good, loyal Knight...

For all of this to happen, though, he had to find Pagaene. Rouaix frowned at the trees, faltering to a halt again. He'd left the castle and started walking, and now he was in the woods. Slowly, he turned around in a circle. All the trees looked alike, and there was no path. He vaguely remembered there being one at some point, but he supposed he must have left it. What a pity Beltor wasn't with him; he'd had a very good head for direction. But of course, Beltor was dead, killed by The Purity. He rubbed his eyes again. He had to keep walking, he had to find his Knight. Because once he'd found him, The Purity would be destroyed, and all the filthy witches, and then everything could be the way it should in his kingdom, and Rouaix would make sure everyone knew that Pagaene had been a loyal Knight right up until his death.

Which direction had he been traveling, though? He caught at a tree for balance, leaning against it and then, rather inexplicably, sliding down it. He frowned. Didn't he need to be up and walking? After all, he was out searching for Pagaene, his loyal Knight...

Rouaix finally returned to himself some indefinable amount of time later—it was still dark, he knew that much—and found himself staring across a strangely green-tinted fire at a dark-haired man who stared back at him with something akin to amusement.

"Oh, this would be a good tale, if there were anyone to tell it to," the stranger observed in a deep, rumbling voice. "A foolish, greedy King, betrayed by the evil he himself caused to be released, wandering lost in the woods, looking for the Knight he thinks should die saving him." He shook an admonishing finger at Rouaix, and in the fire's flickering light, it looked almost claw-like. "You and I are going to have a talk, King Fool. About knights and sacrifices and what honor actually looks like. And then, if you don't die, perhaps I'll help you find the man you seek." A strange smile curved his lips. "And The Purity as well, of course. You'd do well as a distraction for her, don't you think?"

Chapter 28

"Y ou know this story, no doubt, but I shall remind you in case you have forgotten. You must first remember the origin to understand the parts of the story not spoken in the tongues of men," said the dark, hunched figure. Its clawed hands stoked the green-burning fire with a broken stick.

Jentor's King said nothing as he swayed uneasily from side to side. When he sat on the log and looked into the emerald flames, the man felt a strange sort of coolness forming at the top of his brow. In the back of his mouth, a thirst had taken hold. He clumsily grasped at the water skin on his hip and took a long, cleansing drink. The hooded figure spoke in a raspy, bestial voice, and Rouaix could not deny the deep pit of fear in his belly, nor was not oblivious to the palpable sense of danger wafting through the blackness of the surrounding wood. The strange man gravely unsettled Rouaix, but he felt weak—too weak to run.

"In the beginning of all creation, there were the Wells. From them came the Great Mother, the first being to ever know the breath of life. She reigned in solitude for longer than any man can reason." The hooded one's voice carried like wind whipping across a desolate, barren field.

"She birthed the first men from the Wells. The Founding Kings," said Rouaix after a brief lull in his host's recitation. The dry, cracked feeling quickly returned to his mouth, and he once again sought comfort in a long drink. His head throbbed from the cool, spreading sensation.

"Yes, very good. The Great Mother lay with each of the Founding Kings and begat all nations of men from the fruits of her womb." The hooded figure snapped and cracked the joints of his clawed fingers. "The first age was long and prosperous. The Great Mother saw the Wells bring forth much life into the world, but eventually, as you know, the first age had to come to an end."

"The Wells ran empty," rasped the King, his lips having rapidly dried and split. He tried to speak further but could not bring any words under his command. He put the water skin to his mouth and upended it, sucking down mouthful after mouthful, trying in vain to quench the thirst ravaging his body. The icy feeling in his head now made him shiver.

"Indeed," the dark figure added. "And when the Wells went dry… well, you know of the war that soon followed."

"The Purity was born into our world," said the King. He coughed and wheezed, speaking through lips as dry as the broken earth of a summer drought.

"The last bit of life left in the Wells spawned her. The estranged daughter of the Great Mother, she walked in our world with a singular thirst for life. She embodied the emptiness of the Wells. The Great Mother, in her benevolence, took pity on her suffering daughter and allowed The Purity to drink up the lives of mortals who were vulnerable and deathly ill of age," said the stranger with a peculiar reverence. The flames in the fire circle still burned a bright, haunting shade of green, illuminating the clearing but failing to pierce through the dark shadows the stranger's cloak draped over his face.

Rouaix raked his fingernails down his neck and scratched at the agonizing thirst beneath his skin. He emptied the last of his water skin, but his throat felt bone-dry not more than a heartbeat later, matched only by the unbearable chill. The man threw down his empty water skin and crawled towards the green fire. He felt the dancing tendrils of green alleviating the otherworldly cold, the heat of the fire once again inflaming his burns, but he did not care. He was glad merely to be rid of the biting cold.

"I know the tale. The Purity brought on the age of war. I know the blasted tale," the King growled—an animalistic and wholly undignified sound. "Make your point. I tire of listening to you."

The dark stranger filled the woodland clearing with a menacing trace of laughter. He reached behind the log on which he sat and produced a bulging water skin. With a flick of his clawed hands, he tossed the water skin through the tallest trails of green fire, and the sack made of stitched deer hide landed with a gushy thud beside the desperate King. Rouaix pounced upon it with singular desire and rapidly drained its contents.

"I will finish with my story soon enough. You must be patient for a few moments longer, then all will be clear," murmured the cloaked one. "Death came into being at the hands of The Purity. She quenched her thirst with the lifeblood of the sick and infirm for a time, but her appetite grew. She began to drink of those still young before their time in this world had reached its end. The Great Mother took offense to her daughter's rebellion and decreed that The Purity would destroy no more life."

Rouaix had finished the second water skin and left it an empty husk on the ground beside the fire. His belly felt nearly full to bursting, but still the thirst would not abate. Though weak and sickly, he managed to stand up on shaking legs. He peered past the green embers and tried to distinguish the features of the man behind the flames.

"I know of my Mistress," the King rasped. "She thwarted the Great Mother's decree by laying with the Founding Kings. She planted the seed of murder in each of them and so set all nations against one another. She made man kill man, and it was she who reaped the spoils." He staggered and swayed, then stumbled towards the hooded figure.

"So the Wells were replenished with the blood of many men. The Purity drank deeply in the waters stained red," the dark stranger said, standing level with the weakling King. "And that is where the story ends for most and our written history begins, but there is more, as I promised."

"More?" whispered the King lips now bloody from his thirst. The fire in the clearing showed the man for an emaciated ruin, barely discernable as human. The King inched his way toward the hooded figure as if inexorably pulled into the vortex of a whirlpool.

"In the age of war, many died," the hooded one continued, "but not just those slain on the battlefield. The age made many widows and orphans, yes, but the children whose lives were claimed created something truly remarkable."

"What madness is this?" Rouaix fell to his knees before the shadow-clad stranger. He looked at his skeletal hands, covered in skin split and devoid of moisture. "Help me, I beg of you."

"Soon, Your Majesty. You have been most courageous and loyal," the figure replied. "The mothers of the children taken during the age of war wept. There was never any name given to those who lost their children. The sorrow they came to know was too great for words, and the tears these childless mothers shed were plentiful and tasted sweet to The Purity. So plentiful, in fact, that these tears took seed in the earth and ran a vast river. The river would form a new Well. A nameless Well for a nameless sorrow, and from that Well—" With a clawed hand, the thing pulled back the hood of its robe for the waning King to see what lay beneath.

Rouaix's foggy eyes went wide in terrified disbelief at the sight of what the green fire illuminated. He tried to make sense of what he saw, but his mind threatened to break at the impossibility of it. The King looked into nothingness. The creature had a neck of leathery grey skin and a full head of thick, flowing black hair. Where a face should have been, there was nothing, only an empty abyss staring back at Jentor's horrified King.

"From the Well of deepest grief came a faceless thing bred of a nameless sorrow, and so would The Purity come to find her paramour." The shadow laughed, the sound seeming to fuel the green flames. "I thank you for your servitude to your Mistress and my mate, but you are of no further consequence."

Rouaix wanted to scream, but the contents of his belly loosed themselves in place of words. The King let out a profuse spew of water turned to blood inside him. He thrashed and writhed on the ground as every last drop of life vacated his body. As he retched and gargled, the wicked magic finished its work upon him. After several violent moments, the King lay frozen in death amid a large pool of blood.

The clearing lay calm, and the color of the fire transformed from supernatural green to a mundane orange. The shadow thing folded its claws across its chest and emitted a predatory purr. Soon thereafter, the pool of blood encircling the King's corpse bubbled, then boiled. The blood moved and took shape, and in the span of a few heartbeats, The Purity had been conjured from the red puddle to stand in the firelight over the skeletal body of King Rouaix Godfrey XVII.

***

"My love," said The Purity, exuding perverted adoration as she regarded the faceless one.

"I have rescued you from the wickedness of our enemies. It hurt me to see them banish you to the dreaming realm," hissed The Faceless with reciprocated vile affection. "The magic taxed my powers, and the offering was costly." It gestured to the body of the King.

"We must pursue the impure one and her allies. There is little time for us if we are to see them undone," said The Purity.

"On the contrary. It is they who have little time. It seems the blood of a sacrificed King was not without some unexpected benefit. Our offspring will come into this world before any other finds the chance to oppose us," the Faceless one said.

The Purity looked down in response to her lover's curious words, regarding the fullness of her belly and the monster lying within. "You are right. Our child is coming faster than anticipated, and when it does, our rule will be bloody and grand." She gave a revoltingly maternal caress to her enlarged stomach. "Come with me. We must prepare a fitting reception for our progeny."

"As you wish, my love," said The Faceless as it followed The Purity from the clearing. The pair left only smoldering embers, blood, and darkness in their wake.

Chapter 29

"He can't be far," Carrick said as he knelt beside a broken branch still smelling of freshly snapped pine. Uul leaned on his staff and peered deep into the forest, obviously tired from the expense of magic it had taken to rush their raft back from the island in hasty pursuit of Kenyth's now-abandoned boat. His dogs licked their lips behind him and snapped at flies. "Have you stopped to ask yourself why he leaves such a noticeable trail?"

"My brother has always been careless. Today it will lead to his end."

"Perhaps," Uul replied. "Or perhaps there is something far more nefarious at work here."

Carrick rose to his feet. "The only evil in these woods is

my brother."

"Does your brother have the power to sap the trees of their color or wither the grass until it is brittle and broken?"

Carrick noticed the condition of the forest for the first time since they had set off after The Priest. Uul was right. Those trees not already sporting twisted, naked branches possessed a certain dullness, as if the color had been rapidly drained from them. The leaves were not green but green-gray. The typically lively brown bark was not brown but grayish-brown. The grass beneath his feet snapped and turned to dust when he kicked it.

For a moment, fear struck Carrick's heart, but he dismissed it with a wave of his hand. "Eslyd and Pagaene have the stones and are likely in Freywyn as we speak," he said. "The blight will be healed any minute now. No one but I can solve the problem of my brother."

"But the severity of this disease has increased exponentially," Uul said. "I fear that—"

"The presence of evil in the world dulls the light of all good things. My brother carries evil within him, therefore my focus at this very moment is snuffing him out."

Uul picked at his staff and stared at Carrick for a long moment. His dogs, all six of them, locked eyes with Carrick as well. The sight of fourteen eyes fixed on him unsettled Carrick deeply.

"You have something to say, wizard? Say it," Carrick said.

"I fear this fixation on your brother is not beneficial. It is rooted in revenge and malice, not in a desire to bring about any good. Your need to kill him stems from an evil root inside you. And that root is currently aflame with the same dark fire The Purity has set upon this wood."

"You question my resolve to do good?" Carrick growled. His hand moved to his sheathed short sword.

"I do not," Uul said. "I am merely suggesting that the land appears much changed since our journey to the Lake of Destiny. I fear The Purity may be blighting more than the earth and the trees. I fear she may be darkening the souls of—"

An agonized scream—deep, guttural, and human—cut the wizard short. He, his dogs, and Carrick all snapped their attention in the direction of the pained howled; it was not far.

"Kenyth," Carrick said. He drew his short sword and sprinted towards the shriek. Uul and the dogs followed on his heels. After no more than a few moments, they came across a clearing ringed by trees and dense underbrush. In the center of the clearing, the Priest knelt, pawing at the earth. He released another anguished and sustained cry. Ravens with intelligent eyes circled overhead.

"There's the black-hearted monster," Carrick said. He began to rise from his hiding spot in the underbrush, sword at the ready, but Uul held him back with a firm hand on his shoulder.

"Patience," the wizard urged. "Do not let Her get the best of you."

They sat and watched the Priest grope at the dusty ground. He appeared to be searching for something infinitesimally small in the fine motes of dust. He dropped the dust he clutched and scooped up new handfuls. Then his hands glowed with golden light. The dust rose from his hands and hovered in the air for a tense and quivering moment before crashing limply back to the ground.

"No, no," the Priest cried, tears rolling from his eyes. He clawed up handfuls of more dust, the golden light emanated from his hands again, and once more, the dust fell lifeless to the ground.

"Monster!" Carrick shouted as he broke from Uul's grip and charged The Priest. He swiped at Kenyth's head, but the Priest ducked and tumbled out of the way. When he rolled to his feet, he had drawn his own sword and glared defiantly at Carrick.

"You…" the Priest said. "You dare disturb me here?"

"I will kill you wherever you perform that profane black magic," Carrick spat back.

The Priest lunged at Carrick, slashing furiously. Their swords clanged as the Priest struck blow after blow, each of which Carrick parried. Ravens perched in the nearby trees cawed as they took to the heavens and circled overhead.

"Do you know what happened here? Do you know what She did to him?" the Priest said between blows.

"I'll have none of your tricks." Carrick struck back with a slash of his own. The Priest blocked, and the two swords locked, bringing the men only inches apart.

"The vision," the Priest said. "It was meant for Eslyd, but I saw it as well. His Holiness… that demon… She… She…"

For the briefest instant, the fierce gleam in The Priest's eyes dimmed. Carrick shoved hard with as much force as he could muster, and the Priest reeled backwards. When his heel caught a rock and he fell hard to the dust, Carrick pounced and pinned his opponent's sword beneath his boot, holding his own weapon to The Priest's throat.

"Please," the Priest said, "before you kill me, let me try to find a scrap of him. A drop of blood, a bone chip, anything I could use to bring him back."

Carrick laughed. "Why would I allow you to use your black curse to bring back that Abdita-killer? So he could hunt down more of our kind?"

"That man was more family to me than you ever were."

Carrick pressed his blade deeper into The Priest's neck, drawing a few drops of blood. "I'm more than happy to arrange your reunion," he said, then raised his sword high. He plunged down with all his might, emboldened by the added strength of years of anger and anguish. The sword plummeted straight for The Priest's neck.

A flash of fur and teeth streaked across the dusty clearing and knocked the sword from Carrick's hand. The dog stood between him and his weapon, snarling and crouching, prepared to attack.

Carrick glared across the clearing at Uul, stunned by this betrayal. "Dirty wizard," he spat.

Uul took several slow steps towards Carrick. His robes billowed in a rising wind. "This man, your brother, is in mourning for a dear friend," he said. "No matter what evil he may hold inside him, it is certainly not as great as the evil you would perform if you were to murder him here."

"I will rid the world of him."

"And damn yourself in the process?" Uul replied. "She is bending you to do her will, and you are too blinded by rage to see it. He—" Uul leveled a gnarled finger at the Priest "—is one of the few people she fears. He bears the one gift that can destroy Her, or do you not remember what the bear told us? I know not how Her influence has grown so mightily in the time we have been gone, Carrick, but it has certainly grown strong enough to sow darkness in your heart."

"It is because She killed His Holiness," the Priest sputtered. "She devoured him and all his power. Now she uses that power to increase her hold on this world."

"She has absorbed His Holiness?" Uul said. "This is grave news."

"Grave?" Carrick asked. "Maybe to a wizard and a kin-traitor. But suffering and death are all that man ever brought to the Abdita. I say good riddance."

The Priest let out an enraged roar and, struggling free of Carrick's grasp, landed a punch to his chin. Carrick stumbled backwards, and the Priest regained his fighting stance. "He was trying to stop Her long before you," the Priest said. "It is why I joined him. To protect this world. To protect the Great Mother."

"How dare you speak her name, blasphemer," Carrick cried. He dashed toward his sword, and Uul's dog lunged at him. But Carrick dodged, and the dog only caught a piece of cloth from his sleeve. In a single movement, he rolled, picked up his sword, and wheeled upon The Priest. "I care not what words you or the wizard may use to twist me up. I will end you here, brother." He charged the unarmed man, hacking wildly with his sword as if to strike down anything remotely capable of hindering him from his single deadly purpose.

"Stop this madness!" Uul shouted. But Carrick was lost in his rage, blind and deaf to all around him save The Priest. He slashed once, and the Priest barely dodged as the blow glanced off his wrist plate. The second strike hit home, sinking deep into The Priest's leg. Blood spurted from the open wound, coagulating into thick clumps as it hit the dusty earth. The Priest grasped his leg and crumpled to the ground.

"Carrick!" Uul shouted. But Carrick ignored him and drove his sword down with all his strength towards The Priest's skull. "Stop!" Uul's voice echoed in the clearing, suddenly thunderous beyond human capabilities. His eyes lit with a hot violet fire, and a blade of purple energy crackled forth from his staff. It sizzled through the air and struck Carrick in the side, knocking him far across the clearing. "Fool," Uul grunted and huffed toward Carrick. "You impudent, stubborn… no. No."

Uul's hounds joined him at Carrick's side. They sniffed at the open wound freely pouring blood into the dust. The man's ribs were shattered. More than one had penetrated his lungs.

Uul held Carrick's head in his lap and began to summon a healing spell. But before he could even utter the first phrase, Carrick let out a heavy breath and went limp. His heart no longer beat.

"No… no," Uul stammered. "I didn't mean… I never meant for…"

A heavy and weary hand rested on Uul's shoulder. "You did what was necessary to protect him," the Priest said. He clutched his leg and winced at his own bleeding wound.

"But I… I… You must bring him back," Uul pleaded. "You can. I know you can."

"And how would my brother take to that? Restored by the very magic he abhorred. He would surely kill you for suggesting it, kill me for doing the deed, and then kill himself out of sheer hatred. It is better this way. You did him a great favor."

"Favor? I murdered him."

"You said it yourself. She had infested his soul. How long ago, I know not. But you prevented Her from permanently claiming him. Now, he will rest with the Great Mother and be at peace."

"And what will you do?" Uul shouted, his hounds suddenly snapping from their despondence and snarling in anger. "Now that your hated brother is dead, will you go in peace?"

The Priest grimaced and shook his head. He knelt beside

Carrick and closed his brother's eyes with the gentlest pass of his hand. Then, he untied a drawstring bag from Carrick's belt and emptied the contents of the bag into his hand—the broken shards of Carrick's athame.

"You ask if I will go in peace," the Priest said, staring down at his brother's shattered blade. "I ask you, how can I? She claimed His Holiness, the man who was like a father to me. She turned my brother's heart against me. She has cut me deeper than any blade ever could. And you ask if I will go in peace?"

The Priest clenched his hands around the jagged remains of Carrick's athame. Trickles of blood shimmering with a golden light dripped from his palm. As they hit the earth, several green sprouts blossomed in the dust.

"On the contrary, wizard," the Priest said. "I will go to war."

Chapter 30

The White Dragon settled down into the soft moss, folded his great wings, and waited in the clearing near the top of Kreajo Mountain, surveying the realm stretching out before him. The emerald green of the Freywyn forests in the east rolled gently down to meet the Ravendale River, which snaked in a slow amble, glistening brightly in the early dawn light before it split into tributaries like a giant azure hydra, forming the Graskin Delta that fed the Great Drancon Sea beyond.

To the north lay Parkovia and the Shrine of Verity. A low, soft growl rumbled through him as he mourned the loss of his son Fritjof once again. He closed his eyes, forcing away the replaying scene of death in his memory, and remembered his son in his carnation of Khati, his ever-close companion over the years. He felt this loss deeply but knew he would see his son again amongst the stars one day.

His senses told him that a presence had silently joined him in his mourning, hidden in the shadows of the forest encircling the clearing.

'Come forward, old friend,' he said softly to the presence. *'We have nothing to fear from each other.'*

The figure stepped lightly out of the darkness and halted a few paces from the dragon. It was fully cloaked in a long, dark, hooded cowl, its features hidden. "It has been a long time." A smooth, amber voice reached the dragon's ear, and he turned away from the view to regard his company. Long, feminine fingers reached up and pushed back the hood.

'It certainly has been, Muave.' The White Dragon nodded in respect, and Muave reciprocated with a bow of her own. *'Ser Pagaene has successfully retrieved the stones,'* he said. *'But of course, you already knew this. Your ravens have been watching.'*

A smile spread across Muave's face. "Yes, they told me. This is good news."

'Yes.' The dragon looked back in the direction of the Shrine.

Muave stepped closer to share the view. The honeyed horizon promised the coming of a resplendent dawn. "We are on the final leg of the journey to cleanse these lands and fulfil the prophecy," she said. "They just need to bring the stones back here now, back to the Mother Well, so we can complete the ritual. I have already sent a messenger."

He felt her gentle hand on his flank, flinched away from her touch, and stood to pace the clearing, in the center of which was a Sacred Well. It appeared as the others—small, made of stone, and seeming to crumble under its archaic age. But this was the first Well. It was the Well that had given birth to the Great Mother, and it was the source of life for all other Wells across the realm. Its location was a carefully guarded secret, its grounds protected by ancient magic hiding it from all but the highest forms of magical beings sworn to keep it secure.

Muave touched the ancient stone in reverence, and her face glowed from the soft gold light haloing around her fingertips. The White Dragon paced the clearing, keeping his eyes fully on Muave, his tale flicking a little with each step.

'Why did you choose them?' he finally asked.

Muave pulled her hand away from the Well and looked up at him with a small frown. "What do you mean?"

'Why them to carry out this task? Why those particular persons? Why my son?' He stopped and regarded her with an interrogating peridot eye.

Muave pursed her lips. "You know why. The Great Mother showed them to me. She chose them. I was merely her vassal."

'She chose Carrick, your brother?'

"Yes. What bothers you, old friend? Speak to me plainly, as we always have."

'There's something tainted in your brother. A darkness has enveloped his soul. I saw it leaching from his aura. Tell me you did not already know about this.' A deep growl reverberated from his throat.

Muave turned away from him, silent for a moment. "It is not darkness in him but the guilt of what he did to his brother, and this he always carries. He refuses to make peace with it, and it drives a resentful anger in him." She turned and looked back up at the dragon. "He is not tainted by darkness. He merely harbours despair."

The White Dragon raised his head and looked down his long snout. *'That is false.'*

"It is the truth," she implored. "What we did to our brother was wrong. It was childish and cowardly. We were young, we were scared of this new power, and we chose to let fear govern our actions. We ostracised him. I have since seen the error of my ways and have only wanted Kenyth's return. But Carrick—Carrick has always been the stubborn, hard-headed one. He could never make peace with it and admit that he had been wrong. It leaves a black mark on him now. That is what you see."

The White Dragon brought his head down and turned his face to one side so their gazes were level. *'You lie. That is not the root of his darkness. I see the same darkness has tainted you. How long have you been serving her?'*

"I have served the Great Mother all my life."

The dragon snapped his neck back. *'Lies again, old friend. Tell me, how long has she had a hold over you?'*

"I… I don't understand what you mean."

'The Purity,' he roared. *'How long have you served her? I saw her darkness at the Shrine when she manifested. I recognize it as the same darkness in Carrick, and I see that darkness in you.'*

Muave retreated backward, shaking her head and protesting her innocence amidst his accusations. "I am a High Priestess, loyal to the Great Mother. My life is hers. You are mistaken, dragon, but I will forgive your insult, as the death of your companion must be clouding your mind in its grief. Remember, Pierce, that it was I who sought you out after your reincarnation to tell you of your sons. It was I who first informed you of Fritjof's death. I will forgive you your outburst, but I will not forget." She spun on her heel and stalked across the mossy clearing.

The dragon laughed, stopping her in her tracks. *'Look where we are, Muave. Why do you think I called you here?'*

"This is the place where the prophecy will end. Where the Mother Well will refill the others and return magic and peace to our lands. This is the final step in our task," she spat. "It is only natural for you to call me here at this time."

'True,' said the dragon as he strode around the clearing again, keeping his eyes on her face. He watched her walk, carefully keeping the Well between them as they circled. *'All magic is amplified in this place, don't you remember?'*

"Yes." She eyed him cautiously.

'Oh, old friend, did you forget I can see into people's souls and know the truth of them? I admit my Sight has clouded some with the destruction of the Wells, but here, I am no longer blind.'

"Then look at me. Look into me and see that I am the same Muave you know. The High Priestess loyal to the Great Mother."

He paused mid-step. *'I am looking at you. Your enchantment to hide the truth is strong, but my Sight is clearer. I can see it, the darkness wisping from you like dark smoke. Your magic struggles to hide it even now.'*

He changed his Sight and looked deep into her heart. The mirage of a white, pure soul hiding the truth flickered more intensely now. Its faltering increased as it struggled to push back the dark power wrapping around her heart, billowing ashen tentacles. The magic weakened under his scrutiny until, with a final, trembling flicker, the cloaking enchantment shattered, spilling forth the rotten core she carried.

'There. That's the truth of it, old friend,' he said grimly.

He returned to normal sight. Muave still stood before him, but the darkness now shadowed her demeanour, sharpening her features and oozing cruelty. A thin-lipped grin ripped across her features as she chuckled. He shivered at her transformation.

"Yes, you have discovered my secret, but you are too late. You can do nothing to stop it now."

'What has she promised you?'

"A new dawn. For too long, the Great Mother has neglected her children and allowed war, greed, and suffering to ravage our lands." She stepped away from the Well and sauntered toward him. He held his ground. "The Purity will cleanse this realm and birth it into a new golden age of magic."

'You're a fool for believing her promises and a traitor to your kind.'

"No. You are the fool, old friend." She punctuated the words with a sneer. "We have allowed the erosion of our power unchecked. Mortal man has had too much control, and now the world of magic is dying. The Purity offers us a chance to restore that balance."

'If you want The Purity to succeed, why did you send your brother, Eslyd, and my son to retrieve the stones used in the ritual to defeat her?'

Muave chuckled once more, the timbre of her voice echoed sharply by the coarse caws of the ravens, who flocked into the trees around them and roosted like ebony sentinels.

"The stones will be used in a ritual, yes. Not to defeat her, but to protect her. She is heavy with child—with the new world—and will soon bear it to this realm. Here will be the cradle of this new age. The stones' ritual will protect her at her weakest, and the magic of the Well will bring forth her creation with wondrous power. This power will restore and strengthen the Wells across the land. Only someone worthy could retrieve the stones for her, and I served her by sending out the one person who could complete this task. Your son, Ser Pagaene. Of course, I knew it had to be him. The Purity told me herself, but I needed someone to push him forward. Esyld was a convenient tool. My brother was sent with them to ensure they didn't get themselves killed before they could be of use. Once the stones were retrieved, he was to kill Ser Pagaene, take them for himself, and bring them to me. Esyld would return with him, by force, if necessary. Her blood will be sacrificed for The Purity's ritual. So now we have the stones. I am sorry for the loss of your second son." There was no true remorse in her words, only eager cruelty.

The White Dragon roared in rage. *'You will not succeed, witch.'*

"I already have." She laughed.

'I will destroy you.' The White Dragon reared onto his hind legs, bared his teeth, and spread his wings wide. The barrel of his chest glowed carmine as the fire boiled with rage deep inside him. Around them, the crows took to the air and flew like sharp missiles, whipping up the wind and pricking his body with thousands of cuts.

Muave raised her hands, changing the long fingers into gnarled claws, a purple light shining from the tips. "Time to die, old friend," she screamed.

Across the realm, the earth shifted with a crack, and a bright flash of white light blinded all.

Chapter 31

The setting sun cast sharp-edged shadows over Freywyn, yet the villagers did not stand about visiting at the end of the workday, nor did anyone prepare the evening meal. In fact, the village seemed too still and empty, and the gloomy reticence among the people they passed raised doubts—doubts which only grew as Pagaene and Esyld trudged along the village road.

A stern-faced man hauling a heavy bundle moved aside but showed no further interest in the travelers. A dull-eyed woman passed without so much as a glance. Huddled in a circle near the cabin of the Elders, a group of the children whose joyous laughter and curiosity had won over Pagaene's heart during his last stay stood whispering.

The palpable tension worried Pagaene, but Esyld seemed either oblivious of the villagers' odd behavior or unsurprised by it. In any case, Pagaene remained wary.

As they approached the children, he recognized one of the girls by a shock of rosy hair and matching cheeks. She flinched when Esyld addressed her.

"Blessed be, youngling," Esyld said. "Can you tell me where to find Muave?"

The girl glanced up at first Esyld, then Pagaene. Confused, her eyes darted between the two visitors until her face lit up with comprehension. "Forgive me, honored... um... maiden," she said. "I didn't recognize you."

"Understandable," Esyld said with a lenient smile. "I wear a different face. Now, regarding my question..."

The girl swallowed and looked down at her feet. "Muave and the Elders are gathered at the Mother Well, waiting for you." Each of the children in the small group shifted as she spoke the words, as though they'd been waiting for her to deliver that message. None of them met Esyld's eyes.

Esyld thanked the girl and beckoned Pagaene to follow her. She led the way down the quiet street until abruptly pulling him aside into a narrow recess between two sheds.

"What?" Pagaene uttered, perplexed, but Esyld silenced him with a raised finger.

"I used the Sight on the younglings," Esyld replied. "They know very little, but some of their parents are leaving soon. There is such a cloud of despair and betrayal hanging over this place, I can hardly bear it." She paused a moment, covering her mouth with her hand and shaking her head. Then, enlivened again, she added, "Give me the stones."

Pagaene opened the compartment in his arm and handed her the small bag. Esyld selected a single ruby-colored stone and returned the bag to him. She bent and picked up a pebble from the ground. In one hand, she clasped her Nightstone amulet and the ruby. In the other hand, she held the pebble. She closed her eyes, took a deep breath, and stood still.

When she opened her hand again, the pebble had turned smooth and red. Its appearance roughly matched the sacred stone. "Put it in your false arm," she said, handing him the true ruby stone.

"Why?" he whispered.

"If I am wrong, all we risk is looking foolish. But if I am right…" She pressed her lips together and shook her head. "We cannot give Muave the stones.

Pagaene nodded and did as asked. Esyld dropped the false ruby into the bag with the other sacred stones and tucked it into her pack. Then, she helped him pull his sleeve over his wooden arm. She looked up at him, her Maiden's face creased with worry, and opened her mouth to speak.

They both flinched when a brilliant flash of white light startled them. Pagaene turned his back to the light, shielding Esyld with his body. When the glow faded, they turned to seek its source, shielding their eyes with their arms.

Eslyd gasped. "Mount Kraejo," she said. "The Mother Well."

Chapter 32

Muave flicked her wrist. A shimmering dome of emerald energy deflected the White Dragon's fiery breath. She squinted against the brightness until it faded into a dull imprint on the backs of her eyelids. She smirked. "Give this up, Pierce. You cannot win."

"I will kill you, witch." The great beast reared, swiping at her with a foreleg. The massive, clawed foot crushed down into the soil, ripping large chunks asunder.

"Too slow, old friend," Muave taunted. "*Hrafn*, attack."

The ravens swirled around the dragon, pecking at his scales, clawing at his eyes. Their squawks filled the air. Plumes of searing breath erupted from the dragon's mouth as he snaked his head one way and the other, trying to burn the annoying birds alive.

A coruscating beam of onyx tendrils lanced into the dragon's ribs, searing the scales a cloudy charcoal. The White Dragon bellowed, toppling over onto one side. He panted, shaking his head to clear it of the wave of nausea sweeping over him. Another beam of onyx grazed the connecting joint of his right wing. Roaring, he lashed out with his tail, sweeping it through the air like a club.

Muave flattened herself against the ground, then scrambled back to her feet. Her laughter echoed around the White Dragon. "Is this your best?" She grinned, searing the dragon's scales with a third onyx beam. Pierce's roar resounded across the sky. He shook his head and snarled at the witch.

Rearing once more, he let loose a jet of fire, blanketing the clearing. Hundreds of raven claws and beaks tore into his flesh, their throaty caws echoing in his ears.

"I am through fighting you, old friend." Muave sneered. When she pressed her palms together, a crackling sphere of violet energy erupted between them. She drew her hands apart, the energy stretched, and she gripped a wavering violet sword. Dashing towards the stricken dragon, she screeched and threw the sword, which struck the underside of his throat and stopped only when the tip punctured the back of his neck.

Wide-eyed, Pierce choked. A bubble of rich, thick blood burst from his mouth, staining his scales a deep crimson. He fell forward, his body crashing into the charred clearing.

Muave stalked toward him and gripped the sword to yank it from his throat. The White Dragon gasped and reach toward her with one forepaw. She grasped it tenderly, brushing her cheek against one claw. Tears trickled from her eyes. "I am sorry, old friend. But there is no other way. This world must end, and you with it."

She thrust the sword through the dragon's eye, shoving the blade deep into his brain. The White Dragon's body spasmed, then lay still.

Chapter 33

T he final blood moon of the harvest loomed over Esyld and Pagaene's heads as they ventured forth along Mount Kraejo. Although the sun had not yet set, the moon was high in the sky, albeit hidden behind large patches of gray, fast-moving clouds. They ascended the smooth slope through sparsely charred ground, fallen leaves, and bushes spotted with a deep crimson. Spying down on them from the trees, ravens cawed and plucked at their own feathers. Some of them picked on pieces of flesh neither Esyld nor Pagaene could identify. The closer they came to the Mother Well, the larger the number of the birds surrounding them.

"So many of them. How peculiar," Esyld said. She looked up at them once more and tread more cautiously.

"Not really. This mountain is known for its ravens, among other things. I thought you knew that," Pagaene replied, pulling down the sleeve of his prosthetic arm absentmindedly.

"Hold on. I'd like to see farther down the path." The pair stopped in their tracks. In an attempt to exploit the mountain's power of intensifying magic, Esyld raised her arms to the trees in front of them. Violet energy emitted from her palms, and flocks of ravens flew away, cawing loudly. Still, no matter how much she focused her gaze, she could not see through the thick gray mist ahead. Instead of seeing through the trees, her vision blurred.

"This is odd. Here of all places." She gave up trying. "Let's continue."

After a few moments, Pagaene asked, "What if the prophecy is untrue?"

"What?"

"Muave told me a destiny awaited me of which I was not yet aware. But perhaps she lied. What if there is no destiny to discover? Suppose, instead of fulfilling my place to defeat evil, I'm merely meant to be a sacrifice?" He spoke quickly in an uncertain tone Esyld had not heard from him before.

"Remember the dream you had of the Hamadryad. The nymph who told you you would defeat The Purity. And even if Muave lied, others along our journey supported the prophecy you seem to forget. But let's not talk about this now. This is not the time for doubts." Esyld held tightly the strap of the bag containing the sacred stones and hurried her step. Then she noticed the unsheathed dagger on the left side of Pagaene's belt. "I see you carry the keris."

"I wanted something of my brother's. Something of Khati's. Even if that something is the weapon she used to take her own life."

Esyld nodded, her gaze never leaving the deathly-sharp instrument. "May I hold it?" She received a cautious frown in reply. "Briefly. I promise to return it." Feeling the Knight's hesitation, the Maiden softened her voice and inclined her head. "Don't you trust me?" This time, he pulled the asymmetrical dagger from his belt, held it by its sharp blade, and offered her the handle. "Thank you."

Esyld spent a few moments admiring the keris. It had made such a journey, used for both good and evil. The Meta knew that the time had come for it to be used again. With her back to Pagaene, she bent on one knee, rolled up her sleeve, and brought the keris to her wrist. If the Knight saw the single drop of blood falling on the ground, she would never know, for he said nothing.

Shortly after, Esyld and Pagaene sensed the forms of living beings gathering in the mist around them. Esyld stood slowly, offering him the keris' handle for him to take.

"What did you do?" he asked, almost frightened, placing the dagger back to his belt but concealing it this time within his clothes.

"I've summoned bardoul. Like the one that—well." She pointed at his wooden arm, which Pagaene brought protectively up to his chest, momentarily covering its brass knuckles with his other hand. "Don't worry. This time, they will not come for you." The direwolves emerged through the fading mist, their sapphire eyes glowing intensely but aimed at neither their summoner nor her companion. Something else drew their attention. Then the fog dispersed, and the direwolves approached the clearing, growling at a sword-wielding, female shape in the distance. "They've come for her," Esyld whispered, her eyes fixed on her once old friend.

***

At an exquisite grove of eternal power, the sound of water flowing out of huge rocks and pouring out onto endless streams could even lull a demon to sleep. Giant sequoia trees with thick branches and short, prickly leaves in all the colors of the spectrum decorated an immense forest. The massive plants, roots shallow and lifetimes spanning thousands of years, stood hundreds of feet tall—so tall that, from the ground, one could only see the faint shadows of the birds circling its tip. Though similar to the others, one tree stood out among the rest. A single crack in its spiral trunk, wide enough for two humans to walk side by side, led to the depths of a mysterious cave.

An undefined blue essence spread on the cold floor of that cave, breathing heavily but with a steady rhythm. The longer the essence remained inside the cave, the more the cold spread from within its center toward the colorful grove outside.

"Soon it will all be over. And soon it will all begin." The cloaked figure spoke softly in his deep voice, caressing the essence's watery tendrils with his green, claw-like fingers. "Our offspring, the ruler of all, is only moments away. We have only to wait for the Meta's blood to kindle the sacred stones under this final blood moon of the harvest. That spark will ignite destruction." The Purity stirred, but The Faceless covered her mouth, not letting her speak. "Save your energy, my love. You will need it. Let the Mother Well speak for you instead." The Purity closed her eyes. The Faceless was right. Soon, it would all be over.

***

Uul and the Priest advanced through the forest. Even though they had buried Carrick's body in haste, they had prayed over him and blessed the soil with which they'd covered him.

"I will never forgive myself for his death," Uul said, petting one of his half-dozen dogs.

"It was an accident. You know this as well as I. You saw the darkness in him. He was helpless."

Before Uul could reply, he dropped to his knees and grasped at his head. A terrified scream escaped him, and he jerked once more in unseen agony.

"What happened?" Kenyth tried to grasp at the wizard's head to take a look, but Uul rocked back and forth too aggressively for the Priest to approach without risking injury to either of them.

"I'm blind," the wizard shouted. "I cannot see!" Uul's dogs barked around him, also trying and failing to get near. When Uul brought his forehead to the ground, his rocking eased. The dogs licked his face and barked playfully again, but Kenyth did not relax, unsure of what to expect next.

Uul reached out for Kenyth, who helped him to his feet.

"I know where we must go," Uul whispered. "I saw it. Something terrible will take place at the Mother Well. The Purity is there."

"Mount Kraejo? We'll never reach it in time."

"We will not." Uul petted his dogs with a sigh. "You will."

"I can't leave you here on your own. We must stay together. Who knows what lurks in this forest?"

"I will not be alone, young man. I have my army." Uul looked at his dogs. "But there's no time to waste. My vision was clear. You have the power of Rebirth, Kenyth. And I know your magic moves you faster than mere walking. You will be useful at the Mother Well sooner than later. I'll try to find another way to reach you. Now, go! Quickly!"

Kenyth wanted to ask more questions, but he had agreed to trust Uul and his alliance in order to fight The Purity. "I'll meet you there," he said, reaching to pull his athame from his satchel.

"If all goes well," Uul whispered just as the Priest disappeared from the path.

***

As the Gray Wizard let his dogs lead the way, two serpents, burning, acid paste dripping down their open mouths, crept silently through the muddy grass behind him. Without sensing any danger nearby, Uul and his dogs marched toward Mount Kraejo.

***

Behind the mist, Muave stood proudly at the clearing, the edge of her sword pointing toward the ground. With her free hand, she seemed to be petting something else upon the ground. Though the High Priestess acknowledged her presence with a broad smile, Esyld chose to keep some distance between them.

"My friend." Muave bowed her head at Esyld, but the

action was not reciprocated. "Ser Pagaene," she repeated, successfully this time when the Knight returned her gesture. "I am so glad you've come. As you can see, the moon is almost in position, and the ceremony can begin. I knew you would be the one to save the magic realms. And you, Esyld. You've discovered the power connected to your new face. It has made you strong again, your blood and spirit at their best once more. It must have been quite an experience for you." She paused. "Where's Carrick?"

"Carrick… didn't make it," Esyld replied. "I'm sorry."

"What do you mean?"

On the blade of Muave's sword, Esyld saw dried blood and small pieces of white dragon scales. "It was an accident. He protected us on our journey. You must be quite proud of him."

"I shall pray for him," Muave whispered. "His loss was not in vain." Ravens cawed all around them, but the bardoul remained hidden among the last cloud of remaining fog. But that, too, would clear in seconds. "It is time. Let us begin." The High Priestess of the realm turned her open palm upwards. A circle of violet light emitted from her hand, reaching all the way to the moon. "The sacred stones."

Great Mother, protect me, Esyld prayed and approached Muave. When only one step remained between them, she noted an unlit pentagram within the circle of Muave's light-emitting palm.

"Place a stone on each point," Muave ordered, clenching her sword in the other hand. "It does not matter which, as long as they are all placed."

Fully on guard and prepared to strike if necessary, Esyld did as she was told. When she placed the first stone on one of the points, the corresponding triangle of the pentagram lit up, taking her by surprise. The ravens cawed louder.

"Good. It is working," Muave whispered.

Placing the second stone on another point led to another triangle illuminating. With each triangle, the violet light intensified. Esyld had kept the false stone for last.

"One more. Just one more, and then you'll be a hero, Esyld." Muave stared at her palm and dragged her sword a little to the side, marking the ground. Noticing her movement, Pagaene placed his hand on his own sword, prepared to unsheathe it, should it come to that.

Esyld removed the final stone from the bag, which she dropped from her hand, and the growing wind that had cleared the mist carried it away. At long last, Esyld could clearly see the Mother Well. It was made of the same rough stone as her own Sacred Well, but this one was covered in bright green weeds and protected by a strong ivy embrace. She wondered if she would survive betraying Muave to discover what the Well held inside. But then her gaze shifted farther into the clearing. The figures circling the clearing were indeed the Elders, but now that the fog no longer hid their current state, she saw them for what they were—mere husks of themselves, the life drawn completely out of them. Pale, hairless, and frozen in place, each Elder had been struck through and left with a gaping hole in their gut, where a faint tinge of violet, the same color as Muave's wavering sword, still remained. A few feet away, the carcass of the White Dragon had become a makeshift nest of ravens.

"Now, the last one," Muave said, obviously growing anxious and unaware of what Esyld had seen.

With a slightly trembling hand, Esyld placed the final fake stone on Muave's palm. Not only did the remaining triangle not illuminate, but all the others faded, ending the connection with the moon.

"What have you done?" the Priestess asked, her eyes narrowed to slits. "You fool. You have no idea what you've done!" She raised her free hand, first to the sky, then down to thrust her open palm at Esyld.

Before Esyld could react, hundreds of ravens descended. Sharp beaks pecked at her face and body. Unable to send them away, and with a damaged and bleeding face, all Esyld could do was cover her eyes and mouth with her hands. When Pagaene unsheathed his sword and prepared to dash forward, Muave cast thorn-riddled vines, entrapping him around the ankles.

"I will save you for later, Knight," Muave spat at Pagaene.

"This one ends first." The Priestess then ordered her ravens to fly higher. Clutching Esyld's skin and clothes, the ravens lifted Esyld through the clearing and over the Mother Well. Struggling in unbearable pain, Esyld uncovered her mouth and yelled, "*Daos-kunne, aanval*!" Her Nightstone amulet fell and landed upon the well's ivy ledge, its long chain hanging against the cold inner stones. Just before losing consciousness, Esyld heard the howling of the Alpha bardoul echo through the mountain.

Chapter 34

The cave trembled at The Purity's screams, and debris hailed down on the maleficent couple. The Faceless shielded his lover from the dust and pebbles as best he could, but she was too distraught to appreciate the chivalrous gesture. Her glistening blue surface shook from the effort of delaying the inevitable, and her watery tendrils coiled around his arm—so tightly, they would have shattered a mortal man's bones.

"I cannot wait any longer," The Purity panted, and her every breath released white vapor into the air.

"You must..." The Faceless began but stopped when a purple beam pierced the cave's entrance. The light drew a bright triangle on his companion's belly, and within its boundaries, The Purity's outer layer burbled and frothed. The Faceless man would have smiled if he had lips.

"It has begun, my love," he whispered, and her anguished wail proved it came not a moment too soon.

A second beam entered the cave, closely followed by a third, and they all burned deep into The Purity's widespread substance. She howled with pain, and the tendril around her mat'es arm pulled the father-to-be so close, her coldness numbed his chest.

"This. Is. Your. Doing," The Purity hissed between shallow gasps.

"I take pride in your agony," he said, firmly patting her tendril.

It slipped from his arm when the fourth beam hit the birthing mother. She convulsed, her center cracked open like a burned pie's crust, and a dozen small tentacles wriggled from her womb. As The Faceless inhaled the scent of putrid decay, he wished he were able to weep with joy.

"Have a bit more patience, my beautiful daughter," he said, gently stroking one of the appendages that instantly wound around his finger and attempted to prick his skin with its poisonous spikes. Once the ritual was completed, neither shield nor spell would deflect his daughter's attacks. But right now, her skin and barbs were as soft as a kitten's fur.

From somewhere beneath the knot of tentacles, a few eyes blinked at him, each a different color. The proud father uttered a content sigh. Just one more beam, and his daughter would take her first step into the realm of mortals, drain the lifeforce from her first witch, putrefy her first human. He could almost see her glorious future, reflected in those curious eyes.

Yet the last beam never appeared. Instead, the other four disappeared, and The Purity, exhausted and starved of the sustaining magic, collapsed onto the ground. Her essence oozed away through cracks in the stone, and a few tendrils connecting mother and child threatened to tear their half-born daughter apart.

The Faceless had to act quickly. He cut his daughter free with his claws, but when he severed the last tendril, the tiny doom-bringer uttered a mewling cry, quivered, and fell limp. Only then did he realize the mistake; his daughter had left the womb too soon, and she could not yet exist without maternal support. Shocked, he clutched the babe's gelatinous head, lifted one of the many eyelids, and watched her life's spark recede into oblivion. And thus, his offspring's future ended before it had even begun.

From afar, the noise of cawing birds and howling beasts gave voice to The Faceless' grief; his own had abandoned him. He stared at the little corpse, paralyzed by an amount of pain he had never thought possible.

Eventually, a soft murmur wafted through the cave. "Is she strong? Will Nuodai fulfill her destiny?" The Purity asked.

"No," he answered in a toneless whisper. "You failed." He gathered his dead daughter in his arms, stepped out of the cave, and cast a ball of green fire to set the grove ablaze.

***

A demonic cry cut through the cacophony of battle noises. The terrifying sound froze Pagaene's blood but luckily not his sword arm. Driven by rage and concern for Esyld, he dauntlessly hacked away at his thorny shackles. The hard vines deflected some of his blows, and more than once, the blade nicked his skin, but the pain only fueled his fury.

When he finally freed himself, Esyld's motionless body, held by the ravens' talons, hovered over the abyss. They could drop her any moment. Pagaene had no plan, little hope, and probably not enough time, but he raced across the clearing to save his friend.

He ran past Muave, still locked in mortal combat with the bardouls, when an elongated shadow fell from the moonlit sky. At first, Pagaene's heart leapt with joy; he thought it was his father coming to their aid, but the shape was not a dragon's. Without slowing, the Knight stole another glance at the strange shadow. It almost resembled…

"*Fylloma Aegis!*" a familiar voice boomed, and a giant tree, spreading its branches like wings, dove into the cloud of ravens holding Esyld's life in their talons.

"No!" Pagaene yelled and pointed his sword at the flurry of black feathers and green leaves, as if his blade could also summon magic. Unsurprisingly, it did not.

Yet, as the scene cleared, the tree-bird emerged from the impact, devoid of its leaves but carrying a grinning Kenyth on its back, an unmoving Esyld lying in a makeshift basket under its belly.

His mouth agape, Pagaene watched the strange rider circle the clearing and descend before him.

"Quickly," Kenyth urged, offering a helping hand. "Climb up."

Pagaene did as asked but not without taking a closer look at the unconscious Abdita. She was breathing, but her face—the same face his mother had worn—was caked with blood.

"Will you save her?" he asked Kenyth, barely hiding his disdain for the Priest who had crossed them on so many occasions.

"What do you think I'm here for?" Kenyth scoffed, and as soon as Pagaene sat behind him, he clapped his heels into the trunk's sides. The tree-bird took off and circled the clearing once again, providing Pagaene with a strategic overview of the mountaintop.

Beside the Well, Muave and her remaining ravens fought the last bardoul, and there was no doubt they would win. Nevertheless, it was not her impending victory but the big lump at the clearing's edge that made Pagaene's heart plummet. In a dark pool, most likely blood, lay the White Dragon, his scales glistening in the moonlight and a gaping hole where his eye should have been.

"She killed him," Pagaene gasped, too shaken to produce more than a hoarse whisper. When he received no response, he dug his fingers into Kenyth's arm. "Your sister murdered my father!"

Kenyth darted him an indifferent glance over his shoulder and nodded. "She is a traitor."

The pragmatism in the Priest's admission did nothing to soothe Pagaene's anguish. "What are you going to do about it?" he growled.

Before Kenyth could answer, a gut-wrenching howl drew

both men's attention to the ground. Muave had killed Esyld's last bardoul. The Priestess looked up, flashed them a triumphant sneer, raised her arm, and was about to speak when she too was interrupted.

Portentous thunder rolled across the sky, and a savage hiss arose from the Well. Bewildered, Muave turned—just in time to witness a pillar of green fire erupting from the shaft. The flames shot so high, they seemed to singe the moon. Muave's ravens took flight, leaving nothing but the echoes of their terrified shrieks behind, and even the tree-bird recoiled from the blaze. Yet the Priestess held her ground. Pagaene suspected it was horror rather than bravery that rooted her to the spot while a cloaked figure emerged from the pit. The man held a dark bundle in his arms.

Muave fell to her knees. "My Lord," she pleaded with a shaky voice, "it is not too late. I sense the final stone is still nearby. I can complete the ritual!"

Instead of an answer, the cloaked man dropped his bundle at her feet, and it unfolded into a greasy mess of tentacles, eyeballs, and flesh. It was the most hideous thing Pagaene had ever seen, and its foul stench turned his stomach, even from his place in the sky. Where the dead abomination touched the ground, the grass withered, and the soil turned to dust.

Muave swallowed. "My Lord…" she whimpered.

"Your sword," the cloaked man commanded. The Priestess offered it with trembling arms and glanced up at her master. He weighed the weapon in his hands and without warning thrust it through the stinking corpse and into the ground.

The High Priestess flinched.

"You failed," the cloaked man remarked almost casually, retrieved the sword from its gruesome sheath, and examined the blade. Pagaene wasn't close enough to discern any details, but the rotten smell had worsened by far. Therefore, he wasn't surprised when Muave retched. The man took a step toward her and lifted her chin. "You know the punishment for failure, don't you, witch?"

"M-my Lord," Muave panted, her face so sickly in color, it rivaled the hue of the flames. "Have mercy!"

The cloaked man chuckled and touched the sword's tip to Muave's head. She made no attempt to flee.

Pagaene touched Kenyth's arm, but the Priest remained as rigid as his sister. The taut muscles of his back, however, betrayed his tension.

"You expect me to bestow mercy upon my child's murderer?" the cloaked man asked. He shook his head and dragged the blade slowly across Muave's brow. He only grazed her skin, barely enough to draw blood, but where the violet-tinged steel cut, her flesh instantly blackened and rotted away. Like spilt ink, the decay spread across her face, and Muave hardly had the time to scream before it reached her throat. Within a few seconds, her body had moldered and crumbled to dust.

Except for a groan, Kenyth showed no reaction.

Nevertheless, the soft sound was enough to get the cloaked man's attention. He lifted his head and curled a clawed finger at the Priest, daring him to attack.

To Pagaene's surprise, Kenyth complied. With a fierce battle cry, he sent the tree-bird into a steep dive and charged the enemy. The cloaked man, however, had expected the brash move. With well-practiced precision, he shot a lance of green flames at the wooden bird.

Kenyth evaded the first missile, but when a second came their way, one of the branches caught fire. Pagaene attempted to put them out, yet the magic flames neither yielded to his cloak nor the water from his flask. With deadly hunger, they ate their way up to the trunk. "We must retreat," he yelled at Kenyth, and the Priest brooked no argument.

Thus, they rushed off, with more green lances on their tail and a trail of smoke in their wake.

The tree-bird collapsed into a heap of sticks the moment Kenyth set foot on the meadow. They had landed near the forest edge, closer to Freywyn and Mount Kraejo than Pagaene would have liked, but their burning mount had left them little choice. And there was no sign of the cloaked man's pursuit.

While the Priest attended to Esyld's wounds, Pagaene scouted the area. When he returned, he was delighted to see Esyld sitting by the fire. Her natural face covered in a green paste, she cradled the remains of the Maiden's face in her lap. He fought the urge to pick it up himself and stow it away for safekeeping.

"What now?" he asked.

Kenyth reached for a twig and tossed it into the fire. "We didn't exactly lose," he said, but Esyld's groan belied his words.

"How so?" In Pagaene's experience, retreat was hardly a sign of victory.

"The abominable child is dead, and we gained time," the Priest argued.

Pagaene darted him a doubtful look. "What about The Purity?"

It was Esyld who answered, and she sounded utterly exhausted. "I can sense that she remains in the sacred grove, but she is weak."

"Then how do we kill her?" Pagaene asked.

"We can't," Kenyth said. "Death cannot be defeated, nor should it. Everything in the Great Mother's creation has its place."

"So we do nothing?" Pagaene spat at the Priest. "Is that what we risked our life for? Nothing?"

"That is not what I said," Kenyth replied. "We must ensure the restoration of order. To accomplish that, we must imprison The Purity in the sacred grove, where she may feed on the blood of the sick and elderly. Just as the Great Mother had intended."

"To seal the grove, we must seal the Mother Well," Esyld added.

Pagaene nodded. "How?"

Esyld shook her head. "I don't know."

Kenyth heaved a deep sigh. "I do… or rather, I did. The Prime Order foresaw most of what happened today. It was His Holiness himself who planted blessed ivy around the Mother Well. If we could make it grow, it would close the portal between the realms forever. But we need all the powers to do it. We need an Abdita, a wizard, and a Rebirth user. I don't remember the details of the ritual—but we need the three together for magic powerful enough to seal her in."

"Then what are we waiting for?" Pagaene asked and jutted his chin at Kenyth. "You can grow vines. You can make trees fly. Isn't that what you do all day?"

The Priest uttered a mirthless laugh. "There are two flaws in your assumption. First, The Faceless still guards the well."

"Fine. We'll have to defeat him," Pagaene decided. "Who is he?"

"Isn't it obvious?" Kenyth asked, but his companion's scowl prompted him to continue. "He is death's companion and the father of poisonous decay. The one who will never forget and never forgive. He is born from the river of mourning, and I call him The Faceless because his face is as empty as his soul." He paused for a moment. "Can you really not guess his identity?"

Pagaene furrowed his brow and shook his head.

"Revenge incarnate," Esyld whispered. "That's who he is. And he just lost his child."

"Revenge," Pagaene echoed. "A sentiment I understand. I lost my father and my sister."

"I lost my siblings, too," Kenyth murmured.

Pagaene folded his arms and squinted at the Priest. "You might have been able to save Muave," he said. "Yet you didn't even try."

"It would have been pointless," Kenyth muttered. "She was doomed the moment she allied herself with The Purity."

"And what was the point in charging your sister's killer after she died?"

Kenyth angrily puffed out his breath. "I aimed for the Well, you fool. But it would have been in vain. Without the sacred stones, the ivy will never be strong enough to destroy the portal, and you two just handed them to our enemies."

Pagaene gasped and glanced at Esyld, but her eyeless face couldn't meet his gaze. He tilted his head and looked at Kenyth instead. "Say, Priest… How many do you need?"

Kenyth frowned. "The more the better."

"Would one suffice?" Esyld asked, her voice quivering with new hope.

"Hardly," another voice added.

Pagaene and Kenyth jumped to their feet, reaching for their weapons, but they both relaxed when the new arrival limped into the light. He leaned heavily on a gnarled staff, and two dogs trotted after him. Pagaene rushed to greet his grandfather, clasping Uul's arms and looking the old man up and down. "Are you hurt?"

"A scratch, nothing more," Uul answered and gave his grandson a friendly pat on the shoulder. "But we have more important matters to discuss. It seems you have a plan, but you will need more than a single sacred stone to enact it. Perhaps with a Nightstone and a skilled wizard, we can finally end this madness."

"Do you have a stone?" Esyld asked as Uul glanced at her. "Mine is on the edge of the Mother Well."

Uul cursed and looked to the ground for a moment. Then he nodded and said, "Then our first step is to retrieve it."

Chapter 35

Pagaene, for one, was less than enthused about Uul and Kenyth's plan; it was not that he doubted the strength, power, or intelligence of his companions, but rather that the plan itself required far too much luck to proceed in their favor. As a Knight and commander, Pagaene never would have carried out such a haphazard plan of attack—the one that had dragged him into this whole mess non-withstanding, of course. Unfortunately, he was outranked and outnumbered in this group—the sole member of the party that had significant hesitations about tomorrow's battle. Esyld had chided him gently. Pagaene took watch and tended the fire so the others could sleep, knowing he would have trouble enough doing the same.

The wind blew gently through the forest, offering a jovial whistle to offset the erratic melody of Uul, Kenyth, and Esyld's breathing. The silver light from the moon lit the brass of Pagaene's fake arm so it shone brightly, a counterpart to his dour mood. Pensively, he opened the secret compartment and withdrew the ruby sacred stone. In the light of the fire, it warmed beneath his fingers, offering its own steady glow that bathed his hand in pale, scarlet light. He tossed the stone from one hand to the other, watching it shine as it danced through the air. Finally, he set it on the ground beside him.

When he thought of the quartz stone still hanging from his neck, he pulled it from his shirt, ducked out of the circle of the chain, and held the stone before him. He tilted it left and right, examining it in the firelight. It had been pure when the Symorcian bear had given it to him—nearly clear. Now, it was fractured inside and shot through with a sickly gray-green. It was spent, used up from deflecting the power of The Purity and saving his life.

Against his will, he felt a surge of gratitude toward the shapeshifter. He ran a finger along the scabbed scratch still on his cheek where the bear's claw had drawn his blood, testing him. The bear had recited the prophecy, and though Pagaene had put little stock in the prediction, he couldn't help but recall it now, when the final fight was so near.

He sighed and stared into the dark of the forest. His eyes glazed over as images played in his mind—a burning fire; a hand holding a stone; a short wall with blood dripping down the edge. Again, he heard the voice of the bear, clear in his memory. '...*if Her forces are able to fan its flames.*' Pagaene frowned.

He felt a tap on the shoulder and started; Uul stared at him, a friendly smile on his face. "I see you've been very attentive at the watch tonight, grandson. Lucky for you, it's your turn to sleep and mine to guard. Get some rest. Tomorrow will be hard enough as it is."

Pagaene stood absently, mind reeling, still thinking of the unbidden images; they seemed so disparate. What could they mean? He tucked the stone and the quartz pendant on its chain back in his arm compartment before shutting it with a gentle click. The leaves on the trees rustled about them as if the forest itself sensed something, a change in the world it could not quite name but whispered all the same.

"The dogs work quite well for pillows. Shaggy mutts." Uul's voice was strained despite a clear attempt at good humor and affection, as though even the mention of his slowly dwindling team of companions caused him some form of pain. Pagaene eyed his grandfather, considered saying something comforting, or at least inquiring after his well-being. He still didn't know what had happened to Uul before his return earlier that day. He didn't know what had hurt him or caused him to lose more faithful mongrel companions. The fire popped, and the moment passed, grandfather and grandson breaking eye contact as the silence grew long and awkward. The opportunity for deeper familial connection burned away.

Instead, Pagaene tentatively looked to the nearest dog before settling beside it and carefully lowering his head onto the warm, soft fur. From the corner of his eye, he caught Uul's wide smile. He tried to sleep. As he shut his eyes, visions in black and red danced across his eyelids, a deep, growling voice, echoing over and over in his dreams. '…*if Her forces are able to fan its flames.*'

***

Pagaene peered through the bushes at The Faceless sitting on the edge of the Well, which was barely visible through the gnarled thicket before them. Kenyth, to his right, pointed with a grim set to his mouth, and Pagaene followed his finger. The Nightstone amulet, the subject of their mission, sat less than three inches from The Faceless. *What luck*, Pagaene thought wryly and with growing irritation. This morning, when he'd once again stressed his opposition to what he had indelicately termed a 'suicidal tactic', he had been shot down harshly by Uul.

"The world is at stake, and we have no room in this party for cowards," the wizard had said.

Pagaene, hurt by his grandfather's insinuation, had acquiesced and followed silently behind Esyld as they'd left their makeshift camp. Now, he refocused his attention on the amulet once he saw Esyld's lips move in a silent whisper, setting into motion the first part of their plan. Standing only two or three feet away from him, her voice barely brushed his ears as the wind carried it away, commanding the life of the mountain to her bidding.

Thin tree roots broke slowly through the dry ground surrounding the Well. The Faceless sat on its outer wall, peering into the grove below and oblivious to the forest surrounding him. The roots snuck along the ground, carefully controlled by Esyld's magic. A few white tendrils reached the Well stones and began their ascent. Only a few more inches, and they would grasp the amulet, pulling it back to Uul and the others—giving Uul the power he needed to grow the Blessed Ivy and seal The Purity in the Mother Well forever.

At a signal from Uul, Pagaene quietly opened the compartment in his arm and drew out the sacred stone; it was cool and sharp in his hand. He closed the compartment with a quiet click—and The Faceless whipped around with a snarl.

"Come back to play?" He jumped from the wall, and Pagaene watched with a gasp of horror as the Nightstone was swept back towards the Well opening by the quick motion, snagging at the last moment on a stone and dangling above the hole. His heart beating fast, he took a step out of the cover of the forest and into the clearing, only to be chased back by a jet of green flames issued from The Faceless' hands. Uul and Kenyth charged out, each attempting an offensive maneuver to distract their enemy and buy Esyld a few more much needed seconds.

"Your attacks only make me stronger," The Faceless hissed at them, batting away their magic as if it were child's play. "I will have my revenge!"

Esyld stepped into the clearing, pushing more strength into the roots as she encouraged them up over the wall of the Well, coaxing them towards the amulet. She was almost there, sweat beading her forehead and her body shaking with exertion. They were so close; Pagaene watched, transfixed, as the momentous importance of each second seemed to slow time.

Several things happened at once. Esyld gasped with triumph as a thin root wrapped around the chain of the amulet. Uul, distracted by the noise, turned towards her. The Faceless smirked, and Kenyth yelped as a bolt of green fire singed the air, hitting Uul square in the chest. Pagaene reached out with his hand, belatedly, as though he could have pulled the fire back with the sheer force of his anguish.

His grandfather's eyes barely had time to widen with pain before he crumbled to dust on an exhale, swirling away in the same wind that carried Pagaene's roar of agony. The whole clearing went silent, still, until The Faceless softly chuckled. "How does it feel? To have your own blood decay before you?" it whispered, and Pagaene saw red, clutching the stone in his fist so tightly it cut into his skin. Blood dripped through his fingers to the ground. *Revenge*, his mind whispered.

"Steady," Esyld told him, and he was vaguely aware of the roots pulling the Nightstone amulet back towards her. Not that they could use it now. Not without Uul. It was over; hopelessness mixed with his anger, his pain. *Revenge*, his mind urged again, stronger, and somewhere in the back of his consciousness, another voice, deep and gruff, tried to warn him of something but was cut off. His heart beat in time with the chant forming inside him, and he felt new power careening through his blood. His body burned with it, the flames of his despair licking new wounds into his grieving soul. *Revenge!*

Kenyth had dropped to the ground, searching—for what, Pagaene didn't know. The Knight took a menacing step towards The Faceless as it turned its evil attention towards him. He saw the hands rise in the same formation that had just wiped his grandfather from existence. Twisting lines of red and black superimposed over the scene before him; he saw a burning fire, outlined in red but forming green in the hands of The Faceless. He saw his own hand, holding the ruby stone that glittered with his blood, still outstretched before him. Green flames streaked across the clearing towards his chest, but Pagaene made no move avoid them. Esyld gasped, Kenyth shouted, and Pagaene held the sacred stone steady in front of him, his entire being little more than focused suffering. *Revenge. Revenge.* The green flames reached him, and his hand exploded into a brilliant shower of sparks with a loud boom that echoed through the woods, the air around them shattering and throwing everyone to the ground.

The Faceless flew back against the Well, hitting its head; black blood seeped from the wound and down the stonework. Pagaene himself stumbled backwards before slamming into a tree trunk. The stone, swirling with red and green, burned into his skin. He cried out in pain as his own flesh boiled into blackened ash, his fingers shriveling, the stone embedded in his palm as if it were an ornament. He waited for the decay to take him as The Faceless weakly lifted its head, grinning slowly. The decay never came. His mind filled with confusion. The world felt far away. The chant of, '*Revenge, revenge,*' still rang distantly in his ears.

Pagaene blinked, feeling angry and confused and hollow. He slowly uncurled his bloody red fingers to stare at the stone in his palm. Kenyth watched in mute horror, and the Faceless stood again slowly, cautiously, before speaking with barely-contained zeal. "Welcome, Child of the Prophecy."

From the depths of his mind, someplace that felt completely separate from him, he heard the words of the scroll the night before—but no, this time, it was the whole prophecy. He remembered it now, as it had been spoken by the Symorcian bear.

'He will heal this land… defeat Her… rein Her in and hold Her in balance with life. But there is also a darkness in him… that may consume him if it goes unchecked or if Her forces are able to fan its flames.'

"*If Her forces are able to fan its flames,*" he whispered and saw once more the red and black visions of the outstretched hand, the burning fire, the blood on the Well. He clutched the swirling green and red sacred stone, his eyes flickering the same colors, and felt the power singing in his blood, signaling his own Rebirth. He felt wildly out of control yet more commanding of his own fate than ever before. He knew it now; this moment was his destiny.

Chapter 36

"Yes," Pagaene said. "I am the Child of Prophecy."

He stood, and with a swoop of his hand, Kenyth was pulled to his feet by an unseen force. He shuddered once, then froze in place. Pagaene narrowed his flame-colored eyes at the Priest, then whirled to face Esyld.

"Stop!" he commanded, and Esyld found herself unable to move. Pagaene curled his fingers toward her, and Esyld's stomach lurched when she felt the Nightstone slip from her grasp. Helpless, she watched it float through the air to Pagaene, who opened the compartment on his false arm and allowed the stone to drop inside just as Anguis and Caedus stepped into the clearing.

Both creatures sported a ghastly humber of gashes, covered

in dried blood, and they each wore new, furry black mantles around their shoulders.

"Welcome, Brother," they hissed at Pagaene, then glanced from Kenyth to Esyld and smiled. "Very good. The Purity will be pleased."

"I wondered what had happened to you two," Pagaene said.

"Ah, yes," Caedus replied, stroking his mantle. "We had some trouble with the wizard."

"Weakling," Anguis spat. "Barely fought back."

"Turned tail and ran, he did," Caedus said.

"Couldn't bear to watch us split open his mongrels." Anguis laughed. "Filthy animals made much better mantles than they did protectors."

From the bottom of the Sacred Well, a deep moan rose and washed over the clearing. Anguis and Caedus spun towards the sound. "What is happening to her?" they demanded in the same voice.

The Faceless spread his arms wide, his hands clenched into fists. "My blood has found her. She has drunk of it and regains her strength. She will soon be ready to rejoin us."

Pagaene looked from Kenyth, whose eyes were frozen wide open and filled with hatred, to Esyld. She tried to beg Pagaene, *Don't do this.* But he merely stared at her coldly, blinked once, then turned away to face the Well. Though she could not move a single muscle, Esyld felt her heart break inside her.

As if the creature had pulled the thought from Pagaene's mind the second the Knight made his decision, The Faceless cried out in terror and rage. Pagaene raised his blackened hand, the sacred stone fused into his palm, and unleashed a wave of roiling green and red flames, hitting Anguis and Caedus square in their backs. The Symorcian Brothers were knocked off their feet and landed face-down in the dirt, dead before they hit the ground.

"What have you done?" The Faceless asked.

Pagaene lowered his hand and stepped forward. "I am the Child of Prophecy. This is true," he said. "But Prophecy merely suggests what may come. It does not account for Free Will. I am first, foremost, and forever a Knight, as was my father before me. I alone decide my fate, and I will never, *never*, weild my sword for evil." With a sweep of his arm, he released the invisible binds on Kenyth and Esyld.

They dropped to the ground just as Uul's two remaining dogs broke of the treeline, snarling and howling. They raced straight to The Faceless and leaped upon him before he could raise an arm in defense.

"Come!" cried Pagaene and raced to pull Esyld to her feet. She stared up at him with her eerily eyeless face and an open mouth, but he merely shook his head. "Hurry." A second later, Kenyth joined them, and without another word, they raced into the forest.

Esyld stopped to stare at him. "How—"

"There's no time," Pagaene said. "Uul's dogs won't last long against The Faceless, and not long at all if The Purity recovers. I'm sorry for what I put you through, but I hope you understand."

"I do," she said, leaping over a fallen tree. "But I don't know how much it matters without Uul."

"I think," panted Kenyth as he ducked under a limb, "you two seem to have forgotten I weild the power of Rebirth." He held up his hand, and in his palm twinkled a tiny white bone fragment. Esyld inhaled sharply, and the Priest closed his fingers around the item once more. "I found this in the grass. Give me time, and I will resurrect your grandfather, Pagaene."

"Good fortune," Pagaene exclaimed. "With Uul and the Nightstone, we may just succeed in ending this."

"Yes," Esyld agreed. "But not while The Faceless protects The Purity. He will do anything for her, and I don't know if even the Gray Wizard, let alone the rest of us, have the power to defeat the two of them together. And when—" Esyld's unfinished sentence hung in the air as a vision pushed into her mind.

He has what you need.

Esyld gasped to hear the Great Mother's voice once more. She wanted to ask where the Great Mother had been, but her thoughts were completely overpowered by the rest of the vision.

Esyld didn't realize she had stopped running, and when Pagaene and Kenyth begged her to continue, she did not hear them.

Instead of the forest around her, Esyld saw the Lake of Destiny and the beach where they had fought Anguis and Caedus. Bright-red blood still stained the sand and chunks of driftwood that had melted under the Symorcian Brothers' acid. *This must have been just after we fled on the raft*, she thought. *Why show me something that has already happened?* Then she noticed something half-buried in the sand—something with long, dark-brown hair…

A man appeared on the beach, apparently having followed their footsteps. When he reached the thing with the long, dark hair, he stooped and retrieved it, then gently brushed the sand away. Tucking it into his cloak, he turned, and Esyld finally recognized him.

"Esyld?" Kenyth said, tugging at her arm and releasing her from her vision. "Esyld! We must go on!"

Esyld pulled her arm from Kenyth's grasp and shook her head. "No. No more running. We already have everything we need to defeat The Faceless." Her eyeless face turned on him, aligned as though she stared into Kenyth's eyes. "Or rather, *you* do." She held out her hand to him. "Give me her face."

Kenyth took a step back. "How… how do you know about it?"

"What are you saying, Esyld?" Pagaene asked. "What face does he have?"

Kenyth maintained a believable mask of shock until Esyld'd unwavering attention broke through, and he lowered his eyes. "I discovered it as I was tracking you, and I thought perhaps I could use it against you." He reached inside his cloak and retrieved a loosely rolled scroll of skin and hair. He handed it to Esyld but spoke to Pagaene. "Please forgive me."

Pagaene wrinkled his eyebrows in confusion, then looked down to what Esyld had carefully spread across her palms. At first, he could not make sense of the thick smear of flesh, but then it slowly revealed itself to him. "Is that…"

"It is Tilly's Mother face, Pagaene," Esyld whispered. "The very one cast aside on the beach of the Lake of Destiny when we were attacked by the Symorcian Brothers. Kenyth had it with him all along."

"Yes, but—" Kenyth began, but Esyld silenced him.

"We have no more time for apologies," she said. "The Great Mother sent me a vision for a reason, and I think I know why. But we must hurry, for The Purity grows stronger the longer we tarry. Kenyth, you must resurrect Uul. We need him to defeat her and lock her in the Sacred Well. Pagaene and I will deal with The Faceless."

"How?" Pagaene asked, unable to take his eyes off the face in Esyld's hands.

"I will explain as we move," she replied, then turned to Kenyth. "You may have saved us all. Now go. Return Uul to us."

Kenyth nodded once and clutched the bone fragment in his fist to his heart, then turned and ran through the woods toward Freywyn.

Esyld turned in the opposite direction, back towards the Sacred Well, and said, "Let us face our destiny, Pagaene." They ran.

***

"The Faceless was born of mothers' tears as they wept for their slain children," Esyld explained as they retraced their path through the woods. "Deep inside of him, there remains eternal mourning and suffering. It is what sustains him, but it will also be his undoing." Esyld brushed aside a curtain of moss, then turned her face sideways to Pagaene. "Because this creature lacks a face, he has no soul and cannot truly feel the anguish and sorrow of losing a child. His desire to sire Nuodai was born of purpose, not of love. But if we were to give him your mother's face…"

Pagaene's jaw dropped open. "It would unleash the agony within him."

"And destroy him," Esyld finished, just as they broke from

the trees and entered the clearing around the Sacred Well. The sight before them brought them to a terrified halt.

Uul's two remaining dogs were dead. Their bodies had been draped over the lip of the Well, and from large gashes in their necks, blood dribbled down the stones. The Faceless leaned over the Well, watching, but casually raised his head when Esyld and Pagaene arrived. "You're just in time," he said. And in that moment, The Purity rose from the Well.

"Now!" Esyld cried. "Before she escapes!"

Pagaene raised his shriveled hand and unleashed a bolt of red-hot magic arcing across the clearing and striking The Purity. She howled in pain and dropped down into the Well. Her cries grew fainter as she tumbled all the way back down to the grove at the bottom.

The Faceless screamed with rage, and twisting lines of red and black shot from his clawed hands towards Pagaene. Pagaene lurched out of the way just in time, and the magic hit the ground near his feet and exploded into powdered dirt and tree-root fragments.

Keep him distracted. Esyld's thoughts thrust themselves into his head, and from the corner of his eye, he saw her slip away through the cloud of dirt and head for The Faceless.

Pagaene fired another bolt of magic towards the Well where The Faceless still stood, but the creature deflected it with a wave of his hand and in return sent a ball of white fire rolling towards him. Pagaene scrambled out of the way, and the ball thundered past him, striking the trees and setting them ablaze with a roar.

Pagaene fired back with his own green and red flames, but The Faceless ducked behind the far side of the Well, and the flames missed. The burning trees behind Pagaene fed billowing clouds of smoke, burning his throat and eyes, and small embers fluttered into the grasses. Soon, the whole area would catch ablaze. *We need to finish this!* he thought just as Esyld appeared on the other side of the Well, directly behind The Faceless.

She held the face before her, and Pagaene watched her

carefully bend down to pull it over The Faceless' head.

But before Pagaene could even blink, The Faceless had sprung to his feet. He grabbed Esyld's wrist and wrenched the face from her hands. Esyld's mouth opened wide in surprise, and The Faceless dropped the face down the well. Pagaene screamed and darted forward.

"Enough," The Faceless said and wrapped his other hand around Esyld's throat. He lifted her into the air and held her over the Well. Her feet kicked at the open air, and her hands clawed at The Faceless' outstretched arm, but to no avail. Pagaene skidded to a halt and watched, helpless.

The creature flipped a glowing red blade into his free hand and held it to Esyld's belly. The Meta dropped her arms to her side and stopped struggling. Her head drooped, and she seemed to shrink into her cloak.

The Faceless tilted his head back and let loose an ugly, mirthless cackle. "Did you really think you could defeat me? *Me?* Oh, how very foolish you both are. I thought perhaps you would make a decent ally, Pagaene, once you had discovered your powers. But now I see I was merely playing with children. Watch, Knight, as I slit open this witch's body so her blood may nourish my love below."

Pagaene's mind whirled, but he could not think of a single thing he could do to save Esyld. It was over. All over.

Esyld's head snapped up, and in a heartbeat, she pulled something over The Faceless' head.

The creature screamed and tumbled backwards, and he and Esyld both collapsed to the ground. The blade was lost in the grass as The Faceless writhed and clawed at the face he wore—the Mother face—but it was stuck fast. "No," he cried as tears poured down his cheeks.

Pagaene rushed to Esyld and swept her to her feet. "How is this possible?" he asked, staring down at the pitiful creature. "I saw him throw the face down the well."

"You saw him throw my Crone face," Esyld replied. "It had been damaged by Symorcian attacks, but I am quite glad I tucked it away."

On his knees, The Faceless heaved with sobs. "All my children," he moaned. "All my children… lost. Oh, my heart breaks. I cannot bear it!" He looked up at Esyld and Pagaene, and the agony in his new eyes almost brought Esyld to anguish. "I cannot bear this," he whimpered. "I cannot. No one should endure the death of their child, and I… I feel the deaths of *all* children. Please, end this."

Pagaene shook his head. "You must atone for your atrocities."

The Faceless covered his eyes with the palms of his hands and shook as he cried. Esyld wavered beside Pagaene, and she did not need eyes for him to see that she warred with the completion of their task and her inherent need to comfort those in pain. Before either of them could react more, The Faceless lurched forward and pulled himself up over the lip of the Well.

"My love," he yelled down. "Come to me. Come feast on me and end my suffering!"

Esyld and Pagaene grabbed The Faceless and pulled him off the Well's ledge, but it was too late. A great wail rose from the depths, echoing off the stones until it reached the top. Then The Purity burst forth and spilled over the lip of the Well and onto The Faceless. Esyld and Pagaene were thrown to the ground, their flesh singed by a mere brush with The Purity's presence.

The Purity covered The Faceless entirely, and from underneath her, Pagaene heard him rasp, "Consume this body. They have given me a face, and it has weakened me. No longer can I protect you. I give my life for you, so you may live. Please, my love. Do it now!"

The Knight scrambled away as fast as he could. The Purity undulated and swelled, like a great snake consuming a meal, and Pagaene felt the waves of heat rolling over him as though he sat too close to an oven. He rose to his feet and turned to run but found himself facing a wall of fire. The trees around the clearing were burning, blocking his escape. He spun back and saw, on the other side of where The Purity lay, Esyld also whirled frantically about,

her mouth open wide in horror.
They were trapped.

Chapter 37

T he flames danced across the fallen branches of the sacred grove. No matter how far or how fast Kenyth ran, the untamed, magical fire seemed to follow. He swung his head from side to side in search of a suitable sapling to ride, but the swirling tide of flame leapt from tree to tree as if blown by an unnatural wind. There would be no reaching Freywyn before the flames consumed it and everyone there.

When he reached the next clearing, he dropped to his knees and drew his athame. He whispered a spell of protection over the blade before plunging it deep into the earth before him. The conflagration split and circled him, cutting him off from any possible escape, but the athame's magic kept the fire from closing in completely.

Sweat dripped from his brow to his trembling hands. The spell could keep out the worst of the inferno, but the enveloping tower of orange flame was nearly blinding, and the oppressive heat seared his lungs with every breath.

Kenyth trained his eyes on the ground to keep them from streaming as he retrieved the bloody shard of bone from his pocket. With one hand on the hilt of the athame to help him draw strength, he placed the fragment on the ground and covered it with his other palm. A gentle, golden light glowed to life under his touch as he called forth the power of Rebirth.

'Stop!'

The bellow cut through Kenyth's concentration and echoed inside his skull. The gruff, masculine voice couldn't belong to the Great Mother, nor to The Purity.

"Who's there?"

'The man you summoned with your magic. It is I, Rassa Met Uul, and I bid you, stop!'

Kenyth clutched the bone in his fist and released the athame. He opened his hand and spoke to the shard. "I mean to bring you back to life. If Rassa Met Uul truly addresses me now, why would you want me to stop?"

'There is no time.'

"Which is why I must hurry," he replied, closing his hand. The soft glow lit his fist from within as he called the power once more.

'No! There is no time!'

There was every chance this was some desperate ruse by The Purity, but the voice and presence pulsed with a familiar energy. The young man let out a weary sigh and released the gathering power. "I need a wizard to defeat The Purity, and Uul was our wizard. If you were truly a friend to this mission, you would not hinder me."

'Death has shown me many truths.'

"Speak plainly, spirit, or be gone," Kenyth replied, though he felt far less forceful than he sounded.

'There are things here, creatures of power as old as time itself, and they have revealed the truth of the prophecy to me. It has been passed down for so long, the words have been garbled, misinterpreted.'

The voice paused, and the young man unfurled his fingers. He regarded the shard warily, but so many other truths had become falsehoods in the past few days... "Go on. But be quick about it, I beg you."

The deep voice took on an almost childlike awe. *'It is so clear now, don't you see? You already have a wizard in your midst. Pagaene, the Child of Prophecy, has my blood in his veins. He has his mother's blood in his veins. And the shapeshifter spoke of his destiny. He possesses the power of Rebirth.'*

"The prophecy was never about three people," Kenyth gasped. "Unless... unless it foretold the coming of one who could wield the power of three."

'So stop wasting your time with me, lad. You must tell Pagaene to take the Nightstone, to lay claim to every aspect of himself, or the world will fall to shadow and death. You must make him see.'

"I won't manage even two words. The Purity will kill me the minute she sees me. It took you this long to open my eyes, and Pagaene is far less receptive."

'You must trust the Great Mother to help you. It is a desperate gamble, but it is the only way.'

***

Esyld's heart pounded in her chest. The scent of burning trees and the heat at her back overwhelmed her senses, sending her into a tailspin of nausea and panic. Kenyth might have been able to help them, but he had to have reached Freywyn by now, consumed by his task of resurrecting Uul. She hoped he'd hurry, that he'd return in time with what they needed, but what was she to do until then?

Pagaene seemed to panic too from the other side of The Purity's writhing mass. Scowling, he opened his palms and released another crackling stream of flames. It hit The Purity with a hiss like water on hot oil, and the mountain of darkness and hunger shivered and moaned, then swelled impossibly huge. Pagaene continued his attack, issuing strike after strike of red and black, his face contorted in terror and rage.

Esyld watched him, breathless. The Knight expelled such energy with his newfound power, and The Purity consumed every bit of it time and again. What once had resembled a mother had now become a roiling form of need and destruction, feeding on The Faceless' sacrifice and Pagaene's hatred alike. The mere seconds it took to realize what was happening felt far too long, and when Esyld finally put together the pieces, it was almost too late.

"Pagaene, stop!" She would have run to him if she could, but the space between the blazing forest at her back and the bulging form before her was rapidly shrinking. Pagaene shouted, then turned to face her with horror. He collapsed to his knees, his body jerking, and as if of their own accord, his hands continued their fiery attack. It seemed he couldn't stop—and she was sure he wanted to—his efforts to fight The Purity now adding to the strength of the dark force between them.

***

With a giant gurgle halfway between a swallow and a growl, The Purity lurched upwards, shifted, and morphed into a form that again roughly resembled a woman, though her figure rose above the trees. She leaned toward Pagaene, and he scuttled backward until his back hit the rough stone of the well.

"Child of Prophecy," she purred. "Do not fear me."

"Pagaene!" shrieked Esyld. "Ignore her poison. She'll—"

"Silence." Though the fire roared only a short distance away, The Purity's calm whisper carried on the breeze.

As the Knight looked on, the Abdita clutched at her throat and gulped for air. Pagaene cried out in wordless horror, and The Purity knelt by his side and tried to soothe him. Esyld's true face, once so horrible to him and now a familiar comfort, contorted in anguish as she struggled for breath, but Pagaene's head began to swim. The seductive voice of The Purity coiled around his body, imbuing him with an artificial calm.

"The witch is none of your concern," she cooed. "You used to hunt witches, my darling. You know their treachery."

"Treachery…" he echoed, his head lolling to one side. Somewhere in his hazy awareness, he knew he should be fighting the strange pull of her words, but his heavy limbs pinned him to the ground. On some level, he saw The Faceless' blade in the grass. Though within reach, it was far beyond his grasp.

"If they had not so jealously guarded their power, I never could have come. The power of the Abdita is bound to Life, but Life cannot conquer Death. Life and death need each other to exist. Only Rebirth can defy Death, and the Adbita have shunned and derided that power in favor of their own. They depleted their ranks as they turned on those with the ability to defy me and cast them out. Now, their greed is their downfall."

"Downfall…" The glow of the flames withdrew from his vision, the heat leaching from his body. A strange but nourishing coolness coursed through him. He could only watch, helpless, as the evil thing turned to Esyld's writhing figure.

"Do you see it now?" The Purity snarled.

After a flick of the entity's hand, the Abdita finally drew in a few ragged breaths. "No," she choked. "Our ways, they protect us. They protect the kingdom."

A titter of mocking laughter rose about the crackle of burning wood. "I am sure that is what they told you, poor thing," the woman-creature simpered, then her tone harshened. "But their corruption invited me right into their souls. Muave, Carrick, and so many others before them. Wake to the truth, Meta. I have been *free* for quite some time now, even if I could not roam where I wanted. You have only just begun to see the blight lain on this land, in the hills and fields, but it has been in the heart of your people for far longer."

"Longer…" Pagaene repeated softly. The flames seemed a distant memory, replaced by the soothing fog rolling in around him.

***

Esyld struggled to rise, but The Purity pushed her back down. "What have you done to him?" she cried.

"As *you* have deprived me of my mate, I am forced to find another."

"Another…"

"I—" Esyld quieted, watching the flames in the forest behind Pagaene. They curved out away from something, deflected by some invisible shield. In the same instant, she saw the hazy fog drawing up around Pagaene, the telltale sign of a dreamscape.

"Kenyth," she whispered. But, already The Purity was turning back to Pagaene. She would see the fog, break the dreamscape.

The Purity let out a deafening roar, like waves against rock, and everything darkened until there was nothing. No, not nothing, Esyld realized. The Purity had somehow also consumed the light around them, bringing everything into a circle of harsh, freezing darkness. The burning trees were gone. The Sacred Well was nowhere to be seen. The Purity and her lover's body seemed nonexistent, and all Esyld heard was her own harsh breathing— until she heard Pagaene scream.

"Pagaene!" she called, fumbling in the blackness. His reply came wordless, his terror removing from him the ability to answer her sufficiently. She did not know if he was injured, or dying, or taken by The Purity beyond the point of return. The knot of dread tightened in her stomach, restricting her existence, and then she remembered the Great Mother's voice.

You have everything you need.

She thought that had been Tilly's old Mother face, which had accomplished exactly what Esyld had intended. But it still hadn't stopped the monster before her now. It hadn't been enough. What she needed was time, and she prayed to whoever would listen that Kenyth was able to reach Pagaene, to share whatever message had led him back without Uul. But there had to be something more she could do right now.

The image of Tilly's Mother face flashed in her mind, followed by the memory of The Faceless caught within the Mother. She'd used the face's power when she'd tied it to The Faceless, but its work wasn't done. Neither was hers.

Desperately, with everything she had, Esyld turned inward, searching for her Abdita core—what made her what she was. It wasn't just the magic or the connection to the sacred groves within the Wells and the faces contained therein. It wasn't just what she could do. It was who she was, where her lifeforce came from, and consequently *what* she was—physically.

Esyld did not need eyes to see. She'd been using her Sight as humans did for so long, she'd almost forgotten this fact. The Abdita had no eyes; The Purity's light-consuming darkness could not reach her. Not like it had Pagaene … not quite.

She felt all her energy pulling in on itself, folding and morphing, and a warmth boiled up from both the pit of her stomach and deep within her mind. Sending this source of her power outward, she found everything suddenly clear again, pulsing with a dark red light.

Light twisted and refracted in her vision, but Esyld saw The Purity's hulking mass before her, undulating as it still fed on The Faceless' energy. Within the darkness around them, the trees stood as mere blackened husks, almost contorted in agony now that the fire had left them. She saw Pagaene on the other side of the clearing, huddled into himself. And beyond him, in the blackened forest, Kenyth braced on his hands and knees, fiercely sending out his power despite the lingering flames which licked at him through his failing shield. The dream fog struggled to reach Pagaene, pushed back by a force that must have been invisible to Kenyth, though Esyld could see it was The Purity's darkness.

Esyld felt her connection to the Mother face now worn by The Faceless. She hoped she hadn't lost too much time. Then she found it, there—just a flickering of life still throbbing beneath and within the creature soon to birth darkness upon the rest of this world. If she could just reach out, touch that thin filament of existence, she could…

The world lurched around her, and Esyld felt her essence leaving her Abdita body, shooting full-force into the black creature before her. It took half a second for her to regain her awareness, but when she did, she realized she now sensed the world through the Mother's face.

She almost left The Faceless' body—what was left of it. She almost retched right there, though there was hardly room for her to draw breath. But she stopped herself, clutching tightly to The Faceless' last ounce of life within her mind, and expanded to fill his physical form. The squelching, growling sound of The Purity feeding upon her lover now drowned out every other noise, and Esyld thought she would quickly forget what silence was like—what it was to hear birds singing or laughter of those she knew. She thought she might forget everything but the hungering need of The Purity now encompassing her, threatening to devour every last inch of her power and her consciousness.

But she didn't. Even with her physical body left behind in the clearing, Esyld remembered what she had to do. She had to fight. She had to buy Kenyth more time. She had to keep The Purity in this place just long enough for someone else to destroy the darkness. Even if that meant she had to stay within The Faceless' dying husk one second too late.

Esyld stretched. She bucked and jerked, twisted and writhed beneath The Purity. It felt as if she fought five men, all reaching toward her with gnarled claws made of her own despair. Remembering the face she wore now, if only briefly, she drew upon the Mother's strength—the body's physical capabilities for creation, for protection. For giving life. And life was the opposite of everything The Purity intended.

Cries of anguish, wails of agony, screams of loss and pain—they pummeled her from all directions, coming from everywhere around her as The Purity seemed to realize just who had entered her lover's sacrificial body and just what she intended. Esyld felt tears streaming down the Mother's face, felt her strength falter. But The Purity had realigned her focus, now contracting

258

herself even farther towards Esyld to be rid of what must have seemed a dangerous parasite. And if The Purity now aimed to crush Esyld within her darkness, that meant the creature had no energy to spare for growing. It would buy them time.

The battle felt like fighting the very air around her, through water, with neither sight nor sound and very little from which to draw more strength. Esyld opened her mouth to scream, kicking and lurching, and some dark tendril shot down her throat to choke off the noise. Thrashing wildly now, she had no idea if she would make it out of this. The Purity was too strong, too hungry, and Esyld felt more foolish than she ever had in her life for thinking she could do anything to stop this dark thing. She felt herself growing cold, growing faint, and she desperately wanted just to give in and let The Purity finish what she'd started.

***

The curtain of darkness lightened into a swirling gray fog. For a moment, Pagaene's whole existence became a dizzying gray. The mist ebbed and flowed until it had formed into the interior of a cozy cottage. Birds chittered outside the window, and bright, merry sunlight poured in. He looked down to discover he had somehow ended up in a bed, a cheerful quilt pulled all the way to his chin. On the other side of the room, a fragrant stew bubbled away over the banked coals in the hearth. A woman bent over the pot and dipped a wooden spoon into the soup. She breathed in the scent before tasting it, then turned to a sideboard to retrieve some herbs.

Pagaene tried to speak, but it came out as a croak. The woman turned, a delighted smile on her face. "Oh, good! I wasn't sure I would have this ready by the time you arrived. But I'm just adding the finishing touches now."

He blinked at her dumbly, then realization struck. "M-mother?"

Tilly chortled as she ladled a healthy portion of stew into a wooden bowl. "Yes and no, dear. Yes and no. You see *your* mother, but I am in fact *all* mothers."

"You're the Great Mother?" he asked in awe and shifted to a sitting position. "You've finally returned? You're here to save us?"

"Eat your dinner. You'll need your strength."

"But I—"

"Eat up like a good boy," she scolded gently, pushing the bowl into his hands. "And I'll tell you a story."

Pagaene obediently took a bite. The tendrils of heat trickled down to his belly, spreading its rejuvenating powers far beyond his stomach.

"Once upon a time, there was a man. He was so brave and so good, the King made him a Knight. The man was proud to serve his King, to make something of his humble beginnings." Tilly rested a smooth, gentle hand on his cheek. "But he was more, so much more, than just a Knight."

"I think I know this story," he said after swallowing another heaping spoonful.

She smiled sadly, and her hand dropped to her lap. "All but the end."

"Does he... do I... win?"

"That is up to you, my dear."

Pagaene looked down at his hands, unmarred by the use of magic here in the dream. He flexed the pink flesh he knew lay blackened and shriveled in real life and uncurled the fingers of his missing limb. "I can't, Mother. I am not strong enough," he quavered, uncharacteristic tears trickling down his cheek as the faces of his fallen comrades flashed across his vision.

"You are far stronger than you know."

"I am an abomination!" he cried with a child's petulance. "And worse, not even a successful abomination. On the other side of this vision, I lay beneath a spell I cannot break. The magic I inherited from you... it isn't strong enough. I have already failed, Mother."

"The Purity still fears you, or she would not try to bind you. You are not an abomination, my son. You are a miracle. You are the Child of Prophecy."

"And what good has that done anyone?" he raged. "Khati, my father, my grandfather—I found my family just in time to watch them all die because I was too weak to protect them."

Tilly's gentle face took on stern lines as she stood. Hands on hips, she looked down at Pagaene, and he shrank as a person only can beneath a mother's withering gaze. "And you would dishonor their sacrifice by giving up? You would dishonor me?"

All Pagaene's anger leached away. "What can I do? I am depleted, used up. The magic, it's killing me. And we have lost our wizard. How can I hope to defeat The Purity without Uul? It takes three to bind her."

The vision of his mother stepped forward and took his hands in hers. She lifted one to her lips and laid a tender kiss upon it. "You are Abdita, and you hold a sacred stone." Her head bent a second time as she brought the other to her face. "You are wizard, and the Nightstone is within your grasp." With his hands in hers, she leaned forward and pressed her forehead against his. "And from your power, this land will be Reborn."

**

A hot shock ran through Esyld's exhausted body, and her essence was flung out of the roiling mass, pummeling back toward her physical Abdita body. She prayed she'd given Kenyth enough time to reach Pagaene.

When she re-entered herself, the force of it threw her backward through the air to land sprawled upon the dirt of the clearing with bone-cracking force. She cried out for Pagaene.

**

Esyld's terrified scream pulled him from his mother.

The smell of burning corpses and the heat of the flames told him he'd left the vision. As his eyes adjusted, he saw The Purity shrink down to near-human stature to stand over a bloodied and burned Esyld.

"He can't help *himself*," she sneered. "He's not going to help *you*."

He focused all his will into moving what remained of his good arm, and he dragged it across his body. His leaden fingers found the latch to the compartment on his false limb, and as they touched the Nightstone, The Purity's spell receded. When the ruby and the sparkling rock met, a surge of power coursed through his blackened arm. For the first time since the journey had begun, he believed he could succeed.

"Goodbye, witch." The creature undulated, her eyes sparkling with savagery as tendrils of boiling water reached out for Esyld. With a jerk, The Purity looked down at her chest in disbelief. The blade of The Faceless protruded several inches through her sternum. She cackled. "Is that the best you can do?"

"No." Pagaene gripped the hilt with his wooden hand, but as he brought the other and the stones to rest against it, the laughter stopped. He closed his eyes and poured every ounce of pain and loss into the blade, but under it all lay a current of hope for a better tomorrow.

The Purity's flesh melted into quicksilver and expanded into a churning column rising far into the air. She let out a cry of anguish, but the roar of the water swallowed it as her being burst away from the blade. The tide of water spread in all directions, dousing several small fires that continued to burn away stumps and bushes.

Pagaene smiled wanly at his companion before collapsing to the ground at her side. "It is finished."

"No," Esyld replied. "You must trap her in the Well."

"I… I do not know how."

The Abdita pulled herself onto her wobbly feet. She half-dragged Pagaene to the Well. "Place your hand upon it. I will show you. By the Great Mother, your hands!" she cried. He looked down and found the expanse of blackened flesh was gone, the missing limb had regrown. Her voice quieted with her wonder. "I have never seen this breed of power before."

The water of The Purity slithered across the charred ground, puddling and coalescing.

"Show me how to end this," Pagaene rasped, putting his hands against the stone wall. "Now!"

She covered his hands with hers and gave him wordless instructions through the bond the Maiden's face had fostered, and their shared trials had deepened. He nodded his understanding and closed his eyes. When next he opened them, the water streamed across the ground. Rivulets of shimmering wet climbed up the side of the Well and spilled down to the sacred grove.

With his hand against the Mother Well, he felt the deep agony of the land, the disease spreading itself across the kingdom he loved. Pagaene gritted his teeth and pulled harder. The silvery sheen of The Purity gave way to an oily slick as his magic sucked out the contagion, and it slithered from every corner of the realm. It rushed into the mouth of the Well, leaving a trail of new growth in its wake as the land was made new and unblemished once more.

When the last droplets crested the top of the Well, ivy coiled up the side after them, and he dropped his hand. The Nightstone tumbled from his grasp, and Pagaene welcomed the darkness that crowded Esyld's face from his vision.

Finally, he could rest.

Chapter 38

A strange hum with no cadence buzzed in the back of Pagaene's mind. It grew louder and louder until finally it stabbed at his eardrums, and he awoke with a shock. "Who goes there?" he shouted into the dark.

The humming stopped. "Look who's awake."

Shuffling footsteps drew closer, then something was lifted from Pagaene's eyes. He winced against the slap of daylight and blinked as a man's face came into focus. He swallowed. "Healer?"

The man chuckled softly. "Did my singing wake you? I wish I had thought of that earlier. You've been asleep for nearly a week."

Pagaene tried to sit up, but his head spun, and he fell back against the bed. "I'm still alive, then?"

"I would hope so, or this has all been a massive waste of time for me." Healer sat on a stool beside Pagaene and lay a cool cloth on his forehead. "This will ease the dizziness."

Pagaene closed his eyes and took a deep breath. "Esyld. Where is she? Is she…"

"She's only just left your side, Pagaene. I expect she couldn't tolerate my singing, either, but once she realizes I've stopped, she'll return."

Pagaene managed a weak smile. "And Kenyth?"

"A few new scars to match his hands, but otherwise, he is well."

"And The Purity? Did we succeed, Healer? Is she contained once more?"

This time, Healer paused. "Perhaps I'm not the one to answer that."

Pagaene tried to sit up again, but his arms wobbled and could not support his weight. He moaned in frustration. "I must go. I must ensure the task is finished!"

Healer rested a massive hand on Pagaene's shoulder. "No, Pagaene, you must rest." He smiled. "Let me tell you a story. I promise you will like it better than my singing."

Pagaene swallowed back a mouthful of bitter bile. "Perhaps that is best," he whispered.

"Good," Healer said. "This story begins many decades ago, when I was just a lad. I had arrived in Jentor to begin my training as a Knight—"

"You were a Knight?"

Healer looked at Pagaene. "We all have past lives, do we not?"

"Indeed," the Knight said. "Please, continue."

"I joined the same time as another young man, who quickly proved himself a soldier of no parallel. No sooner had we completed our training and received our shields than he was begging to be put at the front of the lines in every battle, to lead the charge against any and all of King Rouaix's enemies. Human, monster, it did not matter. This young Knight was the strongest, bravest, and most loyal person I had ever met. And, for some reason that remains a mystery to me, he became my closest friend. When I fought beside him, I was the finest soldier I could be. He brought out the best in me, in everyone." Healer cocked his head to one side. "Have you guessed his name?"

"You speak of my father," Pagaene said. "Pierce."

"Aye, you're a quick learner," Healer said. "Yes, I knew your father. Pierce was the gem of the King's army, the greatest soldier to ever fight for Rouaix. And when the King learned Pierce's father was The Gray Wizard of Nightstone, well! There was nothing but stars in the King's eyes for him, I tell you.

"But things changed when your father married your Abdita mother. Rouaix thought your father bewitched at first, but after you and your brother were born, there was no denying your father's love for your mother, and Pierce's fidelity was questioned. To prove his loyalty, Pierce volunteered for a dangerous mission to slay a beast terrorizing far-lying villages. The fool's errand could only end in death, and no one else would accompany him. But he was my dearest companion, and I could not let him venture alone."

Healer slowly lifted one pantleg to reveal an atrophied calf with a fist-sized chunk of missing muscle. "The monster would have killed me if not for your father," he said as he covered his leg again. "The man sacrificed himself for me, for his King. It was the most noble, courageous thing anyone could ever do, but it mattered not to King Rouaix. He told his soldiers that Pierce's death only proved he was no longer fully committed to defending his kingdom and that his name must never be spoken again. I could no longer serve a King who had so dishonored my friend. I left Jentor and accompanied Pierce's body back to his homeland. It was here I met the Abdita for the first time and realized my calling was not to fight but to heal.

"And there you have it, Pagaene." Healer sat back and appraised him. "Your father saved my life, and I have now repaid the debt. A good story, yes?"

Pagaene's head swam. "I... I..." He slapped his hand on

the mattress. "Why didn't you tell me this before? Why didn't you tell me you knew my father? I've known nothing of him my entire life, and now—"

Healer shushed him. "Don't wind yourself up. It's not good for the brain." The man spoke softly. "Stories are told when they are meant to be told. And I have many more stories about your father, which I shall share with you in due time."

"And though I deeply wish to hear them," Pagaene said, "I must now discover what happened with The Purity." He pushed himself up from the bed, but his vision blackened, and he again fell back.

"Rest, Pagaene," Esyld said. Her soft footsteps entered the room, accompanied by an unfamiliar thumping.

Pagaene turned his head towards her and blinked away the darkness. When he finally saw her, his eyes filled with warm tears. "Oh, Esyld…"

"I am well." She leaned heavily on a wooden staff, and her arms and legs were wrapped in bandages. She smiled and shook the staff carved with the figures of friendly snakes. "Tirieus, the man who made your arm, has made this for me. I asked him if I should look for any secret compartments, but he insists it is a staff and nothing more. I am not sure I believe him."

Pagaene chuckled. "I will help you look when I am well again." He reached out for her, and she hobbled closer to grasp his hand. "You must tell me, Esyld. Is it over? Is The Purity gone?"

She took a deep, trembling breath. "I hear her, Pagaene," she whispered. "At the bottom of the Sacred Well. I go there every day to ensure the vines hold her inside, and every day, I hear her."

"What does she say?" Pagaene asked, his heart thumping. "Does she attempt escape?"

"No." Esyld shook her head. "She cries. She cries and she begs her mother's forgiveness. And when she hears me, she begs me to ensure she is never again released. She asks me to grow more vines, and I do, but it is not enough for her. Her imprisonment is not her punishment." She squeezed Pagaene's hand. "Her guilt will eternally bind her. No one will ever have to fear The Purity again.

I am sure of it."

Pagaene nodded grimly. "Then our task is complete."

Healer clapped his massive hands together. "Who's hungry? I make a marvelous stew." Pagaene's stomach grumbled in response. It embarrassed him, but Healer merely laughed. "A week of beet juice and marrow soup will leave a body hungry for meat. Please excuse me, and I will get started." Healer rose and opened the door to leave, just as Kenyth walked in.

"Kenyth," Pagaene said. "I'm glad you're here."

Kenyth's right eyebrow had been replaced by a knobby pink scar, and peeling blisters covered his cheek. "Just barely, but I am here."

"We would not have succeeded without you," Esyld said.

Kenyth shrugged. "And perhaps none of this would have happened if not for my role in it. I need to apologize to you both, on behalf of my sister and myself. If I had known…" He choked on the last words, then shook his head. "If I had known," he tried again, "how much devastation, how much loss… my brother, Carrick. Your whole family, Pagaene. So many people died to keep The Purity at bay. I know I am partly responsible."

"Kenyth," Esyld started, but he held up a hand, and she fell silent.

"Please," he said. "I will have to make my peace with it on my own." He turned to Pagaene. "I have come to tell you that the remains of The White Dragon were found on Kreajo Mountain. The fire burned away everything but his bones. They have been turned to marble."

"Marble?" Pagaene asked.

"I have been in contact with your grandfather, Pagaene. Once when I was sent to resurrect him in the forest and again after we'd found the dragon's bones. He has asked that we use the marble to build a temple dedicated to those who have given their lives for our task. With your permission, we will inscribe the names of our lost friends and family on the walls, so they may never be forgotten."

"Yes, of course," Pagaene said. "As long as the first names

inscribed are those of my mother and father, Mathilde and Pierce."

"As you wish," Kenyth said.

"And the Abdita elders who were betrayed by Muave?" Esyld asked.

Kenyth solemnly nodded. "None shall be forgotten."

A bright, glowing light filled the single window. "What is that?" Pagaene asked.

"Let us find out," Kenyth said. He looped an arm under Pagaene's shoulders and pulled him to a sitting position.

Pagaene's head swam for a moment, but then he said, "I'm ready," and allowed Kenyth to help him outside.

The first creatures he saw were Khati's white horse, a fine mist dissipating in the air around her. She stood with the other mounts of Freywyn, but all had paused in their grazing to stare. He followed the animals' gaze.

The townspeople kowtowed around the figure of a beautiful, glowing woman with ebony skin. Her long dark hair flowed in the air around her face, though no wind blew. She wore a gown of ivy and flowers, and when she greeted them, they all knew her.

"The Great Mother!" Esyld slid down her staff to her knees, but the Great Mother stopped her.

"No, child. I wish to speak to you as an equal today." Esyld stood. The Great Mother looked at Kenyth and Pagaene, who had both cast their eyes to the ground. "I wish to speak with all of you. Raise your eyes, my sons." They did, and she continued. "The destruction my daughter has wrought is tremendous. But now, because of you three, she will be the balance to Life, not the end of it. Now that she is contained once more, it is up to you to heal this world. You each have proven your worthiness and capability, and I have tasks for you all."

She faced Kenyth. "Priest, you will be the spiritual leader of the people now. You will assume the position once held by His Holiness and guide the Prime Order as it returns to its original purpose—to preserve the sacred trinity of Life, Death, and Rebirth. Teach the people how to respect and care for each other, and for all life, from the tiniest sapling struggling in the ground to the new King who will take the throne in Jentor.

"I am sorry for the loss of your brother and sister. But you, more than anyone else, understand what it is like to be cast from your family and to see how ignorance, intolerance, and greed can corrupt the purest of hearts. You will devote the rest of your life to remolding the Prime Order as a religion that spreads love and harmony."

Kenyth clasped a fist to his heart and nodded. "I will, Mother."

Next, the Great Mother turned to Pagaene. "Knight. Descendent of both Abdita and wizard, you have the ability to heal this land as prophecy has stated. You will travel back to your home in Jentor, and as you go, you will heal the forests, the fields, and the cropland. You will sow the lands with fertile seeds, and you will cause dry rivers to gush with new water. You will be the first King in a lifetime to teach tolerance and respect for all peoples. You will truly heal this land."

Pagaene blinked. "Mother, did you say *King*?"

The Great Mother smiled. "Of course. There is no one better suited to rule over these lands than you, Pagaene. You will fly a new flag above Jentor, a pennant that celebrates the unification of all the peoples of this land and all the breeds of magic. And to help you in your new position, I give you this." She lifted her hand, and resting on her palm was the Nightstone. It floated through the air to Pagaene, who caught it and squeezed it tightly in his fist.

His legs instantly felt stronger, and he was able to stand apart from Kenyth. "Thank you, Great Mother," he whispered.

***

Finally, the Great Mother turned to Esyld. "Esyld, the faithful. I never doubted you, your strength, or your courage. I chose you for this task because I knew you could reunite Pagaene with his family, strengthen him, and prepare him for his destiny. The bond you two have forged through your journey, the bond that allows you to hear each other's silent words, will keep you close for the rest of your lives. Esyld, as Pagaene rules from Jentor, so shall you rule here as the new High Priestess of the Realm."

At her words, the townspeople collectively gasped and raised their heads to look at her. Esyld's heart fluttered in her chest like a hummingbird, and she smiled down at them. "I will not let you down," she said, then looked back up at the Great Mother. "I am honored, Mother."

The Great Mother nodded once. "Your first task as the new High Priestess will be to assist me in the reparation of the Sacred Wells. I will also need to form new faces to place in the sacred groves."

Esyld cast her third Sight down in to the villagers and saw one young face staring up at her with curiosity and wonder. It was Muave's youngling girl. Esyld took a deep breath. "May I suggest something, Mother?" she asked.

"Of course."

"Might it be possible to create a fourth face? A Child's face? It has been a long time since I felt the unburdened freedom of youth, and I should like the opportunity to feel it again."

The Great Mother was quiet for a long moment as she seemed to ponder this. Then finally, she smiled and nodded her head, her wavy hair curling over her shoulders. "So mote it be," she said. And with that, she plucked a hair from her head and ran her fingers up and down the fine strand. With each passage of her fingers, the hair thickened and elongated until a bulb formed on one end. The bulb grew and grew until it was the size of a child's face, with rosy cheeks and strawberry-colored hair.

"Here," the Great Mother said as she offered it to Esyld. "It is ready for you."

The entire village fell silent but for the soft ticking of Esyld's staff as she shuffled to collect her gift. She took the face and marveled at the warmth and suppleness of its flesh, running her fingers through its fine hairs.

"I believe you will find this stone amplifies its powers," the

Great Mother said, and when Esyld looked up, the sacred, ruby-colored stone dropped into her hand.

Immediately, a warm current radiated from the face through Esyld's body. Without further delay, she attached the Child's face to her own. Her body shivered once, rapidly morphing into the form of a child, and then she was still.

"Esyld?" Pagaene called. "Esyld, are you all right?"

With a clatter, Esyld's staff fell to the ground, and she spun around to face Pagaene. Several seconds passed as they stared into each other's eyes. Then she stuck her tongue between her lips and blew a raspberry at him. Pagaene was struck silent for only a moment before he erupted into a bellowing laugh. The rest of the village joined him, and even the Great Mother had to cover her mouth to hide her grin.

Esyld ignored them all as she skipped out of the village, eager to play in the forest.

THE END

Stealing the Curse
by
J.K Harrison

*H*e who wields Discernment will fall to no blade.

   Sloan read the inscription again. Heaviness settled in her chest, making her heart beat faster. She tightened her grip on the sword and focused on her breathing.

  Cian glanced restlessly around the small hut. "What do you see?"

  "Nothing." Her voice wavered with the effort of lying through a prophecy. Power surged through the smooth sword hilt, radiating up her arm. Sloan could see whole armies fail to strike down any man who wielded the Jade Hilt.

  He tilted his head perceptively. "Sloan. You're seeing something."

  She took a deep breath and returned her focus to her

surroundings. Cian's gaze waited, as deep and enigmatic as the sea. Sloan pushed that aside. "The inscription is true."

A grin, like a flash of sunlight, broke across his face, careless of its affect. Cian pressed his mouth to her cheek, an oblivious, habitual gesture. Then he left, leaving Sloan's hut feeling hollow and dull. His presence always made her feel a little drunk and his departure too much like being hungover.

Sloan pushed herself off the floor to go wash away the weight and burn of the sword. Her legs protested, and her head swam. Staggering toward the open hearth, she had to catch herself on the center post. The spirit bells overhead offered a shower of tinkles she wanted to ignore.

Dipping her hand in a bucket of water did nothing to soothe the sting. She turned it over to find blisters speckling her palm.

"You should not have touched that."

Sloan sighed, massaging her hand. "I know, Grandmother."

She would not have touched it for anyone else in the village, though she did wish it had been anyone else who asked.

Twilight bled color out of the day when Cian leaned inside Sloan's doorway, offering another burst of brightness. Her pallid complexion gave pause to what would have been a passing greeting. "Are you unwell?"

She finished tying the drawing poultice bag before forcing a smile. "Just a little tired."

"Did you cut yourself?"

She glanced at her wrapped hand. "I—yes."

Cian noticed her gaze drift to the sword he still carried. "This? You didn't even look at the blade." He pulled the sword free of the scabbard to admire its gleam in the fading light.

"I didn't need to." She was about to feign another smile when he frowned at her. She knew the words would be useless, like so many things she'd told Cian, but like all the others, she felt compelled to say them. "There is more to the Jade Hilt than what is etched there. Any man who wields this sword brings his own destruction."

He flashed a reassuring grin. "Your kind feel that way about all swords, Sloanie."

Defeat settled into her bones.

The bells announced Grandmother's presence again. "You have known his path since it intersected yours."

"Yes, Grandmother."

"And what is it I told you that day?"

Sloan sighed and wished a simple smudging would chase Grandmother away.

"I am too strong for that, child." The ghost often seemed to know her thoughts. "What did I tell you?"

"That a warrior and a shaman could not walk together."

"Yet you are no more willing to heed my words than the warrior is to heed yours."

"Be gone, Grandmother."

"You let the darkness in, child. Best for you to rest."

Though nothing stirred, Sloan sensed the emptiness in her hut as Grandmother's presence left.

Feverish dreams terrorized Sloan all night; images of death and chaos forged by the Jade Hilt. Each time the wielder fell to the prophecy, they had Cian's eyes, emptied and staring.

The ting of bells pulled Sloan awake when dawn was just a smear of color along the horizon.

"The darkness has found a weakness inside you to feed on," Grandmother scolded.

Sloan ignored the aches throughout her body and the pain throbbing up her arm. "I'll be fine."

"Your poultice did not work. Your mind was too distracted when you made it."

During their long relationship, there had been few times Grandmother had irritated Sloan as much as she did now. She didn't need to be reminded of failures, shortcomings, and futilities.

"A shaman must know her place," Grandmother said gently. "More than anyone in the village, your path must be clear."

"And a shaman is the only one who can help Cian now."

"No." Grandmother's harshness caught Sloan off guard. "Only Cian can walk his path, and he chose it. When he was a boy, he chose his path. Daily, he chooses it. And yesterday, he chose it again when you told him what that sword was, and again when he saw how it poisons you."

"And I choose my path." Sloan rose unsteadily to her feet, the room spinning for a moment as fatigue and illness tried to pull her down.

"Sloan Worldwalker, do not do this."

Waving her hand as if to cut through smoke, Sloan shooed away the presence and turned to pack offerings into a leather sack.

"Let me cleanse it."

Cian's amber brows knotted as he took in the hollowness under Sloan's eyes. "You don't seem fit to cleanse anything this morning. You ought to be resting. Go back to bed, and I'll have Shae sent with tea and broth."

Sloan's glance tugged toward the sword resting next to Cian's mat. The hilt's jade inlay seemed unnaturally dark in the shadow of the hut. "I will not get better until I have cleansed that sword. You don't understand what taints it."

"Even in the height of battle, I did not feel as much a warrior as when I grasped that sword. I didn't feel anything bad in it. Every warrior in Taniga seeks the Jade Hilt, but that is not something a shaman can understand. You ought to keep to consulting smoke and watching birds fly. Warfare is beyond your realm."

"You brought it to me because there are things I understand that a warrior does not. There is a darkness in that thing." Sloan pursed her lips and looked away, continuing with a soft voice. "What will a shaman's ritual hurt to something of such renown?"

Sighing wistfully, Cian turned to retrieve the sword. A patronizing smile broke over his face as he offered it to her. "Do as you like. I suppose you're right about the ritual."

Not even the strongest hunters would enter the Forest of the Restless. Staring at the tall, slender trees, with leaves dark against the sun, fresh sweat prickled out of Sloan's pores, and her chest clenched around her heart. The throbbing in her arm threatened to overwhelm everything else, but she set her jaw and trudged forward.

A silent partner for the entire journey, Grandmother's presence receded as Sloan neared the trees. It left her feeling oddly exposed to the sun's rays beating down from its zenith. The sword, slung against her back, seemed to grow heavier with each step. A welcomed relief from the heat, the protection of the leaves quickly became an eerie chill.

As her pupils dilated, Sloan could see rocks and boulders scattered among the tree trunks. Animals did not trespass here; there were no game trails to help navigate the forest floor. Picking her way carefully didn't stop Sloan from rolling her foot on a stone. A cry burst from her lips when she caught herself on her sick arm, sending a jolt of white-hot pain.

As the throbbing eased to a bearable level, the first whispers slid through the ominous trees to reach Sloan's ears. The still air made breathing hard, feeling too heavy for her lungs.

Sloan righted herself and continued to pick through the trees as the first tendrils of hopelessness wove around her. A shaman could resist longer, but anyone who remained would eventually succumb to the darkness. With each step, she felt the Restless surrounding her, blanketing her with animosity.

The trunks looked the same, but she felt it when she neared the one she sought. Just like last time, it drew her. This time, however, she felt the tree's history—a shadow of what was. Tall and foreboding, the tree stood like all those around it. Despite the whispers engulfing her, Sloan could hear the echo of a creak from the tree's past.

Pulling a breath deep into her chest and ignoring the invasive spirits turned away at her lips, Sloan steadied herself. Everyone here fed off weakness, so she did not allow herself to hesitate before looking up.

Graceful branches, slender leaves, and nothing more obscured the sky. The sun had been bright when Sloan had entered, and it was the middle of the dry season, but from here, she thought the sky could be overcast forever.

Looking like all the others, the branch holding the weight of her mother drew Sloan's eye. Less than ten seasons had passed, but not even the rope remained. She did not know what had become of the rope or her mother's bones; nothing but leaves and rocks littered the ground.

Studiously ignoring the invisible whirl of emotion consuming her and inhaling deeply to slow her heart, Sloan removed the contents of her sack and the sheathed blade. No fire would spark to life here, but she hoped the ground bone and blessed meat would be enough.

"Mother," she called, scattering the bone dust in a circle around her and the Jade Hilt. "I invoke you."

The whispers grew to a muffled howl, but none answered her.

"Mother," Sloan called again, holding out her hand. "With the bond of blood, I invoke you."

Tightening her fingers around the bone handle of her ritual knife, she drew it across her outstretched palm. The glassy blade parted her flesh more cleanly than any steel. Her blood pattered over the cursed sword before she felt the sting of the wound. Even as she knelt, watching the patterns her offering made over the weapon, she felt the gaping of her flesh more than any pain.

A sharp chill cut into the air, standing her hair on end and driving a shiver down her spine.

"There is no mother here, fool," a deep voice growled. "You wield no power among these trees."

She gritted her teeth and stiffened her lips to keep her voice steady. "Blood holds power anywhere." The truth she spoke emboldened her. "I entreat you to cleanse the curse from this sword."

The presence swirled around her but offered nothing else.

Her fist clenched around the cut. "I compel you!"

The air around her split into a roar that bore into her bones. Primal fear and unfathomable anguish filled her with insurmountable hopelessness. Her eyes fell to the black knife she still gripped. Even in the gloom, the obsidian gleamed.

A small bubble invaded the darkness, filling her and pressing against the inside of her ribs. It burst with a sharp pain and something too faint to hear; a little more than a foreign feeling urged her to *run*.

Snatching the sword, Sloan pushed to her feet, spinning toward the way she'd come. She broke through the circle of bone dust, silencing the enraged roar but not easing the despair inside her. Last time, her mother's ghost had been there to help; this time, Sloan had only that old memory to guide her and panic to drive her.

The wash of sunlight shocked her as she burst from the stoic trees and ocean of whispers, but Sloan didn't slow her pace. Half blind, she stumbled along until the Forest of the Restless faded behind her and her pupils constricted to pinpricks.

In the heat of the day, during the peak of the dry season, Sloan was halfway home and drenched with sweat before the chill had dissipated. The sharp cramp in her side finally brought her to a stop, her feet churning puffs of pale dust. Still clenching the sword and knife, Sloan braced her hands against her knees as she gasped for breath and waited for the pounding inside her skull to ease. She expected Grandmother's reprimand to start at any moment.

As her heart slowed and her breath quieted, the silence elongated. The air felt empty around her, and after another moment, Sloan started for home again. Aches throughout her body and the safety of the bright sunlight kept her pace slower now. Perhaps Grandmother had found something better to do or intended to give her the cold shoulder.

Cian wasn't anywhere in sight when Sloan returned, and she was too exhausted to look for him, so she entrusted the Jade Hilt with Shae, his young sister. He might not give her the sword a second time to cleanse, but the bone-deep weariness she felt prevented Sloan from determining that today. She was tired of looking at the cursed thing.

The tinkle of the spirit bells woke Sloan that night.

"It's late for a lecture," she called drowsily. The weight of the proceeding silence pulled Sloan fully awake. "Grandmother?"

"Grandmother is not here."

Iciness stabbed her gut at the sound of the deep voice from the forest. Crawling clumsily off her mat to the open hearth, Sloan's pulse hammered against her ears, muffling everything else except the sound of her breathing.

"You are not welcome here." Her voice came out strong, despite burning her fingertips in her frantic attempts to stir the coals to life.

The orange glow consoled her the slightest bit but didn't keep her hands from trembling when she reached for a bundle of sage drying overhead. Once she had the sage smoldering, the earthy, pungent smoke offered more comfort.

She raised the sage in one hand, using the other to waft smoke around her. "You are not welcome here."

The presence made no reply, but Sloan could still feel it. Angling the bundle of incense downward so it would burn better, she swept through the hut in a widening circle, doing a full smudging. The ancient song came from low in her belly, rising and falling as she moved. Sloan always felt a deep connection to her ancestors when she sang their words, and the weight of balancing the other world with her own settled into a somber determination inside her. When Grandmother had told her that a shaman could not walk with a warrior, she spoke too of the importance of this balance and of how only the shaman could keep it.

Sloan was still smudging her hut when early-morning light streaked through the flaps of her door, illuminating the heavy smoke hanging in the air. She'd gone through enough sage to smudge every hut in the village, but she could still feel the presence defying the sacred smoke and the words as old as her people.

"Sloan." Cian's call broke through the stillness.

"I'm awake."

Parting the animal hides, he waved the sage smoke from his face as it escaped around him. The heavy cloud wasn't enough to distract him from his mission this morning, though. "Shae is ill. We need you."

The girl's face was colorless, except for the lavender rings around her eyes. Sloan would have thought she was looking at a corpse if not for the irregular rise and fall of Shae's chest.

"She does not wake," her mother murmured. "She complained of an aching head last night, and now she does not wake."

"Burn sage next to her constantly. Bathe her in the smoke every hour, and if she wakes, give her pale tea." Sloan rose to her feet and turned to Cian. "Give me the sword."

"Now is not the time to worry about my sword—"

"Give it to me." Something from deep inside Sloan moved through the words, and it was enough to keep Cian from arguing. Sloan took the weapon in her injured hand and walked away from the village again. This time, though, she went to the Blessing Stone, where she could walk the seam between the two worlds. She ought to have come here yesterday, but she wanted to lift the curse from the sword and nothing more. It was too late for that, and now Shae was sick from her foolishness as much as Cian's.

All the ghosts were silent that day, including Grandmother, and Sloan felt the presence from the forest lingering at the base of the Blessing Stone. It would not come into this sacred circle of rock, but it waited for her.

Settling into her seated position, Sloan closed her eyes, breathing deeply and pushing everything from her mind. The crackle of a small wood fire before her was the only thing to break the quiet. A slight wind shifted, blowing the acrid smoke into her face. The smell pulled forth a hazy memory.

When she was a child, before most in the village knew she had the ghost tongue, Grandmother told her stories, teaching her in a way a child's mind would understand. She recalled one about the Angry Man and the Righteous Sword.

As she remembered the story, Sloan's chest tightened, and her heart beat faster. The Righteous Sword fell every enemy it crossed. It discerned justice for each person who came before it, telling the wielder if they deserved to live or die. This knowledge of truth soon conquered entire armies without a drop of bloodshed.

And then the Angry Man possessed it. Scorned by a woman who favored another warrior, the Angry Man drew the Righteous Sword against this man, but the sword judged that the man should live. In a fury, the Angry Man killed him anyway, and then the woman, then everyone else in the village.

When the next dawn rose, the Angry Man realized what he'd done, and sorrow and fear filled him. He fled, running for days, as though he could escape his actions. But the land, seeking justice, moved to stop him. Tall trees rose like prison bars, and stones rolled beneath his feet so he could not run. Forced, then, to face his anguish, the man turned the sword on himself. The Angry Man's betrayal crushed the weapon's soul, its blade drenched in the man's blood, and a cursed prophecy stained the Righteous Sword.

The ancestors were silent; they all knew what Sloan had to do, and it was a path they could not walk with her. The presence in her hut knew too. Yesterday, her blood fell where his once flowed, and they were bonded together now so Grandmother could not return to her. She would not be there to help Sloan heal the village, and the sickness inside Shae would spread to others as long as the Jade Hilt remained.

The sword grew heavier with each step, and the silent presence of the Angry Man dragged against her more and more the nearer she drew to the Forest of the Restless. As the tall, slender trees emerged with their leaves dark against the sun, each step took all Sloan's effort. She tried not to wonder if Cian would miss the sword she cradled more than he would miss her.

For one brief moment, she stood on the edge of the trees, ignoring the way the Angry Man's ghost nudged her, and reveled

in the heat of the sun's rays beating against her.
She pulled in a final, hot breath and entered the forest.

Army of Brass
Chapter 1

The atmosphere in Brasshaven's meeting room was uncharacteristically tense for a weekend in the House of Lords. The assembly of men in their fine garments and powdered wigs made an admirable show of maintaining a sense of stability and dignity, but beneath it, every one of them trembled.

The Lord Speaker, Tullius Von Buren, rerolled the parchment he had just finished reading to his group of peers. He sat down and used a fine lace handkerchief to covertly dab away the beads of sweat that had plagued him throughout his recitation.

"If Fairport is under attack by the Hunter Baron and his Marksmen, what are we to do?" gasped Lord Androcles Von Kemp before taking a sip from the delicate porcelain tea cup in front of him. The question was on every mind in the garishly decorated hall.

After some disorganized chatter among the rest of the aristocracy, Lord Von Buren reclaimed order in the hall with a few raps of his cane against the polished wood of his pulpit. "Undoubtedly, the capital has been made aware of the Hunter Baron's attack, but I will see an envoy is dispatched as well. Naturally, Brasshaven will offer any assistance requested to the crown and our neighbors in Fairport." A chorus of affirming voices swept over the room as the congregation of local noblemen endorsed the Lord Speaker's directive. "The cannons of Fairport have protected our southern border for ages, and not once has a threat of any foreign power, even the Hunter Baron, set foot on our shores. The crown is sure to dispatch the Capital Guard to Fairport, and I imagine this matter will be laid to rest swiftly."

After several more bouts of men speaking over each other, a woman stood from her seat in the rows of benches spreading out behind the comfortable, overstuffed chairs of the noblemen. Elaina Gable fussed with her hairpins the way she always did when thinking about what she wanted to say. The twirling of these pins, combined with the look of dire vexation marked on Elaina's face, finally caught the ever-watchful eye of the Lord Speaker.

"Mrs. Gable, are you quite well? Is there some matter the Tinkerer's Guild needs to bring before the House of Lords?" Lord Von Buren asked, hushing the murmurs that filled the lavish meeting hall.

The Lord Speaker's powerful yet soothing tone served as the spark Elaina needed. "Thank you, Lord Speaker. I wish I could say I am as hopeful as the rest of you about this… this dangerous situation, but I have a fear."

"Please, madam, unburden yourself. You are always welcome to speak in this hall. If you have a fear, then I would certainly like to hear it," he said and beckoned her to come forward.

Elaina pressed her sweaty palms flush against her legs to stop her fidgeting. Her full black dress helped conceal her wobbly ankles as she opened the carved mahogany gate and stepped through the divide separating the commoners from the nobility. She presented herself before the Lord Speaker with the requisite formalities, then took a moment with her eyes closed to find her sense of clarity and poise. When she opened her eyes, she was just in time to see Lord Von Buren's silent nod indicating she should commence.

"My Lords and fellows, I am speaking now, not as the head of Brasshaven's Tinkerer's Guild, but as a former southerner. It is no great secret that I was born and raised on the southern continent where the Hunter Baron rules. Even with the formidable arms of Fairport, I think it is unwise to so readily assume this threat will be defeated with little cost."

As soon as she finished her statement, the brash sound of Lord Himmil Rotterdam's voice arose to refute her warning. "Mrs. Gable, I think you are being entirely too delicate. Fairport's walls and cannons can handle any foe that comes. I can appreciate the perspective you might have gained living among those unrefined savages, but they are clearly no match for sophisticated men of intellect. Best you busy your mind with the gears and cogs in which you are versed. Leave the soldiering to those suited for it," said the fat, greasy man, a patronizing smirk plastered beneath his finely waxed and curled mustache.

It took all Elaina's restraint not to jump into the haughty swine's pulpit, rip the powdered wig from his head, and beat Lord Rotterdam senseless with the accessory. It was not his sexism that cut her the deepest—that was an undeniable reality about the majority lords—but the arrogance the man displayed when it came to talk of war.

"My Lord, with all kindness, and once again speaking as someone who has survived life in the south, I would beseech the House to please consider taking greater initiative in the matter at hand," the Master Tinkerer replied through clenched teeth.

Lord Rotterdam gave a dismissive roll of his eyes and turned his attention to the Lord Speaker. "Lord Von Buren, perhaps it would be in order to post an escort of city guard with Mrs. Gable. Clearly, this news has shaken the fragile thing."

Elaina felt as if she'd been struck in the jaw by the odious man's superior attitude. She was about to launch a civil retort to his statement, but her hand subconsciously fell to her wrist and felt the absence of her wedding clasp around her forearm. The skin where it used to lay had darkened to nearly the same color as the rest of her healthy, tan complexion. She thought of her husband, and the memory of that magnificent man ignited a deep and explosive passion within the her. "Sir, you are grossly overconfident. Even a novice Marksman will shoot out your eye at three hundred yards in any weather. The Hunter Baron is a man of conquest, and he will kill the weak and leave them to rot in the sun. Any prisoners he takes are for sport... like... he will..." Elaina sputtered, eyes welling at the memories of her husband in his final moments.

Lord Rotterdam flushed red with outrage, but before he could reprimand the tinkerer, a cavalier voice emanated from the rear of the meeting room.

"She's right. Southern Marksmen are not to be trifled with," said a young man in a neatly pressed red and tan uniform, wearing expertly polished black boots. He walked into the meeting room through the open double doors without any care of formality or propriety, giving only the most cursory of bows to the assembly of Lords once he was halfway up the room's main aisle. Afterwards, his steely eyes went soft and warm as he looked upon Elaina. "Mrs. Gable, the voice of reason here in Brasshaven, I see. Commendable, madam."

The Herald of the Lord Speaker scrambled into the room behind the man who had just disturbed the proceedings. Sheepishly, the boy stood at attention and announced the man in an attempt to salvage some measure of decorum. "My Lords and fellows, I present Mr. Jack Davenport of the Capital Cartographers Society."

After some murmuring among the assembly, Lord Von Buren addressed the journeymen mapmaker. "Mr. Davenport, a man of the Cartographers Society is always welcome in Brasshaven, but I would thank you to let us tend to our own matters of government."

"My apologies, Your Lordship, but you will want to hear what I have to say," retorted Jack.

"Go on," said Lord Von Buren warily.

Jack cleared his throat, standing tall before delivering the news. "The Hunter Baron has taken Fairport."

A moment of silence ensued, then threatened to turn into panic, but the Lord Speaker spoke before the mood could degrade into anarchy. "Mr. Davenport, I think you must be mistaken. I hold in my hand a letter from the Duke of Fairport, penned barely a fortnight ago. He states that the city is repelling the Hunter Baron and his Marksmen." He held the parchment correspondence aloft.

"That was quite true at the time the note was written. My dirigible left Fairport once the city was overrun. That was three days after the Duke sent that dispatch."

Realization washed over the House of Lords and the common folk; Lord Von Buren was the one to give voice to the thought. "That is unfathomable. You say the Hunter Baron took control of Fairport in only three days?"

The cartographer leveled a steady gaze at the nobleman, his voice heavy. "The Hunter Baron and some eighty thousand Marksmen. They are already cutting timber and laying rail. They will be in Brasshaven before the harvest season."

The Lord Speaker's booming voice rose above the discordant alarm in the assembly at the news. "Eighty thousand? Are you quite sure of that?"

"Yes indeed, Your Lordship. In fact, that figure may be a conservative estimate."

Men shouted and women screamed, while some people ran for the door and others fainted. The Lords fervently bickered with each other over the best course of action, and several long minutes passed before Lord Von Buren managed to regain control of the room. "We must sue for peace. There is no single army, or two armies for that matter, in all the kingdom that compare to a force of that size."

"There is such an army," said Elaina with confidence, cutting through all the bravado of the Lords and the fear of the common folk. The meeting room returned to a more civil state; all desired to learn the tinkerer's thought.

After a long pause, the Lord Speaker coaxed, "Go on, madam."

"The automatons. They could—I know they are currently derelict, but…" She struggled to phrase the notion rapidly forming in her mind.

The obnoxious laughter of Lord Rotterdam and a number of the other lords broke into her pause. "Ha! You hear this? Her plan is to resurrect some overgrown pocket watches and use them to stave off the Hunter Baron," said the portly Lord mid-guffaw.

Elaina did her best to maintain her aplomb. "My Lords, I say we have an army right in our very midst that can withstand any blade or shot. It knows nothing of fear—"

The Lord Speaker silenced her with a gesture. "Mrs. Gable, I can appreciate the sentiment, but… the automatons… they have never moved in all of recorded history. The things are relics of an older world, nothing else. They are little more than a collection of rust and broken clockwork." His words were courteous but clearly no more sympathetic to the tinkerer's idea than his colleague's.

"Your Lordship, I know it requires some faith, but my research into the automatons with the Tinkerer's Guild shows great promise and—"

"You hear this? Faith and promise placed in those gargantuan shambles standing in our valley," Lord Rotterdam bellowed. "These are the hysterical ravings of an overly emotional woman and have no place to be entertained in the House of Lords."

Jack took several passionate steps forward. "Sir, I care nothing for our difference in rank and station. Should you ever speak to Mrs. Gable like that again, on my honor, it will be your choice of pistols or sabers at dawn."

After the cartographer's outburst, the Lord sat and hid an embarrassed face behind his handkerchief.

"Pay him no mind, Mr. Davenport," Elaina said. "I can see that nobody sitting on this side of the room cares for anything I have to say. I will no longer waste my time or theirs. Good day, My Lords," she added in mock courtesy. "Before I go, just realize that any talk of diplomacy with the Hunter Baron is equally as wasteful. That man only knows violence, sport, and bloodshed."

She stormed out of the meeting room and rushed through the cobblestone streets of Brasshaven, grateful her fuming anger stopped her from breaking into tears over the revolting treatment she had just received. Whether the constant disrespect she suffered under Brasshaven's nobility was due in greater part to the fact that she was a woman or a born southerner, she did not know.

People scurried out of her way when they saw the tinkerer barreling down the street. Elaina struggled to stifle the unending stream of colorful words she'd chosen for the Brasshaven nobility in general and her opinions of Lord Rotterdam in particular. Her pace never slowed as she passed the bustling shopfronts of the merchant district and the steaming smokestacks of the industrial quarter. Finally, she reached the observatory platform on the boundary of Brasshaven at the crescendo of her anger.

"Those feebleminded, patriarchal, misogynistic orangutans in waistcoats! They can all get stuffed and mounted in the Hunter Baron's trophy room for their idiocy," she shouted, her voice echoing into the valley sprawling to the south of Brasshaven.

"So, you plan on giving up, then?"

Elaina spun around to see the cartographer approaching and felt a pulse of embarrassment wash over her. "Mr. Davenport. My apologies for what I just said. I know it was not very ladylike."

"No, not ladylike at all. That happens to be one of the things I find most intriguing about you," Jack replied with a flashy smile. "Still, never envisioned you as the sort to surrender,"

"I may be the only one who believes in the automatons, but there's no quit in me, sir. I'll go to the capital and plead my case before the Monarchy Proper if I must."

"I have no question you would, but you won't have to. I admit, I may not believe in them…" Jack gestured towards the south. "But only a fool would doubt you, Mrs. Gable."

He handed her a letter, and as she read the note, her eyes grew wide. "This is direct from the Forgemaster of Brand."

"He will be in Brasshaven by week's end with two score of mastersmiths and three times the number in apprentice forgemen. The Forgemaster's pedigree will be sufficient to bring around the House of Lords. Between your intellect and their industriousness, you will ready an army that can stand against the Hunter Baron."

"How did you manage this?"

"You know me. I'm just so painfully likable and persuasive," Jack said with artificial bravado. "In spite of his time served, the Forgemaster has never actually seen them. And they are a sight to see."

"They are a sight indeed," sighed Elaina, her words laden with reference.

They stood on the platform and looked down at the colossal assembly of constructs filling Brasshaven's southern valley. Even with the heavy tarnish brought on by age, the afternoon sun still glittered off their metallic bodies. Each of the automatons stood as a titanic, ever-vigilant sentry with clockwork eyes, massive blades and shields at the ready. The fleet of watchmen, ten thousand strong, filled the valley with an air of mystery and majesty.

They stood ready for battle to call on them, the Army of Brass.

Army of Brass is CWC's Seventh novel and is set to be published in 2018. Look out for the official release date and excerpts from the ongoing story on the CWC website and Facebook page.

ABOUT CW PUBLISHING HOUSE

CWPH was founded in 2015, dedicated to publishing CWC novels. Due to numerous requests, we have opened our doors to submissions from completed collaborative novels and will work exclusively with collaborative novels written by two or more authors. CWPH has also arranged a number of Anthologies, with more to come. To learn more about our books and our authors, please visit: www.cwpublishinghouse.com